LOVE'S WINDING ROAD

THE GREAT WAGON ROAD
BOOK ONE

SUSAN F. CRAFT

ISBN-13: 978-1-942265-89-4

PRAISE FOR LOVE'S WINDING ROAD

"From one of the finest writers of Christian Colonial Fiction comes a new novel that is sure to please!

In Love's Winding Road Craft transports readers back to a world so believable, they'll think they are in the colonial Blue Ridge Mountains! Don't miss out on this excellent novel!

To have author Susan Craft back, writing her amazing books, is something Christian Historical Fiction fans will be cheering for, as am I!"

— CARRIE FANCETT PAGELS, BESTSELLING
AWARD-WINNING AUTHOR, MACKINAC
ISLAND ROMANCES SERIES

"Where do we put our trust when life spins seemingly out of control? That question lies at the heart of Love's Winding Road, a tender love story set against the ruggedly beautiful but unforgiving frontier of Colonial America, between an Irish settler and a wagon train guide with ties to the Cherokee Indians—the perfect mix of story elements I gravitate toward as a reader. Fans of historical romance woven with adventure, wilderness survival, and blended cultures will welcome Susan F. Craft's exciting contribution to a favorite genre."

— LORI BENTON, AWARD WINNING AUTHOR
OF BURNING SKY AND OTHER HISTORICAL
NOVELS

I dedicate Love's Winding Road to my husband, Rick, who encouraged me to write stories taking place on the Great Wagon Road. We both grew up watching the TV series Wagon Train, with its exciting accounts of our country's rugged pioneer forefathers. Sadly, my dear husband passed in 2017 after a long illness brought about by exposure to Agent Orange when he served in the Vietnam War. He traveled his own winding road through PTSD, and I would like to thank his comrades of the Combat Veterans of South Carolina who scouted the way.

INTRODUCTION

The Great Wagon Road spanned from Philadelphia, Pennsylvania, through Virginia, North Carolina, and South Carolina and ended in Augusta, Georgia. It began as a path carved out of the wilderness by thousands of bison and deer moving from one water source and salt lick to the next. Indians used the footpath for hunting and for warring against neighboring tribes. Hernando de Soto is reported to have trekked part of the trail during his exploration of the Southeast in the 1500s. Europeans, many of them landed gentry, made new fortunes trapping deer and selling the hides along the road. In the 1700s, the road expanded into a major thoroughfare traveled by immigrants, a large number of them Scots-Irish. Colonel George Washington and his troops traversed the road during the French and Indian War. Over time, the Great Wagon Road had many names, among them were Great Warriors' Trail, Indian Road, and Valley Pike.

Come, journey with Rose Jackson, a Scots-Irish lace maker, and Daniel Fordham, a wagon train scout, and their faithful hound, *Tsiyi* (pronounced *Dee-Jee*) as they bestow upon the trail a new name, *Love's Winding Road*.

CHAPTER 1

1753

$\mathcal{D}$aniel Fordham stood with the wagoners huddled around a campfire, but unlike the others, the acceleration of his heartbeat had nothing to do with the awaiting of instructions for the harrowing journey ahead. His attention was not even on his boss, though everyone ceased their nervous chatter as the man stepped forward.

No, his gaze fixed on a young woman across from him, standing between her parents. Her white mobcap barely contained the fiery red curls that spilled down her back. Her black wool cape covered her from head to toe but most certainly concealed a pleasing form.

As half Cherokee, Daniel prided himself on his self-control —inner, as well as outer. Right now, he couldn't seem to get a handle on either.

"Welcome, everyone. I'm your head wagon master, Gavin Kimball, and this,"—Kimball pointed toward Daniel—"is my assistant, Mr. Fordham."

Daniel tipped his hat to the crowd of some twenty would-be settlers.

Kimball, a tall man of solid build, carried an air of confidence about him. Experience and knowledge had etched deep furrows into the sides of his mouth and across his brow. He surely captured the attention of the ginger-haired young woman, who hung on every word the senior wagon master spoke. She had not so much as spared a glance for Daniel, and that rankled a bit.

"I will lead the train, and Mr. Fordham will act as scout, finding the best places for us to ford rivers and streams and to camp at night." He cleared his throat. "Due to some sad circumstances, we're setting out much later in the year than I'd like. But it can't be helped. That means we may run into snow. Don't fret. It's not something I haven't dealt with in the past."

Several of the wagoners mumbled, unhappy with that bit of news.

"We'll leave tomorrow before sunrise. The Ackermans and their daughter, Petra"—Mr. Kimball pointed to the couple and their daughter—"will take the lead. Mr. Ackerman is a cordwainer, which might come in handy as this trail has been known to wear out even the best of shoes. They plan to stay with us until we reach the end of the road in Augusta, in the Georgia colony."

The golden-haired, petulant daughter fluttered her lashes toward the group of single men and then at Daniel. Trouble there.

"Following them will be the McGregors. He's a sausage maker. He's the one whose hog is gonna have piglets any day now."

Everyone chuckled. Some of the men had already taken bets on how much longer the mama hog's legs could hold up her rotund body before she keeled over.

"They will also travel with us to Augusta."

Mr. and Mrs. McGregor raised their hands. The sturdy couple with their gaunt faces and lean builds had an aura about them—they had survived hardships. Their toughness might prove valuable.

Mr. Kimball angled toward the family that had drawn Daniel's notice. "Mr. and Mrs. Jackson and their daughters, Nora and Rose, will follow. Mr. Jackson is a flax farmer who has offered his ropes to anyone who needs them. They will leave us in South Carolina."

The daughter and her parents waved. The girl's lovely smile lit up her face, and when she suddenly cast a glimpse Daniel's way, his stomach flipped over. But which one was she, Nora or Rose? And where was her sister?

"They have two wagons, one driven by Mr. Jackson and the other by his hired driver, Mr. Ward."

Mr. Ward tapped a knuckle to his forehead. A sailor's salute. Of stocky build, he stood only a couple of inches shorter than Mr. Jackson, the skin of his face as weathered and tough as a horse's saddle.

Mr. Kimball swept his arm toward one side of the campfire. "We have seven single men with us who'll take up the rear of our train. Gentlemen?"

One by one, each of them stood and introduced themselves. Miss Jackson exchanged glances with one of them, a lanky, sandy-haired man whose fringed jacket had been patched in numerous places. When the man acknowledged her with a smile, she quickly turned her head, as though embarrassed she had been caught staring. Daniel shifted from side to side and lowered his head. What about him caught her interest?

He focused on his boss's closing comments. "We're a small group, as we're missing three families who couldn't join us. But if we work together, we'll do fine. The road we're taking has been traveled for decades. It started out as a narrow path Indians used when hunting. Over time, the path became a road wide enough for a wagon with room on either side for a foot traveler or horse. Accordingly, our journey should be a smooth one, with some exceptions here and there where the trail narrows. Before we disperse..." Mr. Kimball glanced his way. "Daniel, would you like to say a few words?"

He motioned to Daniel, who acknowledged the prompt to start his part of their routine.

Daniel moved closer to the fire and scanned his attentive audience. Several eyed his copper-toned skin with curiosity. Some considered him a savage. Would they have confidence in him? He had gained the trust of former wagoners and more than likely would again. He crossed his arms, maintaining his casual stance.

"As Mr. Kimball said, I'm Daniel Fordham, and I'm the scout for your train. I've been doing this for five years, and I realize how new and, frankly, frightening the wilderness can be. Mr. Kimball and I will do our best to pass along as much of our knowledge as we can, because we want this to be a safe journey."

He caught Miss Jackson looking at that same man who'd captured her notice before.

Daniel straightened and continued. "We'll be encroaching on territory that belongs to the animals. Some will shy away and run. Like wolves. They don't usually attack humans, but they are curious animals that will be drawn to our campfires. You might see their eyes shining from the forest. Others are dangerous predators. Bears, mountain lions, rattlesnakes, and copperheads. You'll need to be wary of those."

He regarded the faces of the people who counted on him and Mr. Kimball for guidance. As always, the enormous responsibility of his position weighed on him. The very survival of these people hung in the balance. For one reason or another, they had given up everything—all for the promise of a new life, a second chance, or a way to escape prejudice and persecution in a land that offered heretofore unattainable prospects and dreams. He enjoyed his part in helping those prospects and dreams come true.

"Some of you have asked about Indians. This time of year, many tribes have settled in to ride out the winter. Most are friendly and have no desire to bother wagon trains passing through. They will leave us alone if we leave them alone."

By now, his own village's storehouses burst with harvested crops along with a winter's supply of dried meat. Thick blankets stacked under beds and in corners of cabins awaited heavy snows. His Cherokee family and friends concerned themselves with preparing for bad weather and cared nothing for the wagon trains.

"I wouldn't be completely honest with you if I didn't mention that there are also warring tribes that will take a break in the weather to attack settlers, mostly for food, guns, and ammunition, but also to drive them away from land they feel has been stolen from them."

He spoke of the fierce Catawba, the hated enemy of his tribe, who made war throughout the year. In contrast, winter for the Cherokee brought a reprieve from confrontations with the Iroquois to the north, the Chickasaw to the west, and the Muscogee Creek to the south. Which *savages* did these people associate him with? Did they even know—or care about—the differences?

"It's my job as your scout to keep alert to any raiding parties that may venture close to us."

Miss Jackson slipped her arm out of the slit in her cape and reached over to hold her father's hand. Daniel regretted scaring her, but he said what needed to be said. He turned to the third part of the speech he'd given many times—the terrain.

"We will come to some steep hills, so be prepared to help one another. That might mean getting out and pushing, if necessary. Or tying your wagons together to keep your brakes from failing. Heavy rains can swell rivers and streams and turn the road into thick layers of mud, making the way almost impassable. If that happens, you'll need to leave behind some of your belongings."

The wagoners grumbled, apparently taken by surprise with that announcement.

Mr. Kimball tucked his thumbs into his belt. "We're not saying these things to worry you folks, but to give you fair warning of what's ahead. Please know, Mr. Fordham and I will do our utmost to make your journey a safe one. But we can't do anything without the help of the Almighty. So"—he removed his hat—"let's call on Him for traveling mercies."

While Mr. Kimball prayed, Daniel bowed his head and lifted his own words of praise and thanksgiving for God's many blessings and asked for wisdom to make good choices. He opened his eyes to the endearing sight of Mr. and Mrs. Jackson and their daughter circled together, heads bowed, and holding hands. He'd never been taken by a woman as he was by this one. What was this strange draw to her? And would he get the chance to get to know her?

Daniel squeezed his eyes shut. What was he thinking? She wouldn't look twice at a man like him.

CHAPTER 2

*P*oised on the threshold of a dense forest, the line of wagoners grew quiet.

To Rose Jackson, standing with her mother beside their family's covered wagons, everything around her seemed to freeze as if objects in a painting—the people, teams of horses, pack mules, chickens in crates hanging from the wagon in front of them. Even the late-autumn winds stilled and stopped plucking the leaves clinging to the oak trees that towered up to the sky where the morning stars had begun to fade.

Rose's toes tingled inside her sturdy walking boots, and she twined her fingers around her mother's hand. "My heart's racing faster than when we used to climb the cliffs of Gobbins."

Ma gave her a wobbly smile. "Aye, lass. It's fair takin' my breath away. We're a long way from Ulster."

Her mother barely reached Rose's shoulder. Ma was so petite, people had remarked that the spinning wheel Da had fashioned for her looked as though it belonged to one of the little people. But her body was the only thing wee about her. She had a heart big enough to encompass everyone she met. Her voice often boomed with laughter, and back home in

Ireland when she'd chastened her daughters, the children several doors down in the borough had hunched their shoulders.

Rose took a final look over her shoulder at the outskirts of Philadelphia, a strange and fascinating city she would like to have explored. When their ship had first entered the harbor, the teeming ships of every size and color and the tall, spired buildings, inns, and ordinaries had stirred her imagination. Taverns and alehouses with intriguing names such as *Penny-Pot*, *Hornet and Peacock*, and *Crooked Billet* lined the docks. But there had not been time to walk among the crowded streets once her family disembarked from the vessel that had carried them across a fickle ocean. Though the journey had lasted but ten weeks, it seemed a lifetime ago.

Four covered wagons comprised their small train of nineteen travelers, a passel of horses, several pack mules, the very pregnant pig, six chickens, a goat, and a hound dog. Nineteen travelers who should have been twenty-three. The staggering thought brought tears to Rose's eyes.

"Ma, should I try one more time to persuade Nora to walk with us?"

"I don't think it would help. Your sister's grieving in her own way, and that means staying holed up in our wagon and away from folks, with their questions and sympathies. She'll come out when she's ready." Ma patted Rose's arm and called out to her husband, "Connor, here comes Mr. Fordham, the young scout."

"'Bout time," he grumbled, twitching on the wagon seat and swapping the reins from hand to hand.

"Try not to fash yourself, Connor." Ma leaned toward Rose. "He wants to get going. I've never seen him this anxious."

Rose cherished and admired her father, but she had to admit, he was not comfortable with his new role driving a team of horses. As a farmer, he was accustomed to following behind one workhorse plowing furrows for planting flax seeds. A solid, robust man, he had hair the color of coal with a few streaks of white, which he attributed to both his daughters, but mostly Rose. Years of laugh lines had burrowed deep into his sunburned face. Rose adored his laugh that shook his belly. When pressed to describe him, his friends would say that he loved the Lord, worked hard, and took great care of his family.

Rose leaned in to her ma to keep her da from hearing what she said. "Ma, you more than anyone know why he's this way." Being an Old Light Presbyterian had made him a target of hate and persecution. "He complained to anyone who would listen how much he detested being a tenant farmer and especially resented being forced to pay tithes to the Church of Ireland. That was dangerous for us too." How many times had he come home from the pub beaten and battered because of those sentiments?

Her mother tucked in her chin and gaped at her. "You knew about all that?"

"Of course, Ma. Bless you. You tried to hide it from me when I was younger, but I'm twenty now, and neither of you raised me to be stupid." Rose wrapped a stray curl around her ear, but the tendril popped free as if it had a life of its own. "I don't think Nora was aware, living apart from us and being so busy with her family and all."

Ma's face crumpled. "Oh, Rose. I never wanted to burden you."

"That's in the past." She cupped her mother's cheek. "I'm happy for Da and for you. For a long time, he has yearned for a place where he could be master of his own land. It's within his grasp now. 'Tis no wonder he's so eager and grumpy. He's tired of the delays."

Not to mention, the journey had already cost her and her family dearly. The reason for their departure being put off until this morning pierced Rose's heart like the shaft of light that lanced through the thick canopy of limbs, lighting the ground in front of their wagon.

Movement up the line caught Rose's attention. Guiding his chestnut horse from wagon to wagon, Mr. Fordham made his way closer, stopping to speak to the other drivers on the way. The night before, he had stood out from the other men, maybe because he was the tallest and with a broader, more muscular build. Or maybe it was his angular features or his sable-brown hair bound in a queue that reached his shoulders. She had caught him staring intensely at her, but due to the dwindling firelight, she was unable to determine the color of his unusual, almond-shaped eyes.

Riding along the wagon train, the scout had a presence about him, but his expression remained stoic, unlike one of the single gentlemen whose pleasant, appealing face had caught Rose's attention. A hound dog lumbered alongside his master, seemingly unaware of how close he was to the horse's hooves.

Both Mr. Fordham and Mr. Kimball were the kind of men who inspired confidence—capable, rugged, and experienced. *Sturdy* was how her father described them. Mr. Kimball, the older by about thirty years, wore the garb of a colonist, while Mr. Fordham favored a frontiersman's deerskins.

The fringe of his hunting frock rippled as he saluted her father. "Good morning."

"Good morning, young man. Are we about ready to depart?" Da asked, sitting up straighter.

"We are. I'm just checking over everything. Stick to the instructions you were given last night, and all will be well. Most important is to keep up and don't stop for anything, unless your wagon's broken down. Mr. Kimball is at the lead, and most of the time, I'll be scouting ahead. Should you run into trouble, you can call on that lot." He motioned toward the group of single men on horseback who followed at the rear of their party.

Rose glanced between the scout and her father. How would Da take being told what to do by someone so much younger? The scout's comments the night before about leaving possessions behind had disturbed everyone. Though he'd been matter-of-fact about it, such losses would be personal, even painful. She could not imagine what they would choose. They had packed every inch of their wagons with the bare essentials. Her father had been stingy about leaving enough room for his treasure, a barrel of flax seeds they would plant on land he had purchased in a northeast section of South Carolina called the Waxhaws.

Da merely gave a calm nod. "We'll do our best, young sir."

Rose relaxed her shoulders. Da respected him. A good sign.

Mr. Fordham's dog left his side and circled around her, pressing into her petticoats. He stopped to sniff her boots, and when she leaned down to pet him, the red-and-black-speckled hair across his back bristled. Mr. Fordham spoke to him in an unfamiliar language, and the hound relaxed and allowed her to scratch his velvety red-gold ears. He studied her with eyes like limpid pools of amber.

"What a handsome fellow you are." His master, too, though she wouldn't be saying so.

"Heel, Tsiyi," Mr. Fordham commanded, and his dog quickly took his place beside him. He prodded his horse, and as he passed by Rose and her mother, he tipped the rim of his hat. "Fair traveling, ladies."

Rose's heart tripped. His eyes were the same blue as the jay feather tucked into his hatband. And his accent—English, flavored with an unfamiliar nasal sound. What was it?

"Wagons, ho!" Mr. Kimball's gravelly voice rang throughout the clearing.

Rose faced her mother, brows lifted. "Here we go, Ma. Are you sure you'd rather walk than ride with Da?"

Ma threaded her arm through the bend of Rose's elbow.

"I'm sure. Like you, I prefer walking. That way, I can take everything in. Let me walk as long as I'm able."

Rose took a step forward, knees trembling. "God bless our journey," she whispered.

Da slapped the reins, the horses dug their hooves into the ground, and the wagon wheels groaned and popped as they rolled across a thick blanket of leaves and pine needles. Soon the dense woods engulfed them in an eerie grayness, blotting out the first rays of sunrise. What adventures and challenges awaited them on the trail ahead?

CHAPTER 3

*W*ith every step she took, Rose felt more and more like an alien in a foreign, strange, menacing land. The mass of giant pines and oaks and the abundant underbrush made her slip her arms inside her cape. A morning mist lingered throughout the woods like a shroud. Occasionally, she had to duck under ambitious limbs that stretched out in nature's attempt to repair the gap men had slashed through the forest. She and her mother fluttered around a spider web, their boots making crackling noises among the fallen leaves. Ma gasped and pointed to the tiny face of a fox peering out from behind a thicket. A *rat-a-tat* drummed in the distance, and Rose cocked her head at the unfamiliar sound that echoed her heartbeat.

A twig snapped, followed by the rustle of leaves.

"Ma, I fear we are being watched." She stretched the tense muscles at the back of her neck.

Her mother stopped and listened intently, then shook her head. "Dinna fash yourself. It's the strangeness of it all. Never in my born days have I seen so many trees. Ones I canno' even name. And the colors—reds, golds, oranges, yellows. My arms are fair tingling."

Rose pulled her hood up over her mobcap and tucked her hands back inside her cape. Where was the scout? He'd ridden out of sight, and somehow, his absence created a loss of security.

They had not traversed a mile when she noticed her mother grimacing with each step.

"Is it your hip, Ma?"

Pain etched lines in her mother's forehead. "Aye. A plague on it." She massaged her right hip. "Ach, I was so hoping to walk farther than I have. I hate it, but I think I need to rest a wee bit."

They had already slowed their pace earlier, increasing the distance from the wagon. Rose tried not to panic, but what should they do?

"Anything amiss, Mrs. Jackson?" a voice called from behind them.

Rose turned as the friendly single gentleman she'd noted the night prior approached, guiding his horse with one hand and clasping the tether of a heavily laden mule with the other. Wyatt Benson had introduced himself as a surveyor headed out West.

Ma leaned against Rose. "Aye. I'm afeared so."

Rose curled her arm around her mother's waist. "We need to get her into the wagon, but I don't know. We were warned not to stop."

Mr. Benson secured the mule's tether to his saddle. "With your permission, ma'am." He leaned down, clasped Rose's mother under her arms, and swept her onto his horse in front of him.

Ma sputtered. "Oh, my!"

"I didn't hurt you, did I?"

Red-faced, Ma twisted around to stare up at him. "No. 'Twas more of a surprise."

He chuckled. "Well, let's see about getting you into that wagon. On the seat or in the back?"

"The back, I think. My daughter, Nora, is there and may be glad of the company."

At the mention of her name, Nora appeared in the small opening of the canopy as she unlaced it. When Mr. Benson approached, she quickly popped back inside.

As gently as if handling a child, he lifted Ma over the back board and inside.

"Ma?" Rose called out. "Are you all right?"

Her mother poked her head out. "Right as rain."

"Good. Try and get some rest. Maybe you can persuade Nora to come out and walk with me a while. It might do her some good."

Ma glanced behind her, and her smile turned upside down before she ducked back inside. Oh dear.

Mr. Benson dismounted and stood beside Rose. Only a few inches shorter than he, she spotted tiny flecks of caramel in his brown eyes. His tan face was clean shaven, and he wore his neck-length sandy-colored hair loose underneath his tan wool hat.

"Mind if *I* walk a while with you, Miss Jackson?"

"I'm happy for the company. Two people shorten the road." She matched her steps to his as he wrapped his horse's reins around his hand.

"Do I hear a bit of Scotland in your mother's speech?"

"Aye. Ma says her blend with my Irish da gave them daughters who are stubborn, stoic, and sentimental. In my case"—she pressed her thumb into her chest—"*stubborn* applies the most. But she always ends that with, 'Lord love 'em.'"

He chuckled. "I had the honor to speak with her and your

father last night. She seems...well...a formidable person. Surprising in one so tiny."

"Formidable sounds right. She's the heart of our family."

"I'm sorry she's feeling poorly."

"'Tis an old ailment. It plagues her often, but she's one of the strongest people I know. She doesn't allow it to get the best of her. She tries to hide it from Da, but he knows."

Mr. Benson's brown eyes gleamed—warm and open, not guarded like the scout's. "My mother was the same. Cut of sturdy cloth."

"*Was*...?" Had he known the type of loss her family had?

He ducked his head. "Sadly, she and my father both succumbed to the last wave of smallpox that hit Philadelphia a few months back."

"How sorry I am for you." She barely squeezed the words out as her own grief tightened like a steel band across her rib cage. "'Tis a horrible disease. A few weeks after we landed in Philadelphia, we lost my sister Nora's husband and their little boy, as well as her husband's brother and sister-in-law. You see, on the crossing, we rode out several storms, and none of them had endured the voyage well. They weren't strong enough to survive the pox. Ma, Da, Nora, and I had the pox when my sister and I were children. Heaven only knows what would have become of us if we hadn't."

The sorrow in his eyes mirrored her own. "Your sister wasn't at the meeting last night."

"No. It may be a while before she's ready to be amongst others again."

The rapid drumming sounded again close by, and Rose tilted her head. "What is that? I've never heard such a noise before."

"It's a woodpecker. Beautiful birds with black-and-white plumage. The males have a brilliant red cap. The sound you hear is one of them tapping out a hole in a tree, searching for worms and such. That's how they hollow out their nests too."

Rose's eyes widened. "We don't have woodpeckers in Ireland. I'll be on the lookout now. But I ken there's more strangeness in this country I should be on the lookout for."

He nodded. "Last night, your father mentioned that you're headed for South Carolina."

"Yes. We have relatives in the Waxhaws. We're flax growers. It's very much a family business. Da and others will grow the flax, and some will fashion it into ropes and sails. Ma has a gift for weaving fine linen."

"And you?"

Rose bent down and picked up a stick that she tapped against the brush along their path. "Nora and I hatchel the flax into fine silk strands. We use the gossamer threads to make lace, and we sell much of it to ladies for their embroidery."

"I didn't know flax could be used for so many things."

She liked the way the fine laugh lines crinkled his tan skin. What a handsome face. And such a nice smile. She had not seen Mr. Fordham smile once.

"That's why we need two wagons. We have flax seeds, a loom, and my mother's spinning wheel that take up most of the space in the wagon Mr. Ward is driving. We packed all our personal belongings in this one."

"I met Mr. Ward last night. Pleasant fellow."

"Yes, my father hired him to..." She paused. "To take the place of my brother-in-law and his brother."

She stubbed her toe on a root and would have fallen if Mr. Benson had not grasped her elbow and righted her.

"Oh, my! So sorry about that," she exclaimed, withdrawing from the strength of his fingers through her cape.

They had come to a straightaway in the road. Petra Ackerman glanced back from where she walked next to her family's wagon. Watching them? Rose waved, but the girl spun around and picked up her pace.

Rose turned back to her companion. "And you, Mr. Benson, how long have you been surveying?"

"Three or four years now. I was studying to be an artist when my father insisted I take up a paying trade. So I learned how to draw maps and to survey."

"I would think it a lonely occupation. And dangerous being out in the wilderness." She shivered—for being lost and alone was one of her greatest fears.

"It can be lonely, although we do travel in pairs and fours. I'm meeting some partners at Fort McClain, when I leave the wagon train in a couple of weeks." He lifted a branch for her to walk under. "As for dangerous, it may be so, but it's vital that someone fix the boundaries. Just look at the dispute over the land between Virginia and Pennsylvania. I'm afraid that England and France are headed for war over it."

"You think that's possible?"

"Likely so."

"I wonder what Da will say about an imminent war. He uprooted our family not only to follow his vision of owning land in the colonies but to live in peace in a place where we could worship without bother. I don't begrudge him his dream and have enough wanderlust in my own soul to consider this journey exciting. But none of us had anticipated the horrible cost."

Something brushed against her leg, and Rose nearly toppled over trying to avoid stepping on Tsiyi. She glanced over her shoulder to find his master walking his horse a few steps behind.

"Good morning." Mr. Fordham tapped the brim of his hat and moved to join them.

"Good morning." She and Mr. Benson spoke the words together.

Mr. Fordham's blue eyes grew intense as he looked back and forth from Rose to Mr. Benson. His sudden smile made her heart skip. He *could* smile. What could she do to make it happen more often? Distracted by the dimple in his cheek, she stumbled again and almost collided with him.

"Steady on," he said, scanning the woods.

"Is something amiss? You looked concerned."

"Just being cautious, Miss Jackson. Something you'll learn once you've been here long enough."

Lacy white blooms along the edge of the road drew Rose's notice. "How lovely." She bent to pick one, but Mr. Fordham quickly pushed her hand away.

"Don't. That's snakeroot. It's poisonous. Especially toxic for the horses and cattle." He looked down at her with a stern expression. "A perfect example of what I was just saying about caution. This may be one of the most beautiful places on earth, Miss Jackson, but it holds many dangers. Plants and animals—the four-legged and the two-legged kind."

Another warning to add to her list of worries. But did he have to be so stoic about it? "How do you come to know so much, Mr. Fordham? Are you a native of these parts?"

"Yes, I grew up near here. My parents were my teachers. From my father, who was a successful trapper, I learned navigation and the ways of animals and business. My mother was Cherokee. From her, I learned the importance of family and about nature and ways to preserve it for future generations. She taught me a great deal about people, too—how to judge them by their actions, not their words."

Well, that explained his unusual features and his accent. And the obvious depth of his character.

Mr. Benson pulled on his horse's reins, widening the space between his horse and Mr. Fordham's. "Where do you live when you're not scouting?"

"I have a farm in the North Carolina mountains, not far from my family's village."

Rose bent and picked up a fiery-red leaf. "You must miss it, especially this time of year when everything is bursting with color."

"There's a view from my land that juts out over a deep valley. So beautiful it makes your eyes ache."

She tossed the leaf away. "Whatever made you decide to leave it and become a wagon train scout?"

A muscle in the side of Mr. Fordham's jaw twitched, and he paused before answering. "It's not something I wish to speak about."

Her question must have awakened something painful for him. "Please, forgive me"—she patted his shoulder—"I have made you uncomfortable."

He stared at her hand, then her eyes and back again. "No harm done."

A companionable silence had nestled between them when a movement in the woods made her clasp Mr. Fordham's forearm. "I'm not sure, but I think I saw an Indian."

Amazingly, no surprise reflected on his angular features. "Yes. There are two of them. They've been stalking us for miles."

CHAPTER 4

*a*fter the sighting of the natives trailing them, Mr. Kimball rode up and down the train more frequently than before. The men at the rear of the train moved in closer.

According to Daniel, Indian hunting parties often roamed territories far from their villages. Some might follow wagon trains out of curiosity, remaining out of sight. More brazen ones entered campsites hoping to trade their animal skins for pots and pans or trinkets. No matter the reason, their menacing presence disturbed Rose. Curiosity...trinkets...did Daniel leave out some details?

Once Daniel and Mr. Kimball spread the warning, the heightened tension among the wagoners became palpable, and when they stopped to rest the animals around noon, everyone peered over their shoulders and continuously scanned the forest. Worry remained Rose's constant companion throughout the day. Danger seemed to lurk around every bend in the road. She made sure she walked directly beside her da and remained ready to jump up on the wagon seat at a moment's notice. By the time they made evening camp, every muscle in her body ached.

After the wagons circled around a clearing near a stream, Nora started to pick up limbs and branches for kindling. Though only a few years older than Rose, she shuffled her feet like an old woman. Her shoulders stooped so much from the heavy burden of her grief, she reminded Rose of a wilting sunflower. She'd lost weight, and her brown homespun dress hung loosely. She avoided other wagoners and kept her lovely, heart-shaped face sheltered from them.

"Don't go far from the clearing," Rose bade her sister. What a relief that she had finally ventured out from the wagon. She didn't need to scare Nora back inside.

"I'll be careful."

Rose gathered bedding to make pallets. Her ma and da would sleep under the first wagon, she and Nora under the second. The hired driver chose to sling a hammock between the wagon and a nearby tree.

Mr. and Mrs. McGregor came by, offering to share their eggs. How amazing that the chickens were laying after squawking and flapping their wings most of the day and bouncing around inside crates hung from the side of the wagon. Their pig that seemed ready to burst any moment with piglets snorted and settled down for the night, tied to the wagon wheel. Catching a whiff of the rotund hog, Rose twitched her nose and wished its bed was farther away.

The Ackermans, the German family in the lead wagon, kept to themselves and set about building a fire with the wood their daughter had gathered at the edge of the forest.

While their mother warmed the evening meal, Rose and Nora headed to wash in the stream a few yards away.

"I may join you?" Petra Ackerman called out behind them.

Rose beckoned to her.

"'Tis been a long, long day. Ya?" Petra maneuvered in between them. "I tink we vould never stop."

When they reached the bank of the stream, Petra loosened

her pale-yellow hair that spilled around her shoulders, reminding Rose of dried flax stalks and the gossamer threads she spun from them. Her flawless skin and eyes, blue like the flowers that topped flax stalks in June, put Rose in mind of the porcelain dolls she, as a child, had yearned for in the shop window at home.

Rose and Petra carried their buckets to the rock-strewn edge of the stream, where they scooped them into the frigid water. Rose kept alert, constantly checking their surroundings. She and Nora had agreed to be prepared to take off running at the slightest warning.

What kind of country had she come to, where her body was so tense her muscles hurt and she might jump out of her skin at a moment's notice?

"Since ve vill be close in this journey, I may call you both by your given names?"

Rose and Nora nodded.

"Rose, you spend much time vid Mr. Benson today," Petra remarked, dragging her heavy bucket up the embankment.

"He walked with me for a while." Rose exchanged a glance with her sister, whose brows were quirked in confusion as her own.

"He is very nice to look at. Ya?"

"I suppose so."

"You tink to make him yours?" Petra peered up at her with a sly expression.

What an invasive question. Rose took a moment and motioned for Nora to lean over so she could douse her hair.

"The water's freezing," Nora exclaimed, scrubbing soap into her scalp. "But I have to get the dust and who knows what else out. Ugh."

Rose finished rinsing Nora's hair and sat down to undo her waist-length braid.

Petra looked between them. "You are different to be sisters.

Though you both have blue eyes, Nora's hair is silky, the color of coal. Such delicate, pale skin. You, Rose, have hair like a rusty nail. And your skin already turns blotchy from the sun."

How was she to respond to such bluntness? Rose ran her fingers through her *rusty nail* hair that tended to spring into ringlets, defying even the strongest brushes. Nora's raised eyebrows expressed her own astonishment at the personal observations.

Petra motioned for Rose to pour water on her hair. "Please."

Resisting the temptation to empty the entire bucket over the prying girl's head, Rose complied. Thank goodness, once they had sponge bathed and Rose had washed her own hair, Petra decided to return to her family's wagon.

"What an annoying person." Rose draped her hair over her shoulder and rubbed it with a cloth. "I've never met someone who made such peculiar comments."

"Maybe she's lonely or frightened and is trying too hard to make friends. This country is daunting. I'm glad we have each other."

"Me too." Rose tugged playfully on her sister's hair. "But if she's trying to be friends, I fear she's going about it the wrong way. There's something...harsh about her."

"Let's give her some leeway."

"Oh, I'd never be deliberately unkind to her. But I canno' see us being friends."

"If I'm honest, I canno' either. It's time we got back, I think."

Strolling arm in arm to the camp with her sister, Rose assessed Nora with surreptitious glances. Profound grief had stolen the light from her sister's eyes. Rose adored her and had loved her precious baby boy and husband.

Would she ever see Nora's lovely smile again?

Mr. Fordham stepped into their path, his musket slung over one arm. Rose jumped and her hand flew to her chest. How had the man managed to appear as if from thin air? And...had he watched over them at the stream? Tsiyi left his master's side long enough to make a circle around her.

"Evening, ladies. It might be a good idea if, in the future, you don't stray far from the wagons without an escort. Mr. Kimball or I or one of the gentlemen at the rear of the train can be of assistance. All you need do is ask."

Despite his polite way of addressing them, he had an aura of fierceness. Perhaps that was partly because he was taller and more broad-shouldered than most men of her acquaintance, but mostly because he was armed to the hilt. In addition to his ever-present musket, he had strapped two powder horns over his coat and across his chest. He wore a bronze, half-moon gorget around his neck. No less than two knives and a pistol were tucked into his leather waistband. Another knife was secured to the side of his calf.

"Thank you, Mr. Fordham. We'll heed your advice," Nora replied.

"You have a good evening." He stepped aside for them to pass.

When they arrived at their campfire, Mrs. McGregor was showing their mother how to prepare the squirrels her husband had shot. "My husband canno' believe how bounteous the woods are." The gaunt, though sturdy, woman dipped a floured squirrel into the sizzling lard. "I brought seven of these little critters—two each for your men and one each for the ladies."

"Goodness. Ma's face," Rose whispered to Nora, and they could not hold back their giggles.

They sat in chairs near the fire, observing the encounter as if attending a play. Clearly, their mother was trying hard to be gracious about the generous gift even though she'd never cooked or eaten squirrel in her life.

Ma picked up one of the animals gingerly with two fingers and dropped it into the pan. "A bounty, for sure."

"Spoon the grease around and over until it's golden brown. They don't require much salt," Mrs. McGregor instructed, wiping her hands on her apron. "I'll leave you to it, then."

"Thank you again, Deborah. In the morning, I'll let you know how it went."

"I myself can't abide the things. Remind me of rats with fluffy tails," the woman said over her shoulder as she started to walk away.

Ma sputtered, holding the ladle up in the air and letting the gravy drip onto the ground.

Tsiyi loped over and started licking the puddle of gravy. The dog's master wouldn't be far away. Rose twisted around in her chair, and a smile tickled her lips, for indeed, Mr. Fordham strode through the camp checking on each family.

He stopped near their campfire and sniffed the air. "Squirrel. Smells tasty."

Mrs. McGregor spun around. "Then I have a surprise for you. Come with me to my wagon. I'd love to share my husband's bounty."

"That's mighty generous." He tapped the brim of his hat. "Come on, boy."

Rose suppressed a sigh as he strode away and she and Nora joined her mother. There was something appealing about the man and his dog. If only they had stayed a while.

"I'm happy you've made a friend, Ma." Rose sniffed the fried squirrels. "They do have a nice aroma, almost like chicken."

Ma frowned. "I wish they *had* been chickens or wild turkey. What will your father say? I knew this land would bring challenges, but never in my born days would I have imagined I'd be eating a squirrel."

When they sat down to supper not long after, each of them hesitated, studied the meat on their plates, and waited to see who would take the first bite. Rose held in a giggle.

Da led the way and proclaimed, "Tastes like chicken."

They all laughed and agreed to a person that the squirrels were a success, though not very meaty.

Rose took a plate to Mr. Ward and found him lying in his hammock. "Brought you some supper, Mr. Ward."

In one motion, he swung his legs over the side of the hammock and stood. "Thank you kindly, Miss Jackson."

"It's squirrel," she said hesitantly as he took the dish from her. "But there's lots of gravy and corncakes."

"Fine with me, miss. Many a time when I was on ships, we had nothing but hardtack and water." He tucked into his food with a generous appetite.

"You were a sailor?"

"Yep. Most of my life."

"How intriguing." She studied him as he ate. He tended to keep to himself, but Rose liked his air of reliability. Besides, her father was a good judge of character, and if he had hired Mr. Ward, then he was trustworthy.

He paused, spoon in hand. "It's a young man's calling. I'd finished my last voyage when Mr. Jackson hired me on as a driver. I figured if I did a good enough job, he'd recommend me to others. Besides, these wagons with their canvas tops are like ships on land and make me feel right at home."

She moved next to the hammock. "So that's why you prefer this for sleeping?"

He nodded. "Yes, miss, some habits are hard to break."

"Is it difficult to get in and out of?" She touched the ropes securing the canvas sling.

"There is a knack to it."

"May I?"

He put down his plate on the ground, a furrow appearing between his eyes. "Yes, but there's a certain way. In one motion." He gestured. "Turn your back to it, slide your...yourself into the center, swing your limbs over, and hang onto the sides."

Rose followed his instructions and, once in, enjoyed the sensation of swaying back and forth.

"Good job, miss." Mr. Ward picked up his plate and continued to eat. "You reverse what you did to get out."

Rose tried to slide her legs over the side but swung them too hard, flipping the hammock from side to side. "Help, Mr. Ward! What do I do?"

The canvas closed around her until it spun over and suspended her face down in a tight cocoon. Mr. Ward ran to assist her, but not in time to save her from being chucked out unceremoniously onto the ground.

"Oh! My!" Rose scrambled to cover her legs with her petticoats. She was attempting to rise when Tsiyi bounded up and started licking her face.

Standing next to him, Mr. Fordham held out his hand. "May I help?" His expression told her he was finding it difficult to contain his mirth.

She accepted his hand. "It's all right to laugh, Mr. Fordham. I know you want to."

He guffawed and Mr. Ward chimed in. Soon she was laughing with them.

"You were right that there's a knack to it, Mr. Ward." She straightened her mobcap and rearranged her clothes. "I'll leave you to your supper."

"Thank you kindly for it."

"I'll walk you back to your campfire." Mr. Fordham matched his steps to hers.

Rose inhaled the air that emanated the particularly strong aroma of cooked squirrel which wafted throughout the camp. "Everyone must have cooked squirrel for supper. I guess Mrs. McGregor succeeded in giving away her husband's bounty. She called them vile creatures that are much like rats with fluffy tales."

"Ha! Miss Jackson, you are a stitch."

"Is that a good thing?" She could not make out his expression.

"It's a mighty fine thing. Have a good rest of the evening." He left with Tsiyi loping at his heels.

Rose stared after him for a moment, her heart warm.

Later, she and Nora sat on a blanket near the fire while their mother put the cleaned bowls and utensils into a wooden chest. Smoke from her father's and Mr. Ward's pipes circled their heads as they concentrated on the game of draughts they had set up on a tree stump. The gurgling of the stream and the cheerful fires that dotted the campsite had almost assuaged her tension when she looked up to see a couple of Indians making their way across the clearing.

She sat up straight. "I think they are the ones who have been following us."

They both wore moccasins, buckskin leggings, and drop-shouldered shirts with hip-length, rabbit-skin vests. One wore his soot-black hair in a ponytail adorned with two feathers. The other had shaved his head on one side, and on the other side had draped his locks across his shoulder, secured with a piece of rawhide and strings of seashells.

Mr. Fordham greeted them and led them to one of the campfires to meet Mr. Kimball and Mr. Benson. Fascinated, Rose could hardly stop staring when she realized that the one with the ponytail had sat on the ground facing her. And was staring back.

She stiffened and quickly focused on her father and Mr. Ward, comforted by their close proximity.

Mr. Fordham whispered something in Mr. Benson's ear. Minutes later, Mr. Benson walked over and sat beside Nora, his expression serious.

"Are they the same men who followed us?" Rose asked.

"Yes. You see the powder horns strapped over their shoulders? They're carved with black snakes. That means they are

Catawba. Some of the fiercest and most feared warriors. I won't lie to you, ladies, we must all be on our guard. They can be friend one minute and foe the next."

"Did Mr. Fordham send you to sit with us?" Worry lines feathered the corners of Nora's eyes.

"He did." He leaned closer. "But just as a precaution."

Rose heard only part of what Nora and Mr. Benson said. It was the unexpected, unwanted guests that held her attention. Thankfully, they remained only a few minutes, but her breath quickened when the one who had been staring nodded her way before he vanished into the forest. Her uneasiness remained while she and Nora gathered bedding and lay down on the pallets underneath the wagon.

"I think I'll check on Ma." Rose scooted out from under the wagon.

She had reached the back wheel of the other wagon where her mother lay sleeping soundly when she caught the voices of her da and Mr. Fordham from the other side of the wagon.

"We'll have to make sure someone is with the young women at all times." Mr. Fordham spoke in almost a whisper. "Maybe for a few days, they should ride in the wagons."

"Aye. 'Tis a good plan. Do you truly fear they might be taken?" Da's voice cracked with worry.

"Honestly? Yes. Some tribes are known for kidnapping young women. Some for slaves and some for wives."

"What?"

"Ten or so years ago, the Catawba were almost wiped out by smallpox. They used to number in the tens of thousands. Today, there are less than a thousand. So kidnapping women... of all races...is a way of bringing their tribe back. My own people have kidnapped others."

"But that's barbaric."

Though Rose shared her father's shock, what effect would

his words have on Daniel? It must be painful to be the target of disparaging comments.

"As for the two that visited our camp, it seems that one of them is most fascinated with your daughter, Rose."

The hairs on Rose's arms prickled.

Her father let out a soft growl. "Why is that, you think?"

"Might be that glorious mop of red hair."

Rose bristled. *He likens my hair to a mop?*

"Aye. 'Tis something to behold. And a temper to go wi'it. Takes after her ma, she does."

Mr. Fordham chortled.

How can they speak of me in such a way? I guess it's what I deserve for eavesdropping.

"You have a weapon, Mr. Jackson?"

"A musket, but I've never had much cause to use it. I don't have much ammunition."

"We'll start practice tomorrow. For everyone. Women included. Come with me, and I'll give you some cartridges."

Their voices faded as they walked away. Almost sick with fear, Rose hurried back to find Nora asleep. No need to disturb her. She would hear the news soon enough.

For hours, Rose tossed and turned, throwing off the covers one minute and gathering them over her head the next as even the slightest sound magnified until her goosebumps had goosebumps. Thunder rumbled and lightning danced across the sky, startling her to sit up so fast she knocked her head against the bottom of the wagon.

"What's the matter?" Nora mumbled, leaning up on her elbow.

A strong wind slapped against the wagon canvas, rocking it to and fro, and rain fell in heavy sheets, pounding the ground around them and forming a stream of water that invaded their makeshift bed. Squealing their surprise, they gathered up the covers and jumped into the wagon. Moments later, their parents joined them, and they huddled together while the storm raged around them.

Da wrapped his arm across his wife's shoulder. "I wonder if this is how Noah felt."

Ma cuddled against him. "And what of poor Mrs. Noah? Can you imagine the ruckus?"

They burst out laughing, and Rose was still giggling when she scooted over to tighten the strings of the canvas. She peeked out, and a flash of lightning lit up the campsite, exposing Mr. Fordham, his rifle resting across his arm, sheltering underneath a tree and looking her way.

What a comfort to know he was there. She might forgive him for comparing her hair to a mop. Although he did say *glorious mop*.

She snuggled under the covers and fell asleep, only to awaken a few minutes later with the disturbing thought—tomorrow she would learn how to shoot a gun.

CHAPTER 5

*E*arly the following morning, Daniel sat astride his horse, Wadulisi, with one knee resting across the saddle. From his vantage a few yards into the forest, he watched Miss Jackson and Wyatt enjoying a conversation as they followed the wheel ruts in the road.

Daniel liked Wyatt's open and honest demeanor. He had valuable skills and would make a reliable comrade in dangerous situations. Although he and Wyatt had become friendly, he envied his solicitous behavior toward Miss Jackson. Yesterday he had lifted a branch for her to duck under and pointed out plants and animals that seemed to fascinate her. Now they were together again walking alongside the wagons, so relaxed and at ease with each other, one would think they had been acquainted for a time.

It was not until their meeting yesterday when she'd looked up at him from petting Tsiyi that he'd noticed her cobalt-blue eyes. Her lovely smile, peach-colored skin, and the light dusting of freckles across her nose made a charming picture.

Daniel looked down at Tsiyi, who sat patiently beside the horse. "You like her, don't you, boy?"

Tsiyi stood, leaned onto his front paws, and stretched out one back leg and then the other.

Daniel settled himself on the saddle and slid his foot back into the stirrup. "She's mighty fine. Too good for us—the half breed and his hound."

Anyway, it looked as though she may have set her cap for Wyatt.

As Daniel maneuvered his horse deeper into the forest, he glanced over his shoulder at the wagon train that would be his last. He was twenty-five and had spent the past five years running away from the memories of the tragedy that had taken his parents' lives. His grief, though never far from the surface, had abated. It was time to get on with his life, to settle down, marry, and start a family.

Rebekah, the Cherokee woman who had grown up with him and his Cherokee cousins, represented comfort and familiarity. A marriage to her would be built on solid ground. He had never formally proposed, but he had known her all his life, and there had been an understanding. And yet, since leaving home, he had returned a handful of times and had begun to question if he and Rebekah truly suited one another. He needed to make a decision and soon. Given his own experience with rejection, he wanted to go about it in the right way. Rebekah deserved that much.

He prodded Wadulisi and called out encouragement to the hound that trotted beside him. "Enough dawdling, Tsiyi." As the wagons continued forward, Daniel guided his horse deeper into the woods, with Tsiyi following. "Let's get those blue eyes off our minds and go to work. We need to keep a watch on those Catawba who've been skulking around."

During one of his sweeps around the area, he'd spotted the two men lurking alongside the wagon train while attempting to keep out of sight.

On the prior evening when they had entered the camp, Kimball had asked them straight out, "What brings you here?"

"Hunting," one man had responded, keeping his eye on Miss Jackson.

Kimball had poked the fire with a stick. "It's good deer country."

The man with the ponytail had stood abruptly and motioned to his friend. "We go."

After they moved into the forest, Kimball had tossed his stick onto the fire. "I don't think deer is what they're after."

Daniel didn't either. Those men had been more interested in their defenses—and their women.

He would make it his business to find out for sure. After picking up their trail several times and then losing it again, he caught up with the wagon master while the train stopped to rest the horses. "So far, all they're doing is following along and watching, but I don't have a good feeling about them."

Kimball mounted up and rode side-by-side with Daniel ahead of the train. "We'll have to double up on the guard. Once you've scouted a place for us to camp, you'll need to stick closer...keep a sharper lookout. Get Mr. Benson and the others to take the rear guard. Might be a good idea for everyone to ride in the wagons for a few days. No walkers. And let's get started on the gun lessons before supper tonight."

"Yes, sir."

Daniel spent the afternoon keeping watch, riding up and down the train. Finally, toward late afternoon, he found a place to camp, and when everyone was settled, he spotted Miss Ackerman and the two Jackson sisters walking to the nearby stream.

"Vill you come with us, Mr. Fordham?" Petra called out.

"Yes," he said, "but don't take long. Shooting practice before supper, remember?"

He motioned for them to proceed. He followed and

remained out of sight, leaning against a tree, his musket at the ready. Balancing safety against privacy, he kept his vigil while they washed their hair and bathed. Each was a beauty in her own way, but only one, Miss Ackerman, relied on it to manipulate others. He recognized that trait in her from experience.

He had learned at a young age that beauty and evil often made up the two sides of the same coin. At fourteen, he had accompanied his father to England to meet his family and to decide if Daniel should be left behind to attend school. He'd hated every moment of it—the constraining social rules, the restricting clothes, the artifice, the pain a beautiful woman inflicted only because she could.

How flattered he had been by the attention of one particular woman whose beauty shone like the sun. Besotted, he'd cared not that she was much older. As part of London's elite society, his father's family received invitations to the most exclusive fêtes, where he eagerly sought her out to bestow gifts on her as if she were a queen. Her subtle smiles half hidden behind her fan and her delicate, though strategic, touches had awakened his young body. He'd ached for her and wanted her for his own. But when he'd approached her, she had laughed at his heartfelt proposal.

He'd built up the courage to seek advice from his father and learned that she had been toying with him. Gathered in his father's loving embrace, Daniel had cried out his heartache. It was a terribly painful lesson for one so young and inexperienced.

He'd asked his father if he was not handsome enough for the woman.

He smiled now, recalling his father's response. *My son, you aren't aware of it yet, but even at your young age, you have the look about you that makes women swoon.* He had not known what *swoon* meant, but the way his father said it, it might be a good thing. *But remember, Daniel, it's not your reflection in a mirror that's important. The only mirror you will ever need is the light in the eyes of the woman you love and who loves you.*

Daniel turned his attention again to the young women bathing by the stream. Neither of the sisters could be capable of such cruelty. Rubbing a cloth up and down her arms, the younger one, Rose, seemed completely unaware of how lovely she was.

He shook his head to clear his mind. He had already covered that territory this morning. A woman like that was not for him. His job was to get her safely where she was going, and that was all.

CHAPTER 6

Rose could hardly wait for the camp to settle. All the long day, she had eagerly anticipated gun practice. Mr. and Mrs. McGregor were excused, as both were already proficient with firearms. They stood to the side but offered occasional encouragement and instruction. Mr. and Mrs. Ackerman had let it be known that they would participate only reluctantly. Petra much preferred the instruction of Mr. Benson or Mr. Fordham to Mr. Kimball's. Nora was so clumsy at loading the cartridges, she spilled more gunpowder onto the ground than into the paper wadding.

"Watch closely," Mr. Benson said to Rose and Nora. "This is a lead ball, about twenty-eight grams. It goes in the bottom of the piece of paper...then comes ninety grams of black powder. You keep it all together by twisting the paper into a tail." He demonstrated as he spoke.

"Paper, lead ball, black powder, and twist the paper," Nora repeated.

Mr. Fordham picked up where Mr. Benson left off. "To load the musket, rip the tail off the cartridge with your teeth." And he looked good doing it too.

Rose copied him and got some gunpowder in her mouth. "Ugh! That tastes awful."

"You're not supposed to eat it, Miss Jackson." The wink he gave her smoothed Rose's ruffled feathers a bit.

"Next, we want to prime the gun. See this? It's the hammer." Mr. Fordham tapped on the curved metal piece on the bottom of his own musket. "You half cock it by pushing back on it. Push the frizzen forward. That opens the flash pan. And that's where you'll pour a bit of the powder from the cartridge."

Rose frowned, trying to follow along, but each step became more complicated for her. "Cartridges, flash pans, frizzens, ramrods. There's so much to remember."

"Don't worry, Miss Jackson. It will all come with practice." Mr. Benson held a musket in the crook of his arm. He knew his way around weapons.

"You need to learn this." Mr. Fordham's tone held less patience. "The frontier is a dangerous place, and one day, you may find yourself having to load weapons for yourself or others. It could be a matter of life or death."

"Yes, Mr. Fordham." Rose's shoulders sank. She might not have his approval now, but she'd work to gain it.

When she was finally allowed to shoulder a musket and take aim, it was heavier than she had imagined. "This is like trying to hold a full bucket of water on your outstretched arm."

Mr. Fordham reached around her and steadied the gun. "The ramrod is this long piece of metal that's stored along the channel of the barrel. Take it and shove it down the barrel, pushing the powder, ball, and wadding so that it will catch the sparks coming from the flash pan. When you've done that, replace the ramrod. Lift the musket and pull back on this—it's the dogshead—which will fully cock the gun. Raise the musket and press the butt firmly against your shoulder and fire."

Rose followed his instructions, braced herself, and pulled the trigger. She had thought she was prepared for the blast that reverberated throughout her body. She wasn't. With her ears ringing, she put down the musket and rubbed the side of her face. "Oh, my. That's loud."

Nora covered her ears. "I may stick to making cartridges."

Mr. Benson shook his head. "You'll both be fine. As I said, it will take practice."

After watching Rose's mother struggle to pick up a musket, Mr. Kimball handed her a pistol. "No need for you to aim, Mrs. Jackson. It's much more frightening with you waving the pistol around."

Rose could not help laughing at the sight of her da ducking down to avoid his diminutive wife who grasped the weapon with shaking hands.

Mr. Kimball came to Rose's side. "You're doing very well, young lady."

The wagon master stood over six feet tall, requiring Rose to lean back to observe his face that was a portrait in grays—gray hair, gray beard, gray eyes. His weathered skin spoke of years of hard living in the elements. His commanding presence radiated confidence. He was someone who could and had made hard decisions. Still, there was a gentleness about his eyes and mouth that made him approachable.

"Thank you, sir." She made a slight curtsy. "There is something to the feeling of being able to defend oneself if necessary."

Nora prodded her with an elbow and nodded toward Petra. The silly girl was gazing up at Mr. Fordham as he leaned near and showed her how to press a musket into her shoulder.

"Tank you for being so patient vid me," Petra murmured.

Nora scoffed, leaned down, and whispered in Rose's ear, "Is she truly batting her eyes at him? What a ninny hammer."

"Looks as though target practice is not only going to be instructional but entertaining," said Rose, sending them into laughter that stopped abruptly when Mr. Fordham scowled their way.

CHAPTER 7

nother storm during the night left the trail a slippery pile of muck that stuck to Rose's boots and soaked the hem of her dress halfway to her knees. Several times, she would have landed facedown had she not grabbed hold of the side of the wagon. Sloshing through the mire was her reward for volunteering to walk instead of straining the horses even more. Besides, she needed the change. Her bottom muscles had taken enough abuse from the bumpy wagon seat.

Rose attempted to tug her boot out of the sticky goo that refused to let go. "Hagfish!"

Mr. Fordham happened by as she struggled to keep her balance. He rested an arm across his horse's neck. "Miss Jackson, if you walk directly behind the wagon and keep your feet in the wheel ruts, you'll manage better." His amused expression hinted that he had witnessed the undignified flailing of her arms and probably heard her use her favorite cussword.

Despite standing ankle-deep in mud, she enjoyed being the reason for his smile. "Now that you've seen me at my worst, do you think you could call me Rose?"

His eyes lit, and he sat up in his saddle. "I'd like that very much, Rose. Please, call me Daniel."

"It's a pact, Daniel." His name felt nice on her lips.

"I'd be happy to help you," Mr. Benson called out and halted his horse next to Rose. "Come, ride with me," he offered, holding out his arm.

"I won't be a burden?" she asked, though she longed to get out of the muck.

"No burden, Miss Jackson."

"Daniel and I just agreed to address each other less formally. Would it suit you to call me Rose also?"

"I'd like that."

The frown on Daniel's face indicated he did not.

She accepted Wyatt's outstretched arm and was swept up behind him. Too bad Daniel hadn't had the idea first.

"Put your arms around my waist," Wyatt suggested. "You'll feel more secure."

As she complied, a muscle twitched in Daniel's otherwise-granite expression. He tapped two fingers against the brim of his hat and rode toward the lead wagon.

"I canno' thank you enough. It was rough going." The solidness of Wyatt's back and the warmth of his waist beneath her arms provided a pleasant contrast.

"It's about to get rougher, I'm afraid. I can hear the river roaring from last night's rain."

Rose had turned her ear to catch the sound of the river when the wagons slowed down. Ahead, Daniel had stopped to talk to her parents.

Wyatt urged his horse forward. "Let's see what they're saying."

They drew near enough to hear Daniel. "The wagon you're in will be fine. But you're going to have to take some weight from your other wagon. See how deep its ruts are? The guide ropes across the river won't hold it against the current."

43

Ma clasped her husband's arm. "Not my loom, surely, Connor?"

"We have our orders, my dear." Slipping an arm around her, Da tried to console his wife, who began to cry.

"My mother must be undone. I've never seen her cry this way. She's always so brave," Rose whispered in Wyatt's ear.

"How is the loom packed?" Wyatt asked Da.

"In pieces. In crates," her father answered.

"What if I carry the separate crates across on my horse, Daniel? I might persuade the other riders to help."

Daniel tilted his head as he considered the proposal. "Might work. Let me check with Kimball."

He returned minutes later with the wagon master's approval. Rose felt like cheering. Wyatt lowered her to the ground and rode back to the others who, to a man, agreed to help.

"You see, Claire. All will be well." Da pecked her ma on her cheek. "Now, give me one of your smiles, my lovely."

Ma tittered like a girl. "Away wi' ye."

The men unloaded crates from their wagon and strapped them to the sides of their horses. The sight lifted Rose's spirits —until she neared the river. Churned into waves by a strong current, the muddy water raced by. Branches and limbs popped above the surface—dangerous obstacles to the wagons making their way across the forty feet to the other side. The river's sheer power and noise made Rose shiver.

The McGregors, their faces stoic, waited on the riverbank beside their abandoned mahogany grandfather clock and a mirrored dressing table.

Petra Ackerman and her mother stood next to their possessions—a rocking chair and a bureau. Their wagon had already made it to the other shore.

"It's not fair," Petra wailed. "Doz men are helping the Jacksons. Can they not help us? Vhy must I give up my bureau?"

"Hush, silly girl," her mother responded. "I dislike it as much as you. But even if they tried to carry our furniture across, it would be ruined by the water."

Petra glared at Rose and then spun around.

When it came time for their first wagon to cross, Rose, Nora, and their mother held hands and watched Da struggling to manage the reins. The wagon strained against the ropes that were strung across the swift current that reached the horses' shoulders. One of the horses shied, rocking the wagon back and forth.

Daniel splashed through the water and grabbed the lead horse's bridle, and led the team to the other side.

Ma clapped and laughed. "*Iontach*! Wasno' that something to behold? We are in good hands, are we not?"

The way the water sprayed over Daniel's head and then how he swam his horse through the deeper waters, guiding his mount with such confidence—Rose agreed with her ma's exclamation. It *had* been breathtaking. She also enjoyed watching Tsiyi, who swam the river multiple times, keeping close to his master.

Once the wagons landed safely on the other shore, Daniel, Wyatt, and Mr. Kimball took turns transporting the women who had watched the entire process in awe.

Rose felt confident riding behind Daniel until a strong current swirled around her legs and pushed against the horse.

"Don't worry, Rose. You're safe with me and Wadulisi." He pulled her arms tighter around his waist. She'd ask Daniel later about his horse's curious name.

His ponytail brushed across her cheek. What might his hair look like loose around his shoulders? She tucked her thumbs underneath his belt, curved her body into his, and rested her cheek on his sturdy shoulder.

Wyatt, who conveyed her mother, looked back over his

shoulder and beamed. "What a great adventure, Mrs. Jackson. Don't you agree?"

Ma's knuckles had turned white from hanging on so tight. "Oh, aye, young man. But I dunno' want to repeat it. One time is enough."

"That's the spirit. Hang on." Daniel kicked Wadulisi's sides, urging him up the embankment, where he jumped down, swept Rose from the horse, and steadied her on the ground.

His pupils contracted, accentuating the tiny specks of light blue in his eyes. The aroma of pine needles, tobacco, campfire smoke, and sweat wafted around Rose and tickled her nose.

"Thank you." She swallowed and concentrated on the beads of river water that clung to the blue scarf tied around his neck.

"My pleasure." He lingered, and she liked the feel of his fingers on her forearms. Did he have something else to say? He could stay this close as long as he desired. Her heartbeat hadn't sped this fast when she was near Wyatt.

He finally stepped back, and leading his mount, he walked away to reorganize the wagon train.

Why was it that every time he left her, she felt a wee bit bereft?

CHAPTER 8

Three days had passed since Daniel's encounter with Rose crossing the river, and try as he might, he could not keep her from his thoughts. She had become a dangerous distraction. Despite his efforts to maintain distance, they seemed to be thrown together more and more. He needed to concentrate, especially with the looming menace from the Catawba.

He spent several hours trying to pick up their tracks but could never find them. If they still followed, they were experts at stealth, and that worried him.

However, on one of his wide sweeps of the area, he came across the campsite of three trappers, their horses, and a mule packed heavy with deerskins. Dressed in oily, stained, fringed jackets and breeches, they sat cross-legged around a fire. One of them turned a rabbit on a spit made of Y-shaped wood branches. Yards away, the butchered carcass of a deer hung from a tree limb.

"'Lo the camp," he called out.

They remained seated but never took their eyes off him.

The skin on all three of their heavily bearded, ageless faces resembled the tanned hides they planned to sell.

"Is that dog a mean 'un?" The one turning the spit pulled a knife buried in the sand and wiped it on his breeches.

Daniel glanced down at Tsiyi, who stood beside Wadulisi. "Not unless I need him to be."

The men guffawed and motioned for him to join them. He dismounted and squatted by the fire, rubbing his cold hands close to the flames. Tsiyi lay beside him, his back a little stiff, at the ready.

"This here is Sam McCloud, and this is John Nance." He gave the spit another turn. "And I'm Bill Campbell."

Daniel acknowledged each of the men with a nod. Their resemblance was uncanny—same build, same wizened faces, same air of hard, frontier living.

"I'm Daniel, Mr. Campbell, and this is Tsiyi."

"It's Bill. We don't stand on no ceremony here. So what's your business, young fellow?" He stabbed his knife back into the sand.

"Scouting for a wagon train out of Philadelphia."

Bill took a draught on his pipe. "Mighty late in the year with winter coming on soon."

"Couldn't be helped. There was sickness in Philadelphia that held some families up."

Bill scanned Daniel's face. "You look familiar. What's your full name?"

"Daniel Fordham."

The man slapped his thigh. "Your pa was Edward, right?"

"Yes, sir."

"I knew it. You're the spittin' image of him." He motioned toward the others. "I trapped with your pa and your ma when she was pregnant with you."

"Is that so?" Daniel raised his brows. "You knew my parents?"

"I knew them well!"

Bill smiled, and to his friends, he said, "Fellas, this man's pa was as fine a man as they come. And his ma..." He took another draught on his pipe.

Daniel stiffened his back, unsure of what the man would say.

"Well, she was a Cherokee and as beautiful a woman as they come. Kind too. She stitched me up once when I got tangled up with a bear. Cared for me till I was well."

His friends nodded.

Bill propped his back against the saddle on the ground behind him. "Seems I heard they both met with an accident and died."

Pain that had lain dormant for some time unexpectedly shot through Daniel's heart, and he gritted his teeth. "You're right, sir."

"That's sad." He studied Daniel's face. "I reckon it's not something you wanna talk about."

"No, sir."

"Too bad. Good people like that are worth remembering." He shook his head. "But fancy meeting you out here in the middle of the woods. Life is full of surprises, ain't it?"

"I couldn't have said it better myself." Daniel allowed his shoulders to loosen.

Sensing his master's comfort, Tsiyi relaxed too.

They sat quietly for a while, each lost in their own thoughts. It was a comfortable stillness as it often is when people trust one another and have shared common experiences.

Finally, Daniel broke the silence. "Have you seen signs of two Catawba?"

The men exchanged glances.

Bill grabbed one end of the spit and slid the rabbit onto a

tin plate. "Not two, but a passel of them two days back. They was headed north."

A scream resounded through the forest, sending chills down Daniel's spine.

"Mountain lion." Bill spoke matter-of-factly as he threw another log on the fire. "Been wandering around these woods a couple of weeks now. We been keepin' the flames high and our eyes open."

Sam used his knife to cut a piece of the rabbit and popped it into his mouth. He finished chewing and cut another piece. "Okay if I feed your dog?"

"Sure."

Sam tossed the morsel to Tsiyi, who gobbled it in seconds. "If you got livestock on that train of yours, you best be on the lookout too."

Bill reached into a satchel and took out a frying pan. "You're welcome to stay for supper. I make some mean beans and venison stew."

Daniel stood and brushed off his leggings. "I thank you, gentlemen. But I best be on my way. It was nice making your acquaintance."

Bill grinned. "Manners, just like his pa. Take care of yourself, lad. God go with you."

"And you."

Daniel left them and headed back toward the wagon train. On the way, he discovered mountain lion paw prints weaving in and out of the woods and headed south. He spent half a day hunting the animal without success. At last, he stopped by a stream and waited for Wadulisi and Tsiyi to drink.

"I give up, fellas. And it rankles. I'm saddle sore, cold, and irritable as a bear with a thorn in its paw." He patted Wadulisi's neck. "I know you're ready to head back to the train. And you, Tsiyi, you're wanting to circle around the petticoats of a certain red-haired woman you've taken to." He missed her too.

No Catawba. No mountain lion. How was he going to protect the settlers if he couldn't even track down the threats that stalked them?

CHAPTER 9

*S*itting on blankets by the fire a day after Daniel
returned from a three-day absence, Rose and Nora
stifled giggles at their father's hearty snoring coming from
underneath their wagon.

"Dinno' laugh, girls. Your father is weary." Ma glanced up
from putting another stitch in her husband's sock.

"Sorry, Ma—" Nora started but quickly stopped at a peculiar sound coming from outside the camp. "What is that?"

Rose stood. "It almost sounds like a cat."

Nora wrapped her arms around her chest. "There it is again,
but this time it sounds like a woman screaming for help."

"It *is* a woman, and I think it's Petra."

Across the clearing, Daniel, who had been sitting at his
campfire, grabbed his pistol, jumped up, and darted between
two wagons and into the woods toward the screams, his dog at
his heels. Rose's back stiffened. Just like the man to run headlong into danger.

As Tsiyi started barking and howling, others ran toward the
commotion at the far end of the circled wagons.

A shot rang out from the direction Daniel had taken. *Dear Lord, please, let him be all right.*

Rose spun around. "Ma, where's your pistol?"

"Here." Her mother retrieved the pistol from underneath her chair and held it out to her.

Rose grabbed the weapon. "Come. Let's go see."

Trying to hold up a sobbing Petra, Daniel staggered out of the woods and struggled over the tongue of the Ackermans' wagon that lay on the ground. She clung to him with both arms wrapped so tight around his neck, he fought to keep them upright. The open lapels of his hunting frock exposed the front of his shirt, which was ripped and covered in blood.

"Someone get her off, please," he managed to gasp out, though Petra's grasp nearly strangled him.

Mr. Ackerman untangled his daughter and passed her to her mother. "What happened?"

"Mountain lion." Daniel bent over in an effort to bring his breathing under control.

"Are you hurt?" Rose stared at his blood-stained shirt.

He looked down. "It's mostly the lion's."

"Mostly?" Ma stepped forward. "Here, let me see." She opened the tatters in his shirt to reveal a slash in his skin just above his right breast.

Petra, crying hysterically, threw her arms around Daniel again. "You're hurt. But you killed it! You saved me! How can I ever repay you?"

Ma rolled her eyes at the theatrics. "Mrs. Ackerman, would you please control your daughter?"

The woman tugged Petra toward their wagon. "Come away, Petra, and quit being such a nuisance."

"But, Ma, I could have been killed." Petra continued to wail until her mother shoved her into their wagon.

"Help me get him to his campfire," Ma directed to the men

gathered around. "Nora, get water and cloths. And my medicine kit. Rose, bring your needle and thread."

Rose ran to do her bidding, and by the time she returned, Ma had removed Daniel's jacket and shirt. He sat on the ground near the fire and leaned against his saddle while her mother pressed together the gash in his chest with her forefinger and thumb.

"Anyone have whiskey?" she asked the onlookers.

Several of the men reached into their coats and extended various-sized containers.

Ma whooped. "Well, I'm surely in the right place if I ever hanker for a wee dram."

The others laughed, even Daniel, who immediately seemed to regret it and gave out a moan.

"Pour some over the wound, Rose," Ma instructed. "It's going to burn, young man."

One of the men gave Rose a leather pouch. She pulled out the cork but hesitated. She hated the thought of hurting him.

Daniel winked at her. "I've lived through worse."

She drizzled the liquid up and down the gaping skin. He focused his brilliant blue eyes on her and never flinched.

"That's enough. It's clean." Ma gently touched the open wound. "Rose, sweeting, you've a steady hand. I need you to stitch this up."

Rose flinched. She was considered a master needlewoman, but always with cloth, never with human skin.

Daniel gave her a tight smile. "As I mentioned before, Rose, I've lived through worse."

She wanted to state that she had not, but the encouragement in his eyes sent her to fetch her supplies. She threaded her needle with her finest flax fiber, returned to Daniel's side, and holding her breath, she began the first tiny stitches.

Think of it as cloth. Think of it as cloth. She repeated the words over and over in her head.

Daniel cleared his throat once when she reached the deepest part of the cut but otherwise remained silent until she tied the final stitch, and they both blew out a big breath together.

Ma nodded her approval. "Fine work, daughter."

After Ma sponged the blood from Daniel's chest, she retrieved a small ointment pot from her kit and spread its contents across the stitches. Nora handed her mother a roll of bandages, but her petite mother massaged her bad hip and struggled to stretch the strip of cloth around their patient.

"Let me do that, Ma." Rose wrapped the bandage several times around Daniel's back and chest. His breath fanned her neck. Her own breath came quickly, and the pulse at the base of her neck fluttered. Could he see it? She had never been this close to such a man. She tied off the bandage and stood back, avoiding eye contact, lest he perceive the confusion in her gaze.

Ma closed her medicine kit. "Keep it clean, and I'll see about removing the stitches in about five days."

"Thank you for your kindness. Each of you. I'm grateful." Daniel's voice was pitched low.

Rose accompanied her mother and sister back to their wagon, a hand on her stomach to quell the strange sensations stirring there.

CHAPTER 10

The following days fell into an uneasy routine. The camp began to stir at four each morning. While the men gathered the livestock that had grazed during the night, the women fixed a breakfast of bacon, corn porridge, or flour-and-water Johnny cakes. After the plates and mugs were cleaned, bedding and hammocks stowed, and tents hauled down, Kimbal and Daniel conducted a morning target practice. Then the men hitched their teams to wagons, and everyone ventured down the trail. At nooning time, they stopped to eat, drink, and rest, usually in a clearing or beside a stream previously scouted out by Daniel. All were back on the road after an hour. By six in the evening, after covering about twelve miles, fifteen on a good day, the weary travelers set up camp and settled down for the night, except for those designated as guards. No matter how tired she was, Rose found sleep evasive and often heard the changing of the guards at midnight.

Along the way, they stopped by plantations and small farms where Ma, determined never to cook another squirrel in her life, purchased bushels of corn, turnips, and sweet potatoes.

She was ecstatic to add those to their meals and was especially happy to obtain pumpkins, apples, and grapes. The evening she made apple pies, many of the single men found one reason or other to visit their campsite where Ma, who took pride in her cooking prowess, proudly shared her baking.

Some of the men returned the favor and dropped off rabbits and venison as well as bags of flour and sugar. Ma made sure they understood that squirrels would not be appreciated.

The train came across several settlements where they replenished provisions and purchased hay and chaff for their animals. Some patronized the blacksmith for various repairs. When the timing was right, many attended Sunday services.

On one occasion, a handful of settlers confronted them at the outskirts of their town and were barely civil until Mr. Kimball made it clear that there were no Moravians among the wagoners. Much to Rose's disappointment, they refused to allow the brethren into their communities. For her, prejudice was a terrible word. She'd had her fill of that in Ireland.

During one of their stops at a large settlement of about sixty homes, Rose, Nora, and their mother decided to sell some of their lace and thread. Inside the general store, Nora and her mother went to the back seeking shirts and socks for Da.

"I've darned your father's shirts so many times, I think I've repaired the repairs," said her mother. "His socks are in such a sorry state, I have to look the other way when he takes off his shoes."

Rose approached the owner, who stood at the counter, a lanky man who must not have washed either his thin, oily hair or his stained apron in a while. He greeted her with an equally sour expression.

"Would you be interested in buying lace and embroidery thread?" Rose took the package she'd been holding under her arm and placed it on the counter.

"Maybe. Let me see what you've got."

She rolled open a length of linen and flattened out several yards of lace and put the spools of thread next to them.

"Let me get the wife. I don't know much about lace, but this looks mighty fine to me."

Rose nodded, suppressing a hopeful smile.

"Martha," he yelled. "Come see."

His wife came from the back of the store, wiping her hands on her white apron. Tidier than her husband, she tucked wisps of her wiry gray hair under her mobcap. "Real nice work. I won't touch it 'cause I've been dusting. It's the finest quality I've ever seen, Herold."

"I thought as much. How much are you asking?"

Rose was about to answer when the door opened and Daniel joined her at the counter. He nodded her way.

The owner stared at him and frowned. "What can I do for you?"

"Do you have molasses drops?"

"We're clean out." The man spoke gruffly.

At his obvious lie, Rose pursed her lips. The candy filled most of the jar on the shelf right behind him.

"Then I'll have a plug of tobacco. And before you say you're out, I'm looking right at it." Daniel's voice remained calm, but his expression was steely.

The owner grabbed the tobacco and threw it down. Daniel put it inside his jacket and dropped a few coins on the counter.

He glanced at Rose and at her lace and pulled his hat from his head. "Nice."

This was the second occasion when she had been this close to the scout, and this time, she noticed a light dusting of a mustache. Dark blue rings encircled his vibrant blue irises as he searched her face. A tendril of his sable-brown hair had escaped his ponytail, and she had a sudden urge to tuck it behind his ear.

The owner bristled. "Is this half breed bothering you, young miss?"

Rose's cheeks heated from the anger smoldering in her belly. "This *gentleman* is a leader of the wagon train my family is on," she snapped. She pointed to the jar of candy. "I'll have a dozen of those."

"Yes, ma'am." He wrapped the candy in paper, tied it with a string, and handed it to her.

"Ma," she called out as she secured the cloth with her lace. "Pay for the candy for me, please. I'm going outside with Daniel."

Her mother poked her head around a shelf. "Aye, but what about the lace?"

"This is not a place I want selling our work." She tucked the roll of lace under one arm and wrapped her fingers around Daniel's forearm. "Shall we?"

"Yes, miss." He donned his hat, rippling the muscles beneath Rose's fingers.

Outside, she sat on a bench by the door, and he leaned against a post and crossed one ankle over the other.

She blew out a breath. "Wicked man. Does that happen often...being called a half breed?"

"More than you'd expect in a place crowded with people fleeing that kind of treatment. I don't let it bother me 'cause that's what I am."

"It bothers *me*, Daniel." She leaned forward on the bench and folded her hands in her lap. "I may not be familiar with this part of the world, but I realized when we first met that there was something different about you—your looks, your accent, the language I heard you speak. And then you mentioned that your mother was Cherokee. I come from a people who've suffered greatly for our customs and differences. I so hope this country will be different. I swear, I'll do my part, and I plan to call out hate wherever I see it."

"The look on the store owner's face when you stood up for me..." He chuckled deep in his throat, emotion behind the sound. "You have spunk."

"What? That? You've no' seen the worst of it."

He lifted his brow. "Goes along with the hair, I suspect."

She sent him a look that told him she would let him get away with that comment. "How is your wound?"

He rubbed his fingers across his chest. "Since your mother removed the stitches, it's healing fast. I'll bet there's not a man in this country that has a finer-looking scar."

"Ha! If only you knew what it took for me to do that."

He became serious. "I do know. You saw what had to be done, and despite the fact that you looked as though you wanted to faint, you managed it, anyway. We call that gumption." He clasped the railing on either side of him. "This is a hard country, Rose, but I'm sensing you have what it takes to survive. You'll make someone a fine wife."

Suddenly feeling shy, she opened the candy and offered it to him.

He popped a piece into his mouth and lifted his eyes to heaven.

She followed his lead. "Oh, this is good. I've never had it before."

"My mother used to make it for me. I hanker for it now and again."

"Here." She held it out to him. "You take the rest."

"No, I couldn't."

"Yes, you can." She waggled her eyebrows. "I'm going back inside and getting some more."

He grinned. "You're a kind woman, Rose."

He saluted her, and she watched him walk toward the wagons at the end of town until he was out of sight.

～

*D*aniel perched on the bottom limb of an oak tree. He gazed up into the bare branches at the azure sky and breathed a sigh. Climbing trees brought him joy. Today he sought respite from the exceptionally busy days he had spent scouting out farmers and plantation owners willing to sell their goods to the wagoners, as well as towns and settlements amenable for their train to camp nearby.

He still kept a lookout for the two Catawba whose trail had disappeared after the last thunderstorm. While their tracks had vanished, he had picked up signs of a large party of Indians traveling northeast.

He had visited a trading post and talked to others who had also come across the signs. Several settlers were so frightened of an Indian attack they had abandoned most of their possessions and were headed to fort up with a garrison stationed about thirty miles away. A couple with a newborn son vowed never to return to the wilderness. The terror on the young mother's face had tugged at his heart.

Did Rose indeed have the gumption to survive on the frontier?

He brushed his fingers across his chest where the scar had healed nicely. His pulse raced again as he recalled the enticing aroma of roses in Rose's hair and the feel of her breath on his neck as she stitched his wound. Her fingers had trembled, and fear had reflected in her eyes. Despite her distress, she'd managed well.

He reached inside his jacket, opened the pouch of molasses candy, and popped a piece into his mouth. He would never again experience the taste without remembering how magnificent she had been facing up to the store owner. Maybe his parentage was not a barrier, after all.

He admired everything about her—her kindness, bravery, generosity, and sense of humor.

Was there a special someone back in Ireland? Or was she still attracted to Wyatt? Did her hatred of prejudice extend to marrying a man of mixed race?

He intended to seek answers to those questions.

CHAPTER 11

"What's wrong with Da?" Rose asked as she and Nora hovered at the back of their wagon while their mother bent over their father, who lay inside on a pallet.

"It's the inflammation in his hands. From handling the reins all day." Ma searched her medicine kit. "And I've run out of willow bark." She peered out the back of the wagon. "I see the young master there. Why don't you ask him if he can help, Rose?"

Rose slung a rucksack over her shoulder and walked up behind Daniel, who was conversing with the Ackermans. She waited for him to finish and was about to say something when he turned around.

"What is it, Rose?"

He does have the most arresting face.

She blinked. "Um, my father suffers with inflammation in his hands. Ma treats it with willow bark, but she has run out. In your scouting, have you come across any willows? Black willows...not weeping willows."

"I have. As a matter of fact, there are some along the bank of this stream."

Tsiyi came bounding across the campsite and flopped down between them, breathing heavily. She scratched his ears, and he lolled his tongue to the side in complete enjoyment.

"Could you fetch some for us? She needs about ten twigs the length from my wrist to the tip of my fingers and as big around as my little finger." She swept one hand over the other. "For making bark tea. She needs the same number of lengths, but shorter for boiling. And then she needs thinner pieces my da can chew on when he's driving the wagon."

He stared at her with a quizzical expression.

"I...well, maybe I should accompany you. Let me know when we can go."

"Now would suit, Rose. This way."

She and Tsiyi followed him across the campsite and into the woods along the stream until he stopped abruptly.

"There." He pointed to a tree that towered to the sky with some of its brown feathery branches gracefully draping out over the water. At the base, he jumped, grabbed a limb, and swung himself up. "Tell me again what you require."

"See that branch to the left of you? We need ten hand-length twigs."

He pulled his knife from its sheath, slashed a couple of branches, and dropped them at her feet. "I'll remove the branches here, and we can cut the proper lengths when we get back to camp."

She continued pointing to the branches she wanted until there was a pile of them. "That's enough, I think."

He climbed back down and balanced himself on the bottom limb.

Rose scanned the willow. "It's a braw tree. I used to climb ones just like it when I was a child." She sighed. "How I miss the feeling of freedom I got dangling high above our borough."

He held out his hand. "Come on up."

She glanced over her shoulder, and feeling quite mischievous, she reached up with both arms. He clasped her wrists and lifted her with little effort to stand beside him. She was pressed against him a few moments, and with her heart hammering, she grabbed the next branch and swung herself up.

"Watch yourself."

She climbed higher and higher, her joy increasing with each step.

"That's high enough," he warned.

From her vantage, she observed up and down the stream that rushed over rocks and layers of fallen leaves. "I can see our wagons," she shouted with glee. She breathed in deeply, taking in the sights and sounds that brought her senses to life.

He chortled. "Time to come down now."

Reluctantly, she descended until she reached the bottom limb. Daniel stood on the ground ready to catch her. She hesitated.

"Trust me."

She jumped into his arms which cradled her underneath her bottom and allowed her to slide down his body. She landed on the ground with her face buried in his chest. Ruffled, she stepped away and rearranged her clothing. She straightened her mobcap. She must look a sight.

She lowered herself onto the ground by the roots of the willow and started shoving the twigs into her rucksack. Daniel sat beside her, and as Tsiyi ran up and down the riverbank, digging holes and sniffing here and there, they worked in companionable silence until the sack was full. Daniel whistled, and the dog returned and settled himself between them.

"What a fine lad." She patted him on his rock-hard neck. "I know that Indian names have meanings. Does Tsiyi?"

"It means *canoe*."

"Why canoe?"

"Canoes are crucial to the Cherokee for traveling, hunting, trading. They are solid and reliable. A good name"—he patted

Tsiyi's head—"especially good for a dog who does well in water."

"And your horse, Wadu...?"

He grinned. "Wadulisi. It means *molasses*."

"Ha! I know why you gave him that name." Her favorite candy, now.

"Do you have a Cherokee name? Or am I being too personal?"

"Not at all. It's Waya. It means *wolf*."

"Like the engraving on your ring."

He stretched out his little finger. "It's my father's family crest."

Intriguing, but I'm prying. Much like Petra.

Daniel stood and held out his hand to help her up. "We'd best be going."

Accepting his assistance, Rose glanced at the willow. "I know it wasn't ladylike, but I did so enjoy the climb. Please, Daniel, not a word to Ma. She would have an apoplexy."

He chuckled. "You remain a lady no matter what you do." He picked up the rucksack and put it over his shoulder. "Your secret's safe with me, Rose."

He would guard her secret, but what about her heart if she offered it to him?

CHAPTER 12

A couple of days later, Rose and Nora sat on the bank of a stream near their wagon, washing the breakfast dishes.

"Don't move, ladies, not one muscle," Daniel whispered. He was suddenly close behind them—just a few feet away.

Rose dropped a cup into the water bucket and froze. She glanced at Nora, who hunched her shoulders.

Heavy feet sloshed and stomped in the stream. The closer the sounds came, the faster her pulse raced. A tall, thick tuft of grass growing out of the bank blocked her from seeing what was coming. That Daniel was close by helped her anxiety but did not keep her imagination from running wild.

Was it another mountain lion? A bear? Some other creature that roamed this wild and extraordinary land? Whatever it was, Daniel considered it dangerous, and that was all she needed to remain as still as possible.

The stomping continued until a huge bison bull rounded the bend. He halted the moment he spotted her and Nora. He stared at them with onyx eyes set deep in his hairy, triangular face that ended in a thick black beard. Each time he took a breath, a mist pushed out of his nostrils. Horns grew up and away from his face, made blacker in contrast to the light-brown hump on his back.

Could the beast hear her heartbeat that rang like thunder in her ears?

"There are four more with him. We'll give him a few minutes and see if he continues on downstream," Daniel said in a low-pitched voice.

The beast had taken several steps away when Rose heard someone running and then the cocking of a musket.

"No, Mr. Ackerman. Don't shoot," Daniel ordered.

A musket clattered to the ground.

"Get out of here, Ackerman."

To Rose's horror, the huge animal swiveled back toward them, dipped his head down, and pawed the water with his enormous foot. He snorted so hard, he sprayed a mist all around his head.

"Ladies, carefully, slowly, get up. Bison can hear for miles, but they don't see well. So don't turn your back to him, but keeping as low as possible, move toward me. He's not charging...yet."

Rose struggled to raise herself up inch by inch from the ground. The largest animal she had ever encountered in her life was staring at her with eyes that were slowly turning red. Her body shook so hard she almost fell back down. She glanced at Nora, who was having trouble getting a foothold on the bank.

"What's going on, Ackerman?" someone yelled from the camp.

That loud voice spooked the giant beast. He lowered his head and started up the embankment toward them.

Tsiyi, howling so loud it hurt Rose's ears, hurtled from behind her and headed straight for the charging animal's legs. He circled around, nipping at the bison's hooves and gaining its attention. Daniel stole that moment to grab Rose and Nora by their arms and pull them behind the wagon wheel.

Rose clasped the wheel so tightly her fingers ached. Tsiyi continued to dance around, trying to drive the animal from the edge of the stream and back into the water. He came dangerously close to the horns several times. When the bison swept his head to the side and sent Tsiyi flying off into the air, Rose clamped her hands over her mouth. He landed on his side a few feet away and did not move.

Finally, apparently tired of the distraction, the bison moved away. Without looking back, it lumbered its way downstream, followed by the rest of the herd.

With the animals safely out of sight, Rose scrambled out from behind the wagon, dropped to her knees, and pulled Tsiyi's head onto her lap. Daniel joined her and ran his hands up and down the hound's body.

"Is he badly hurt?" she asked through trembling lips.

"Nothing's broken. But he did get a nip from the horns." He stared into her eyes. "Are you up to some more sewing?"

She gulped. "Yes. I'll do it."

Daniel gathered Tsiyi into his arms, carried him to the campfire, and laid him gently on the grass. Rose's parents, who had been visiting the MacGregors, came running.

"Whatever happened?" Da asked.

"He was attacked by a bison," Nora answered. "He saved Rose and me, Da. He gave us a chance to get away but was hurt for his efforts."

Mr. Ackerman joined them. "Shoulda let me kill that beast."

"We have no need of the meat or the fur." Daniel stood ramrod straight with his hands balled into fists. "They're headed toward a salt lick a couple of miles downstream. Those are more than likely the last of their kind left around here. Between Indians and hunters, they've about been wiped out."

Rose understood and shared his anger, and would have

joined in the argument, but she needed to help Tsiyi, who had gained consciousness but remained still. "Nora, please fetch Ma's medicine kit and my needle and thread."

Daniel knelt and rubbed the dog's haunches, murmuring soothing words in Cherokee.

Rose examined the wound and Tsiyi whimpered. "It will be all right, boy. I'll try my best not to hurt you." She nuzzled his jowls and down his neck, and he raised his head up and licked her fingers.

Rose caught Daniel's eyes, and her heart softened at the pain and worry in their depths. "It's not deep. Maybe needs only three or four stitches. And look...it's on his chest, almost in the same place as yours."

That made him smile.

Speaking words of comfort, she washed the slash in Tsiyi's skin and stitched it together. By the time she finished, he stood up on his own and started licking her face.

"Take it easy, big fellow." Rose held the dog by his ears and kissed him on his forehead. "You are my hero, you know that. Right?"

"Absolutely right." Ma moved next to the hound, which was almost as tall as she. "From now on, our table is your table, and you are welcome to anything we have to eat."

Daniel, his eyes shining with gratitude, ruffled Tsiyi's ears. "You hear that, boy? They are going to spoil you rotten."

Judging by the tears in Daniel's eyes, he might need a little spoiling too. Good thing she was up to the task.

CHAPTER 13

For two days after, Rose worked to rid herself of the shock from the bison attack. The thought of losing Tsiyi upset her. She loved the dear dog. How would Daniel have managed without his treasured companion?

Sitting on the wagon seat beside her ma while her da guided the horses away from one of the settlements, Rose expressed her surprise that most of the towns they had visited were Scots-Irish.

"Listening to their brogue made me a wee bit homesick, I admit. But as much as I miss our homeland, this new place, full of strange sights and sounds ...it's...it's captivating."

Ma patted Rose's arm. "Aye. I feel it too."

The wagon in front of them carrying Mr. Ward and Nora was drawing to a halt.

Following suit, Da brought their horses to a standstill. "It's no' the time to stop for the evening. I hope naught is amiss."

"Here comes Mr. Kimball," said Ma, "and he's not looking happy."

The wagon master tipped his hat. "Trouble ahead. Several trees have fallen across the road—I suppose from the storm we had last night. They'll have to be moved before we can proceed. Sit tight, folks."

A few minutes later, the men who made up the tail of the train rode past them.

"I'm going to go wi' 'em. See if I can help." Da wrapped the reins around the brake peg and jumped down. He searched in their wagon in front of them before hurrying away carrying a saw.

"I'm uneasy about this, Rose."

"So am—"

A hand clamped around Rose's elbow and yanked her to the ground. She landed with a thud and slammed against the chest of an Indian.

"Ma!" she screamed.

Her mother scrambled to the edge of the seat, extending her arms. "Rose! Rose!"

Rose stretched her hand to her mother, but the man threw her over his shoulder and dashed off into the woods. Her head banged against his back, and she pummeled him with her fists and kicked her legs.

Briars reached from the dense underbrush and ripped her mobcap from her head. When a thorn scraped her cheek, drawing blood, she gasped. Another person, still out of sight, crashed through the woods behind them. Enfolded in the hood of her cape, Rose's head dangled and bobbed, slamming against the man's shoulder blades. Blood rushed to her head, and she began to feel dizzy. They moved so quickly that what ground she could see became a blur, and they were soon out of earshot of her mother's screams.

Dear God, help me!

She had no idea how far they had traveled when, mercifully, they stopped. Her captor slung her off his shoulder, and she came face to face with him. Although almost unrecognizable with half his features painted black and the other with a white circle, he was the one who had stared at her at their campsite.

Fury shot up from her toes, and she balled up her fist and drew back her arm to punch him in his nose. But he easily dodged her, and she lost her balance. He gripped the front of her cape with one hand and slapped her face so hard with the other she saw stars.

"We go. Fast. Keep up, or..." He touched the knife at his belt.

He spun around to lead the way, and the other man, painted in the same fashion, dug his fingers into the small of her back and shoved her ahead of him. Along a path they seemed familiar with, she followed. Each time Rose stumbled, she was rewarded by a vicious tug on her hair that had come unbound. Strands of her unruly curls caught on branches and were ripped out so many times, one of her captors stopped long enough to bind it with a strand of rawhide.

Rose's lungs burned from gasping for air. Her feet and knees ached so much she could barely put one foot in front of the other. Countless streaks stung on her arms where stickers had scraped away her skin. Her head pounded from pain where the clumps of hair had been snatched from her scalp. She strained to keep up, but when she slowed down or tripped, she was punished with a shove so brutal she tumbled to the ground, only to be jerked to her feet again.

The blisters that had formed inside her boots had burst and stung like hot coals. Suddenly, nausea overwhelmed her body, and she grasped onto a bush and retched.

She wiped her mouth with the back of her hand, and furious beyond anything she had felt before, she glared at Ponytail. "That is the last straw," she yelled, balling up her fists. "I don't know if you understand, but I cannot go any farther."

He checked with his friend and made a motion toward his knife.

"Threaten me as you like, but I'm not taking another step."

Ponytail sidled close, nose to nose, and ran his thumb along the scratch on her cheek. He stared at the blood, wiped it on his leggings, and placed the tip of his knife against her throat.

To her surprise, memories of Daniel came to her.

You saw what had to be done, and despite the fact that you looked as though you wanted to faint, you managed it, anyway. We call that gumption.

This is a hard country, Miss Jackson, but I'm sensing you have what it takes to survive. You'll make someone a fine wife.

Steeling herself, she waited for a deadly blow, never taking her eyes from his. For one moment, she thought she spotted something close to admiration in them. Maybe he was not such a monster, after all.

He moved his knife away and quickly sliced off a lock of her hair that he tucked into his belt. Without warning, he thrust her to the ground and spoke to the other man, who handed him his gourd canteen. He drank heavily and motioned it toward her. Grateful, she put the canteen to her lips and gulped down the water.

Drawing upon her newfound courage, she stood up and started walking away.

Ponytail jumped up and blocked her.

She pointed toward a tree, and punctuating each word with her finger, she said, "I have to relieve myself."

Her words clearly puzzled him.

She pointed several times back and forth to herself and then the tree.

Understanding of her meaning dawned in his eyes, and he stepped away. But when he moved to follow her, she stomped her foot, wincing from the pain. "Just me."

As she completed her personal business, she thought she heard a howl far off in the distance. The men must have heard it, too, for as soon as she emerged, they grabbed her arm and began their trek anew.

Why had the howl startled them? Could it have been Tsiyi? Was Daniel searching for her? *Please, Lord, let it be so.*

A tiny flicker of hope came to life, spurring her on to ignore the pain in her arms and feet.

After they had traveled for what seemed like miles, the distinct thunder of rapids echoed among the trees. They came upon the bank of a river that churned and rumbled, forming a mist lingering in the air.

Ponytail motioned her toward a tree trunk that spanned the water. They expected her to walk across it? She hesitated and took a step back before she caught a sound—a dog barking.

"Tsiyi! I'm here!" she shrieked and was rewarded with a stunning blow across her ear.

In answer to her frantic call, the hound hurtled up the hill and seemed to fly in the air before slamming against the Indian who had taken her. The man screamed and fell to the ground, desperately trying to get away from his vicious attacker. The grinding, chewing sounds Tsiyi made as he dug his teeth into the man's neck sickened Rose.

The other man pushed her onto the fallen tree trunk, where she gaped at the murky golden-brown water tumbling and roiling over huge boulders several feet below. A freezing spray spiraled up and dampened the hem of her dress.

With glaring onyx-colored eyes, the Indian sidled closer and pushed her again. Her feet threatened to slip, and she frantically gripped a tree limb that stretched out over the water. The man took a step onto the trunk but abruptly stood still and hunched his shoulders. He whirled away and pulled a knife from his belt to face Daniel, who was aiming his musket at him.

Tears filled Rose's eyes, and her heart pounded as hope leapt full-blown in her chest.

Her captor inched closer to her, causing Daniel to drop his musket, grab his tomahawk from his belt, and charge headlong up the hill.

The man's back muscles knotted up as he braced for Daniel's attack. The Catawba thrust one arm up to shield himself from the tomahawk blow and aimed his knife to slash across Daniel's stomach.

For one moment, Daniel made eye contact with Rose. When he jumped back barely in time to miss the point of the knife, she stifled a scream.

Locked in combat, Daniel struggled to seize control. The men wrestled, muscle against muscle, grit against grit, until they fell to the ground. The Catawba's head hit hard against a rock, dazing him for a moment. Daniel took advantage, freed himself from his enemy's grasp, and slammed his tomahawk downward with a lethal blow.

The Indian's skull crunched, and blood spurted from the gash. Rose froze in horror, struggling even to breathe. Daniel, chest heaving, rolled over, jumped up, and ran toward her. The moment she let go of the steadying branch, she lost her balance, and her feet slipped out from under her.

"Rose!" Daniel's shout carried over the roaring water.

She screeched, and with arms flailing, she plunged head-first into water so frigid it sucked the breath out of her. She came to the surface coughing and choking, only to be slammed against a rock.

Rushing waves spun her over and over, and only when her cape snagged on a branch—nearly strangling her before she was able to reach up and untie the string—did the spinning cease for a moment. But as soon as she was free, she whirled through a series of rapids so fast, the trees on either side of the river became a haze.

Her body was captured in a water spiral that spun her round and round until she could hold her breath no longer. She grabbed her knees and balled up in a knot, and the whorl spit her out like a wad of tobacco. Several times, she almost lost consciousness when the rocks battered her body. Somewhere along the way, limbs of fallen trees ripped off her cape and petticoats, and she lost a boot. The frigid rapids numbed not only her body but her mind as well.

How much longer could she endure?

Bruised, scraped, and beaten, Rose ached from head to toe. Completely spent, she sensed a change. A gentle current carried her like a bobbing cork toward a tree that had fallen into the water. She grabbed a limb and pulled herself toward the shore. Each movement was agony.

It took every bit of strength she had to crawl to the water's edge, where she collapsed, unable to force her tortured body to go any farther. As cool sand scraped against her cheek, the world went black.

CHAPTER 14

*R*ose was awakened by a warm, moist, spongy caress across her cheek and opened her eyes to find Tsiyi hovering over her. She tried to lift her head, but arrows of pain shot throughout her body and held her down.

Tsiyi ran up and down the beach, howling and barking so loud it made her ears ring. Someone whistled and then footsteps bounded through the woods and across the sand.

"Thank God!" Daniel knelt beside her.

She struggled to turn on her side, but it was too much.

"No, don't move. Not until I can tell if something is broken."

"My...my shoulder," she mumbled, tears filling her eyes.

His fingers, strong and warm, probed her shoulders and across her back and down her arms. She winced as he explored her lower back and down her legs.

"Nothing's broken, but there's hardly a place on you without a scratch or bruise." Anger tinted his every word.

Memories of the terrors she had endured flashed through her mind, and she began to cry, shaking uncontrollably.

Gently, he rolled her onto her back and cradled her across

his lap. "Hush, now. You've come through it. I'll keep you safe."
He rocked her back and forth.

When her shivers subsided, he sat her up and pulled off her
remaining water-filled boot and her stocking that had slipped
down inside it. He wrapped his coat around her, picked her up,
and carried her across the riverbank to a stand of trees.

Nestled in the crook of his shoulder, she huddled inside his
coat that smelled of pine needles and campfires. His chest was
warm and solid. When he laid her against a tree trunk, she
moaned, bereft at the loss of his comforting arms.

He sat beside her, popped the cork of his canteen, and held
it to her lips. "Drink. I know that water is the last thing you
want right now, but you need to drink."

She swallowed the liquid that was lukewarm compared to
the frigid waters of the river.

The river. The rapids. She trembled.

As if sensing her dread, he cupped her cheek in his hand.
"Sun's going down. Just look at the splendid picture God has
painted for us."

She gazed up at the sky, brilliant with streaks of gold,
oranges, and purples, splashing across the rolling mountains in
the distance visible through a break in the forest—a sight both
glorious and soothing.

"I must start a fire and build us some shelter."

She whimpered.

"Tsiyi will sit with you." He motioned to the dog, which
hurried to Rose's side. "He likes you, and he doesn't take to
many people."

It did not take Daniel long to build a fire near her
outstretched legs, and soon the warmth penetrated her frozen
toes.

The hound stretched out beside her, and she closed her
eyes, listening to Daniel cutting down branches and dropping
them close by. She rubbed Tsiyi's fur until she drifted off into a

haze, only to come awake when Daniel leaned the branches against the tree trunk, forming a tepee around her with an opening facing the fire. After he spread evergreens on the shelter floor, she closed her eyes again, but a sharp pain in her shoulder brought her back to consciousness.

Where is he? He's been gone too long.

As if summoned, Daniel squeezed through the entrance and sat beside her, holding two rocks and a branch with flowers that looked like bright yellow spiders. He stripped the blooms and piled them and some of the bark on one rock and smashed them with the other, adding a bit of water until he had formed a paste. He ripped a piece of her chemise that lay in tatters around her knees and doused it with water.

"This may sting." He pressed the cloth against her cheek.

She groaned. "There is no *may* about it."

He dipped his finger into the paste and grimaced. "This will truly sting."

When the concoction touched the deep scratch on her face, she balled up her fists, holding back a scream. It could not have hurt worse if he had branded her.

"Bravely done. It should feel much better in a few minutes." He frowned. "I'm afraid I must put this on your other scratches. We don't want them getting angry."

"What is it?"

"It's witch hazel. We use it for many things, including treating cuts and sores. We could use blackberry leaves, but this stings less."

"Less?" Rose uttered a harsh laugh.

"Yes, believe it or not."

With gentle movements, he spread the ointment on her arms, legs, and neck. When he dabbed some on several raw places on her scalp where her hair had been ripped out, Rose clenched her teeth until her face hurt. With her hand trembling, she reached up to touch her hair.

"Don't worry. It will grow back. Just thank the good Lord, for though it may be distressing and painful to have lost some of your hair, the strands helped me keep track of you." He paused a moment and peered outside the lean-to, where night was overtaking day. "I'm afraid we'll have to remove your wet clothes."

Eyes widening, she looked down and remembered the sharp branches that had ripped away her clothing. She now wore only her bodice and chemise. Her cheeks heated. She nodded, avoiding eye contact.

He pulled his coat from her shoulders, and she reached for her bodice laces, but her muscles screamed with the effort. She tried again but sagged back against the tree.

"I canno'. I don't have the strength."

He cleared his throat. "Let me, Rose."

She looked into his blue eyes that had grown dark, but by the firelight, she saw only concern. "I trust you, Daniel."

His hand shook as he turned her toward him. He clasped the ribbons, but they would not budge, no matter how hard he tugged. "Your stays are swollen from the water." He grumbled and tried again. "I'm going to have to cut you out of them."

He drew the knife from its sheath and slit her bodice from top to bottom. He took away the soggy garment and threw it outside the shelter near the fire.

"And now, the chemise?"

Rose swept her lashes down. She'd be naked. Modesty or health? She knew which made the most sense. She cleared her throat. "Whatever you think best, Daniel."

He moved around in the entrance to the shelter, taking off his shirt, then holding it over her head. She gulped down her panic and lifted her arms. The coarse material settled around her shoulders, providing a drape. In a matter of moments, her shift was gone and replaced with his shirt.

Taking great care not to hurt her shoulder, he helped her

push her arms into the sleeves and lifted her body enough to slide the garment under her and down over her legs. Still warm from his body, it emanated heat from her neck to her calves. A host of smells wafted from the coarse linen cloth—smoke, tobacco, gun powder, and sweat—a combination not altogether unpleasant.

As if she were a child, he rolled up the sleeves and tied the drawstrings at the neck.

"You must stay warm." He laid her back onto the evergreens and covered her with his coat. "Try and rest."

She stared at his bare chest, noting the scar that had almost completely healed. "But what about you, Daniel?"

"I've lived through worse."

"I've heard you say those words before. And I feel, after what has happened to me, I'll be able to say them too."

"That's the spirit."

"Those two men, the ones who took me... they're both..."

He held her face in his hands and gently drew a thumb underneath the wound on her cheek. "You are not to think of them. Ever again. They hurt you, Rose. We must, each of us, face the consequences of our actions."

Another thought slammed into her mind. "And my family?"

"They're fine. It seems the Catawba only wanted you this time."

He motioned for the hound to lie back down beside her and went outside. She propped up on one elbow and watched him add more logs on the fire. He sat cross-legged on the ground and loosened his hair from the rawhide string. He shook his head and dug his fingers into the strands that flowed down across his shoulders. For the first time, she noticed silver bands on his forearm and wrist and a small leather pouch hanging from a rawhide string tied around his neck.

His arm muscles bulged as he reached forward and cupped smoke into his hands and spread it over the top of his head in what Rose guessed was some kind of Indian practice. He was larger, more muscular, and darker skinned than any man of her acquaintance. Very nice to look at, as Petra had once described Wyatt.

What must Ma and Da and Nora be suffering? They would be desperately praying for her safety...for her life. How happy she would be to be held in their arms again.

Growing weary, she dropped back down and snuggled next to Tsiyi.

Daniel entered the shelter and lay down on his side, facing away from her.

"Daniel." She lifted up the coat. "Let us share the covers."

"I..." he began, still remaining on his side.

"Please. You don't want me to catch cold, do you?" she asked, feeling much less sure of herself than she sounded. "See? I will turn on my side and face Tsiyi. Then, if you slide over with your back next to mine, we will be as pieces of warm toast."

He grumbled but followed her instructions and scooted his back next to hers.

"You see. This is much better."

"Yes, Rose."

"Daniel?" The need to know more about him overpowered her exhaustion.

"Yes?"

"What is the thing you wear around your neck?"

"It's my medicine bag. A type of amulet. It contains things that are special to me."

"What things?"

"They are sacred. A secret known only to me."

Drawing comfort from the feeling of his back next to hers, she huddled closer. "Why did you push smoke across your head?"

He released a heavy sigh. "It's a Cherokee custom, a

reminder for good—thoughts, words, sounds. But it's also a way of cleansing my hair."

"Daniel?" She liked the sound of his name.

He groaned. "Yes?"

"Why not live with the Cherokee? Why a scout?"

"It was a way to make money and...to get away."

Rose tilted her head toward him. "Get away from what?"

He stiffened. "From many things. This is to be my last wagon train. I plan to return to my home in the mountains. Now go to sleep, Rose."

"Very well." She curled up next to the hound's soft fur and relaxed as the fire crackled, but it was the man at her back who kept the heat in her bones.

～

*I*n the morning, Rose awoke with a searing pain in her throat. She gasped and pressed her fingers below her chin. "Oh, it's like swallowing daggers."

She could barely pry her crusty eyes open, and she could not stop the tremors that shook her from head to toe.

Bending over her, Daniel cupped his hand to her forehead and cheeks.

When he frowned, she clasped his forearm. "What's wrong?"

"It's as I feared. You have a fever." He sat back on his heels and tucked his coat around her.

"I'm so s-sorry."

"Nothing to be sorry about. None of this was your doing." He paused, pressing his fingers to his forehead. "I'd planned to build a travois and take you back today, but you can't travel as you are. We've got to keep you warm, and we must get the fever down."

"I'm so cold and my legs...my legs are aching." Rose pulled his coat up around her neck.

"All will be well, Rose. Here's what we'll do. I'm going to build up the fire, and Tsiyi will lie beside you. There're things I need to search for—herbs for tea, fresh water, and something to hold the tea. I'll work as fast as I can—"

"How long?" Rose feared his leaving.

"I'll be within earshot. All you need do is call out, and I'll be right with you."

She clamped her teeth together, trying to stop them from chattering. "All right."

He picked up his canteen. "I'm getting the water right away." He left, but to Rose's relief, he returned quickly. "You're to drink as much and as often as you can."

She clasped the canteen to her chest. "Yes, Daniel. But, right now, I'm so very tired."

"I know you are, but let me see you take a sip before I leave."

Rose complied, then lay back down and closed her eyes. She was vaguely aware of Daniel's comings and goings. She ached all over. Each time she swallowed, she moaned, and each time, Tsiyi cuddled closer. He rested his head on her stomach, and she caressed his ears.

"What a fine lad you are," she croaked.

Daniel returned to the shelter laden with a bundle of large crinkled leaves and shavings of birch trees that he had fashioned into a crude bowl. He scooted behind her and lifted her to lean back against him with his legs sheathing her.

He held the bowl to her lips. "Drink."

She took a sip and gagged. "It's terrible. What is it?"

"It's boneset tea. Good for colds and flu. Lots of things. The leaves are used to wrap underneath bandages when someone has broken a bone."

"Ugh. It tastes as though someone left the bandages in it."

"Ha! I know. When I was a boy, I dreaded getting sick. I knew my mother would make me drink this. And I agree, it's awful, but it works. So let's get as much down as we can."

Rose managed to swallow a few more sips, but a terrible ague attacked her body, and she started to sweat. Dazed, she barely registered what Daniel was saying. For hours, she fought to remain conscious. Each time her stomach churned and she cast up her accounts, she would express her embarrassment and apologize.

"You're ill. No need to be embarrassed. You're doing well, Rose. You'll be better soon," Daniel encouraged as he bathed her face, neck, and arms with a cool cloth.

Sometime in the middle of the night, her fever broke. She fell into a deep slumber only to awaken to find Daniel lying on his back and her head nestled against his shoulder. She had flung an arm across his chest and a leg across his thigh.

It feels quite wonderful. I should be mortified. It isn't proper.

"Hang proper," she mumbled.

She thought she heard him chuckle before she snuggled against him and fell asleep.

And they hadn't moved by the next morning when a shadow fell over them, waking them.

"Daughter!" her father exclaimed, peering inside the shelter.

CHAPTER 15

*D*aniel scrambled from the shelter, to be replaced with Rose's da, who threw his arms around her and kissed the top of her head.

"*A leanbh,*" he whispered.

My child.

Not any longer. The nightmare she had lived had swept away any remnants of her childhood. And yet, when she began to sob against her da's chest, she cried out, "I want my mother."

"Hush, now." He pushed her away to look into her eyes and caress her cheek. "Ach! Your bonnie face." He scanned her arms. "And these?"

She looked at the bloody wreck of her arms and grimaced. "Briars from when they...they had me. Daniel made some salve to put on them."

He pulled Daniel's coat from her grasp and replaced it with his own that he buttoned from top to bottom. The warmth and smells of his wool greatcoat were different from Daniel's. They embodied her home, her safe place.

Her father motioned toward Daniel, who was sitting on a

log across the clearing. "So he dinna do harm to ye, lass? Because if he did…"

"Oh, no! Quite the opposite. He saved my life."

"B-but, your clothes? What happened?"

"I fell." She shuddered. "When I was with the Indians, I fell into the rapids." She shuddered again. "It went on and on, Da. I thought I would die." She gulped against the sobs that shook her. "The branches…the rocks. They tore away my clothes. And then the current carried me here."

Tsiyi poked his head into the shelter and stared at her intently.

She reached out and stroked the hound's face. "'Twas him… Tsiyi…who found me first."

"He's a fine beast. He brought us to you. No telling how long we would have searched." He held her hand. "Come, let's get you back to your ma and Nora. Fair worried they've been."

She winced. "I don't think I can walk, Da. And my shoulder…"

"We'll make a stretcher, Mr. Jackson." A voice came from outside. Rose recognized it as Wyatt's.

Da grabbed Daniel's coat. "I won't leave you but a moment," he said and crawled outside.

From her vantage, Rose watched him give Daniel his coat and then offer his hand. "Seems I owe you a great debt, Mr. Fordham."

Daniel shook his hand and then donned his jacket.

"We found your horse. And also the bodies of the Indians. You weren't injured?"

Rose shivered at the memory of her captors.

"No," Daniel replied.

"Thank God for that."

Two of the men who were part of the wagon train approached, and one pulled her chemise from the side of the shelter. "We can use this for the stretcher." He lowered his voice, addressing his companion. "Do you believe her?"

"It's some story," the other whispered back.

Rose was too exhausted to grasp their meaning and slumped back onto the evergreens.

The trek back to the wagon train was long and arduous. The men carrying the stretcher tried to be gentle, but almost every movement jarred Rose's shoulder, and soon her jaws ached from gritting her teeth. Daniel had taken the lead and stayed out of sight the entire journey. Why had he not come alongside her to see how she fared?

She had time to mull over the comments of the men at the shelter. Did they truly question her integrity? What would Ma and Nora think about her having spent two nights with a man? And the others...would they believe that nothing happened?

All those doubts faded the moment her mother's arms wrapped around her inside their wagon.

"A stór. My treasure," her mother said, rocking her back and forth. "I thought my heart would stop when I saw that savage carry you away. But the good Lord has returned you to me."

When Ma helped Rose out of her father's greatcoat and saw the bruises and scratches that covered her body, she glanced over at Nora, whose eyes widened in shock.

"My poor wee lassie." Ma clicked her tongue. "And what is this?" she asked, fingering the garment Rose wore.

"It's Daniel's...Mr. Fordham's." Her face heated.

"How did you come to be wearing it?"

The distress on her mother's face made Rose want to weep. "Please, Ma, ask Da. He will tell you. I'm too tired to talk anymore."

No one spoke while Ma tended to Rose's wounds and helped her don a clean shift. Her mother pulled the covers up around her neck and kissed her forehead before she and Nora left the wagon. Comfortable and safe once more, Rose fell into a deep sleep.

~

*T*he following days on the trail were like a shadow with nightmares that brought her awake, whimpering and shaking. Other dreams—Daniel by the fire or treating her wounds or lying beside her—woke her to unfamiliar sensations.

When she felt strong enough, she crawled to the open canvas and searched for Daniel. She saw him once on the other side of their campsite, but he never looked her way. She observed him again talking to several men, but his back was turned. Another time, she caught him staring at her, but he quickly angled away.

Why was he avoiding her? The loss of his nearness left a fierce ache in her chest.

CHAPTER 16

$\mathcal{D}$aniel and Wyatt stood together at the edge of the campsite. Daniel readied Wadulisi and prepared to scout, and Wyatt waited to join the back of the train. The wagons had traveled two days since Rose's kidnapping. About halfway through Virginia, they approached the Blue Ridge Mountains. The wagoners wore extra layers of clothing against the chilly winds blowing down from the mountains. Even Daniel donned wool socks underneath his moccasins.

"How is she?" Daniel tightened the saddle's cinch. "You must know. I've seen you at their wagon." The statement came out clipped, though he'd intended to sound casual.

"Let me make something clear, Daniel. I don't have any feelings for Rose, and she has none for me. We are simply friends. Truth be known, I'm drawn to Nora."

Daniel slipped his musket into its sleeve and checked the ropes on the bedroll. "Yes?"

"Yes."

One hurdle out of the way. He had lain as close to Rose as he dared. He'd enjoyed the feel of her, the smell of her. From her responses, she'd savored it too. But physical attraction alone wouldn't see them through the hurdles they would face as a mixed-race couple.

Did he love her? To the heights required for their marriage to succeed? Did she love him enough to leave her beloved family? Was he good enough for her? What about Rebekah? Questions and more questions. His head hurt from the turmoil.

He faced Wyatt. "But you've heard how she's doing?"

"The cuts and bruises are healing, and today she wasn't wearing the arm sling. So I gather her shoulder is better." He held out his hands. "Why can't you go over and ask for yourself?"

"It's best I stay away."

Concern creased Wyatt's face. "Can you tell me why? She's asked about you, and I didn't know what to say."

Rose had asked about him? Dare he hope she missed him as much as he missed her?

Daniel turned away, put his foot into the stirrup, and mounted his horse. "I overheard a couple of the men making remarks about what may have happened when Rose and I were alone. Hopefully, if I stay away from her, that kind of talk will die out. Besides, she suffered...a lot...and I don't want to remind her of it."

"It's not my place to tell you what to do, my friend. But I hope you're right about the talk dying down. Nevertheless, I think Rose wants to see you."

"I value your advice, so we'll talk about it more when I get back." He guided Wadulisi south to seek a good place ahead for the train's next stop. "Take care of them."

Wyatt waved and walked toward the camp.

Daniel waved back. "Come on, Tsiyi, let's do some scouting."

Tsiyi took his place to the right of Daniel, and they started down the road. For ten miles, the road was clear—no obstructions and no streams or rivers to cross. But this uninhabited part of the trail narrowed and provided few areas large enough for a campsite. He scouted the woods on both sides of the road, searching for bear and mountain lion tracks. Finding none, he sat beside a creek that ran parallel to the road, relaxed, and chewed on a piece of beef jerky.

Memories of his time with Rose in the shelter kept running through his mind—rocking her in his arms at the edge of the river, her trust when he removed her clothes and replaced them with his shirt, the feel of her as they lay together, and the way she draped her arm and leg across his body. As if she owned him.

Maybe she did.

She stirred him as no other woman had ever done.

"I need to get back to work."

He mounted his horse and had scouted a few more miles when he inhaled a sweet, metallic odor floating in the air, coming from the east. He knew right away what it was— burning bodies. He had smelled it the first time at ten years old and knew he would never forget it. Carefully, he traced the scent through the woods, where he immediately spied the moccasin prints of a large group of Indians. He tied his horse to a tree and followed the trail, keeping low and creeping between trees, until he came upon the smoking ruins of a cabin.

First, he checked the raiding party's tracks. Thankfully, they had moved farther east, away from the wagon train. Next, he reluctantly studied the ashes and discovered the charred remains of a man and a woman, who must have hidden inside when the attack came.

The sight made his heart heavy. What was their story? Why were they so far out in the wilderness...alone and helpless?

He thought of Rose and was overcome by an urge to get back to the wagon train as quickly as he could.

"Come, Tsiyi. Let's get out of here."

CHAPTER 17

One evening a week after the kidnapping, Rose joined the others who had been called together by Mr. Kimball. She and Nora huddled between their parents and held hands.

"Folks, I've got some serious news." His frown mirrored his words.

Everyone stopped their chatter. Rose spotted Daniel standing opposite her. His eyes met hers, but he kept his expression blank.

"We've been lucky so far. Except for a handful of thunderstorms that hampered our river crossings a bit, we've had great weather. Although it's getting colder by the day. We've made amazing progress, averaging ten to twelve miles a day." Mr. Kimball straightened his back and shoulders. "But, now, there's been reports of Indian attacks close by...within a mile or two."

Nora let go of Rose's hand and put her arm around her waist. Ma stepped closer to them.

Many of the wagoners voiced alarm but quieted when he held up his hands. "I know how frightening this must sound, but it's mine and Mr. Fordham's job to make sure you're safe."

I'll keep you safe. Rose remembered Daniel's promise.

"That being said, Fort Henry is a day's journey west, just over the border into North Carolina. We'll head there and remain until we feel it's safe to continue on."

"How long will that be?" Mr. McGregor asked. "It'll be snowing soon."

Mr. Ackerman spoke at the same time. "What guarantee do we have that we'll be safe there?"

Mr. Kimball held up his hands again. "I just don't know the answers. But, as I said, we'll do our best to keep you from harm."

Nora let go of Rose's waist. "Come, let's get back to the wagon. It's fearsome news, but Da is staying calm and so must we."

Not so easily done, thought Rose, as the fierce look in her captor's eyes flashed into her memory. Before moving away, she searched once more for Daniel, but he had already left.

The next evening, they passed through the gates of a massive fence made of logs that looked like newly sharpened pencils. Rose, who had never been inside a fort before, was disappointed by how rustic it was. She had expected a fortress. Instead, in the center of a huge, flat area bare of any trees stood a weathered wooden building connected to smaller buildings on either side, forming a semicircle. Two-man tents dotted the area on one side of the main building.

Only ten soldiers dressed in brilliant red coats and buff-colored pants stood to attention near the entrance to the largest building. Each carried a musket almost as tall as they were. The polished bayonets reflected the flames of the campfires. One of the two soldiers guarding the gate directed the wagon train to line up beside the fence at the rim of the yard and behind other wagons.

Once settled, the wagoners followed Mr. Kimball and Daniel into the central building. Around forty men, women, and children had assembled in the room. Many stood and some sat on plank benches or on the floor. Rose and her family and Mr. Ward gathered together just inside the entrance.

A soldier stepped into the middle of the group and shouted, "May I have your attention?"

Everyone stopped talking.

"Thank you. I am Lieutenant Taylor. I'm in charge of the garrison until Captain Williams returns with the bulk of our company. I realize you are worried about the Indian situation, but I guarantee you, Fort Henry is a stronghold that has stood the test of time. Our soldiers are the finest among King George's armies." He swept his arm around the room. "We have with us members of a wagon train as well as the occupants of Gibson's Settlement four miles away. To the right and left of this building stand barracks that can hold four people each." He pointed toward a soldier seated at a table at the back of the room. "If you would, form a line in front of our quartermaster, who will assign you to a billet. I wish you a pleasant evening."

Watching the group scramble to form a line, Ma pulled on her husband's sleeve. "Connor, there's too many here. There may be sickness. I say we sleep with our wagons."

Da looked down at her with affection. "Aye, *mo mhuirnin*. As always, you give good counsel."

The obvious love Rose's parents had for each other never failed to stir her heart. She turned to follow them out the door as Petra, standing with a group of young women, whispered something to them, and they all stared at Rose with disgust.

What must she be saying?

The next evening, as the refugees met again in the main building for announcements, a young man approached Rose and with a wink and a bow said, "Gerald Brown, at your service. How would you like to take a walk with me?" He moved to take her arm in his.

Rose slapped his hand. "Go away!"

Faster than her spluttering Da could react, Daniel strode over to the man, grabbed his arm, and shoved him outside. Two of the man's friends rushed out the door.

Wringing her hands, Rose turned to her father. "I think Daniel needs help."

"Aye, lass." Da hurried away.

Rose, Nora, and their mother huddled together, aware that many in the room were staring at them.

"What is happening? Why would that man behave in such a rude manner?" asked Ma.

"I think I know." Nora leaned in toward her mother. "Earlier, I overheard Petra talking to some settlement girls, and I heard her say Rose's name."

Heat sweeping through her, Rose scanned the room, searching for Petra. She spotted her, and against her mother's protests, she marched over and confronted her.

"How dare you talk about me, you hagfish?"

Petra stiffened. "I'm not zee one who acted zee hussy."

"You know nothing about me or what happened. Shame on you, you hateful gossipmonger." Rose poked her finger into Petra's chest. "Be warned. Stop spreading rumors about me, or you will live to regret it."

Rose's mother firmly pulled her away. "Come, dear, let us leave these people."

They started to go, but at the door, they came face to face with Daniel and Da. Daniel had a bruised cheek and black eye, and her father was dabbing his swollen, split lip with a strip of his torn shirt.

Ma bustled her husband outside toward their wagon.

Rose stood in front of Daniel and lifted her hand, almost overwhelmed by a desire to caress his bruised cheek. She scanned the room. People were watching. She dropped her arm by her side and whispered, "I'm sorry this happened, but I do thank you. Very sincerely."

He shook his head and scowled at Petra. "Be on your guard, Rose. I don't think this is the end of it."

~

*D*aniel was right. Over the next few days, Rose and her family were bombarded with such insults and slights, they soon avoided contact with the others. The boiling cauldron of vitriol frightened her. Things finally came to a head when someone punched Wyatt. That evening, he visited the Jacksons at their campfire.

"I don't understand." Sadness and worry clouded Ma's eyes. "Why would they attack you, Mr. Benson?"

"I'm afraid their hate now encompasses Nora. They are smearing her and Rose's reputations. I won't stand by and let that happen."

"My lovely, innocent girls." Ma covered her face with her hands.

Da stood, digging his fists into his sides. "That's it. We must put an end to this."

"But how?" Rose asked.

"I know a way," he responded, "but you may not like it, daughter."

CHAPTER 18

The evening following the altercation over Rose, Daniel and Mr. Kimball sat together near their campfire. The odor of smoke and wet wood from doused fires wafted throughout the compound as wagoners prepared to bed down.

Daniel puffed his pipe, cupped the smoke in his hand, and drew it over his hair. He grimaced. His fingers scraped the edge of his scalp still sore from the fight. "I think I'll do some scouting tomorrow. We must know where the raiding party is headed."

Mr. Kimball tapped his pipe against his boot, emptying out the spent tobacco. "Good idea. I'd like for us to get back on the trail as soon as possible. I don't want to fort up here long enough to get caught in the snow."

Rose's father strode their way, his face set. Daniel stood to greet him. "Evening, Mr. Jackson. How can we help you?"

"Evening. I'd like to talk to you, Mr. Fordham. If I may?" Mr. Jackson nodded to Mr. Kimball. "In private, please."

"Certainly." Daniel motioned for him to follow a few paces toward the fence and behind his tent.

"How's the eye?"

"Getting better." Daniel touched the puffy skin underneath his lashes. "And your lip?"

"Still hurts, but not as much as my heart."

Daniel stiffened.

"I canno' tell you how grateful I am to you for saving my Rose. I'll be forever indebted to you. But I'm sure you're aware of what's going on."

"I regret that I am." Daniel also regretted the worry lines digging into Mr. Jackson's face and the sadness in his eyes.

"My daughter's...both my daughters'...reputations have been sullied through no fault of their own. It's unkind, unfair, and downright unchristian."

"I agree."

"I canno' fight everyone who slights them." He laced his fingers together and spread out his thumbs. "I've prayed and searched for an answer and have come up with a solution."

Daniel sensed what was coming and braced himself.

"Would you be willing to marry Rose?"

"You don't know me."

"I know what I see. A man trusted enough to hold the well-being of people in his hands. A strong, resourceful man who could take care of my Rose and keep her safe."

Daniel folded his arms across his chest. "Are you aware of my parentage?"

"I am not."

"I'm what prejudiced, ugly people call a half breed. My mother was Cherokee and my father, English."

"'Tis of no significance to me. I judge by the heart and how a person behaves."

"You are not in the majority. If we were to marry, Rose would become a target of that same prejudice."

"I'm certain that together, you will forge a strong union."

Mr. Jackson held out his hands. "There is an attraction there, if I'm not mistaken?"

"Yes, sir. I'm very much taken with your daughter. But what does she say about your solution?"

Mr. Jackson ran his hand over his chin and looked to the heavens. "She refused to consider it."

Daniel's heart pounded. *She refused.*

"She seemed more worried about your reaction to being forced to marry her."

Oh. "I'll do it, Mr. Jackson." Daniel balled his fists at his sides. "I'll marry Rose, but I want her to know I wasn't forced."

"Seems I'm in your debt again…Daniel." Mr. Jackson put his hand on Daniel's shoulder.

"When?"

"There's a reverend among the settlers. I'll seek him out. See if he'll perform the ceremony and dispense with the banns." He held out his hand. "If so, the marriage will take place in three days."

Daniel gulped. He shook his future father-in-law's hand.

Rose will be my wife. He smiled at the happy thought.

In three days. His insides shook with the fearsome thought.

CHAPTER 19

"We must marry? That is your way out?" Rose jumped up from the chair near their campfire and waved her hands frantically. She yanked off her mobcap and pointed it at her da. "You've come back here to bring me this news?" She twisted her mobcap and paced from the wagon to the fort wall.

Da winced. "Hatchel down." The familiar, flax-weaving expression failed to settle her. "Your ma and I have decided it is what's best."

"What makes you think I would agree?"

Nora put her arm around Rose's shoulders. "If things continue as they are, someone is going to be badly hurt. Daniel? Wyatt? And what about Da?"

"What about you?" Ma asked. "We canno' protect you every minute of every day. What if one of those ruffians decides to...?" She paused, shaking her head at the notion.

Rose understood their concerns, but the removal of choices slammed down on her tighter than a loom batten. "And Daniel...why would he agree to this? Surely, he would balk at such a dire solution."

Da scraped his fingers through his hair. "I've spoken to him, and he agrees to do the right thing."

"The right thing!" Rose screeched. "But nothing happened. How many times must we say it? Please, say you believe me."

Ma stroked Rose's cheek. "Of course, dear one. But the damage has been done to you and Nora. And Mr. Fordham. We must go on from here free from any more stain or harm."

"But we know almost nothing of each other."

"There is a bond, you must admit, after what happened to you. Many marriages have been made with less. And he's a fine man, as I can see," Ma cajoled.

"Oh, Ma. I thought you would help me," Rose wailed in a voice that sounded pitiful even to her own ears.

"Enough, Rose!" her father yelled.

Rose startled. Her father never spoke to her in that manner.

"It's arranged. There's a minister among the settlers who has agreed to forego the reading of the banns due to the circumstances. It's unfortunate that Mr. Fordham is Church of England. Back home, we would be at odds with one another. But...we are not at home, and this is a new place. No matter. God will be present among us."

"When?" Rose balled up her fists and tried to stop trembling.

"In three days' time." He looked down at her and his expression softened. "All will be well."

But would it? Rose lowered her head. Was Daniel doing this only out of duty, and if so, would he come to resent her? He had said he planned to return to his home in the mountains after guiding this wagon train to its destination. To his family? And did that mean she would have to leave her own...and with a man who might not even want to take her to wife?

~

*T*he next day, Rose and her mother opened a wooden chest in their wagon, searching for the dress she had worn to Nora's wedding. They found the dark-blue silk dress gown folded neatly between lengths of linen.

"It's almost as fresh as when you wore it four years ago." Ma held the gown up to Rose's neck. "Of course, you've filled out quite a bit in the bust, but your waist is still tiny. I can take it out here...and here...and you'll have your lace collar."

The dress stirred memories of one of the happiest times of Rose's life. Had it really been four years? Nora had been a radiant bride in her pink silk gown, a perfect foil for her pale complexion and ebony hair. Her sister's beautiful smile, the one she shared only with her adored husband, had made sixteen-year-old Rose yearn for such a love.

She liked Daniel and could not deny the attraction to him that kept her pulse racing every time he drew near. Would affection and attraction blossom into an enduring love...the kind Nora and her husband had shared? The kind her parents shared? How could it, with such a strained beginning?

Rose brought out the lace collar she had designed two years prior in anticipation of her eventual wedding day.

"Oh, yes." Her mother held the collar. "This will be a lovely addition to your dress. You'll make a bonnie bride, sweeting." Her brow furrowed, and she pressed both hands to her heart. "Speaking of being a bride... We talked once of what is expected of you."

Rose brought to mind the picture of Daniel sitting by the fire, shirtless, his arm muscles rippling as he drew the smoke over his hair that had fallen to his shoulders. Her cheeks grew hot. "I-I...yes."

Her mother relaxed her hands. "That's taken care of, then."

Rose's recollection of the talk was apparently unlike that of her mother's, for the conversation had left her with only a vague notion of what *that* entailed. Of course, she had grown up on a farm and was not completely ignorant of what went on between males and females. But those were animals, and she had a notion something would be very different for her and her husband.

Would her sister be more forthcoming with advice? She thought better of it. Although still in mourning, Nora had agreed to take part in the ceremony, and Rose could not ask anything more of her.

Panic stronger than she had ever known gripped her. Was it too late to stop the ceremony? What would Daniel say? He had been conspicuously absent since agreeing to her father's solution to their problem.

"Ma, I must speak with Daniel," she announced and scrambled out of the wagon.

Outside, Nora and Wyatt stood by the fire. "Wyatt, have you seen Daniel?"

"He left the fort early this morning and didn't mention where he was going."

He has abandoned me!

Nora must have seen the dread in her eyes. "Donno' make more out of it than there is, Rose. He may have had business. Or maybe he had something he wanted to do for the wedding preparations. What say you, Wyatt?"

"I haven't known Daniel long, but long enough to know that he is a man of his word. Patience, Rose. Everything will work out."

"I can see you mean well, Wyatt. But I'm right tired of people telling me that everything will be all right. My life is changing, and I'm being granted no say so in it."

The sense of helplessness overwhelmed Rose. What was more embarrassing—a forced marriage or being left at the altar of a forced marriage? She would be an object of pity. Petra could chew a long time on that piece of gossip.

No. Daniel was a good man...a man of his word. If he wanted out of the arrangement, he would tell her and face her father directly. So where was he?

CHAPTER 20

*A*bout three miles out from the fort, Daniel came across a meadow covered in gentian flowers. The purple-blue hues mirrored Rose's eyes.

What have I done? His life had definitely taken an unexpected turn.

He looked down at Tsiyi. "But with Rose by my side, it will be a good turn. Right, boy?"

He crossed the meadow and picked up a path leading to a trading post a half-day's ride away. He reached the place near suppertime, tied his horse to a tether line, and wove his way around men camped out in the yard. Inside, he hailed the barkeep, who was handing tankards of ale to a young waitress.

"What can I get you, dearie?" The waitress grinned at Daniel.

"What's good?"

"Venison steak and sweet potatoes is halfway decent."

"Then that's what I'll have. And extra bits for my dog."

"We don't want dogs in here," the barkeep mumbled. A menacing man of about twenty stones, his face seemed etched in a permanent scowl.

Spurning the man's intimidation, Daniel rested a hand on his tomahawk. "He's with me."

The man grumbled. "Fair enough, then."

Carrying four tankards of ale, the waitress headed toward a table of men sitting by the fireplace. "Take a seat, love. I'll be out with your food in a few minutes."

Daniel pointed to a table in the corner. "We'll be over there."

The food the woman served him tasted only halfway decent, but at least it stopped Daniel's stomach from rumbling. The warm ale softened the edge of his weariness. After eating his fill of steak, Tsiyi lay beside him, observing the men coming and going.

Daniel paid the waitress and handed her an extra coin that she tucked into the top of her blouse. He perused his well-worn tunic and breeches stained with mud and dark streaks where he had wiped blood from his knife.

"Not very fit for a groom," he said to Tsiyi. "Let's get ourselves presentable."

With Tsiyi at his heels, he wandered across the tavern and into the store that took up the other half of the building.

He rummaged through a pile of light-canvas hunting frocks and found one large enough to close together and secure with his leather belt. The fringed collar-cape draped over his shoulders. The sleeves had short fringe just above the elbows. It was well made with secure stitching and should last him a while. To that, he added a shirt, a neckerchief, breeches, moccasins, patches for his old moccasins, wool socks, and a bar of beeswax and honey soap.

A pile of blankets caught his eye. On top lay an azure-blue one embellished with red silk ribbons.

"Perfect." He folded it over his arm and carried his purchases to the counter.

The proprietor had already tallied up the sale, and his wife was securing his items inside a piece of linsey-woolsey when Daniel spotted a Cherokee rivercane basket.

"This, too," he said, adding it to the pile.

He pulled his gingham market wallet from his coat. "This getting married is about to break me," he said with a smile.

The proprietor nodded toward his wife. "Women will do that to you."

"That so?" she responded. "Well, then, the basket is my gift. And God bless your marriage, young man."

Daniel tipped his hat. "Thank you kindly, ma'am."

Outside, he secured his purchases onto his horse's back and rode away, his heart a little lighter for the kindness and the blessing.

Stars had poked their way through the night sky when he reached his destination, a cluster of hot springs. He built a fire and laid out his bedroll on a flat layer of shale stone. He removed his clothing except for his shirt and slid into the mineral water.

"Ahh," he moaned, enjoying the silky warmth on his sore muscles.

Tsiyi sniffed the edge of the pool and lay down beside the bedroll.

Daniel pulled off his shirt, washed it with soap, and flung it onto a nearby shrub. Next, he lathered his hair and ducked his head underwater. He surfaced and reveled in the cold breeze that wafted across his chest and shoulders while the rest of him remained warm in the bubbling water. Lying against the side of the pool, his arms stretched out over the rocks, he gazed up at the myriad of brilliant stars. The full moon reflected on the surface of the water.

I must bring Rose here. I know she will love it as much as I.

The vision of the two of them lying together as God had made them slammed into his body. The sudden ache was torture. Should he wait to become one with Rose? Give her time? Living side by side with her...without touching her... could he wait?

Trembling with longing, he left the pool and dried off with a cloth before donning his new clothes. After adding another log to the fire, he lay down and pulled the covers over his head.

Sleep evaded him, and the first few rays of sunrise lighting the sky came as a relief.

CHAPTER 21

*T*he mid-morning sun shone brightly on Rose and her father as they paused on the porch of the main fort building.

"All will be well." Rose's father spoke softly, and escorted her to the makeshift aisle formed by people seated on bleachers, boxes, and crates. She repeated his words in her mind.

"I pray you aren't angry with me, dear one," her father whispered.

Da was so dashing in his waistcoat and crisply tied cravat. His worry that she might think less of him made him vulnerable.

"I love you, Da. I always will," she managed to whisper back.

Holding onto her father's arm, she slowly put one foot in front of the other. She clenched her bouquet of gentian flowers so hard the blossoms trembled. She had awakened to the lovely surprise basket of flowers Daniel had left at the foot of her pallet with a stirring note attached. *Today we wed. Wear these for me. They match your eyes.*

Her hair flowed down her back, loose except for the tresses

at her temples, which Nora had plaited and adorned with gentians and intertwined at the back of her head to form braid that fell to her waist.

Her mother waited at the end of the aisle. Across one shoulder, she had donned the blue-and-green sash of the MacKenzie clan. Her face shone with fierce pride echoing the MacKenzie crest, *I shine, not burn*.

To the preacher's left, Nora, beautiful in her pink silk dress, smiled her encouragement. Across her wrists she held the handfasting cloth, a length of pristine white lace, she had used at her own wedding.

Wyatt, serving as best man and as appealing as ever, smiled at Rose and winked.

Not until she approached the wedding party did she dare to turn and face Daniel. Handsome in a new hunting frock, he had draped a blanket over one shoulder. It was the same hue as her dress and adorned with stripes of red silk ribbons.

He had a dark smudge under one eye, a remnant of his recent fight. Except for a muscle twitch in his cheek, his face seemed as if fashioned in granite.

He is angry. He doesn't truly want to do this.

Nevertheless, he pivoted with her to face the preacher.

So many anxious thoughts crowded her mind, she barely registered the words being spoken. Like a puppet controlled by some outside source, she spoke the words required of her. When the pastor took the handfasting lace from Nora and motioned for Rose to extend her hand, she obliged. Daniel reached out his hand, and the pastor bound their hands together. They both pulled away at the designated time, forming the traditional Scottish knot. Two houses had become one.

The preacher admonished them that "a cord of three strands is not quickly broken." Her knees shook, and her pulse raced at the pronouncement that she was now Mrs. Daniel Fordham.

Daniel swept the blanket from his shoulder and held it over their heads, enveloping them in an intimate canopy that made the others fade away. Rose's eyes widened. What was he doing?

With an expression so intense Rose's bones seemed to melt, he spoke to her first in Cherokee and then in English. "With my mantle, I cover you. You are my *udalii*. Our paths are now one. Your joy will be doubled. Your burdens will be halved. In winter, I will warm your body with mine. In summer, we will fall asleep counting the stars in the heavens. We will instruct our children in the ancient ways. We will paddle rivers of life together until the Great Creator guides our canoe to the edge."

Standing close enough to have witnessed Daniel's vow, Nora wept softly. Rose could barely contain her own pent-up emotions. A solitary tear spilled down her cheek. Anything she might say would never match Daniel's stunning declaration.

"Courage," Daniel whispered and stepped back, removing the mantle and allowing the outside to enter again. "This is my gift for you." He removed his gold ring from his little finger on his left hand and slipped it onto her ring finger. "As I told you once, the wolf is part of my family's crest."

"I'm honored." How many other pieces of the mystery that was her husband would she uncover in the coming days?

Daniel curled his arms around her waist and pulled her close.

Caught off guard, she pressed her hands against his chest, but when his soft, warm lips caressed hers, she melted into him and slid her arms around his neck. He nibbled her bottom lip, sending waves of heat through her stomach and down her legs, which threatened to give way. A moment before she was swept into the arms of her family and well-wishers, she caught a glimpse of fire in Daniel's intense blue eyes. Goodness. What would it feel like when they really kissed?

Apparently satisfied that Daniel had made an honest woman of her, the settlers had combined their provisions to present a beautiful wedding feast outside in the compound. One of the soldiers brought out a fiddle, and another played the piccolo. Several couples formed two lines and began dancing a country minuet so like an Irish jig that Rose's da pulled his wife onto the makeshift dance floor.

Nora laughed. "Look at our parents, Rose. I haveno' seen them this happy in a while."

"Aye. 'Tis a joyful sight."

Daniel and Wyatt joined them and others who had formed a ring around the dancers. Caught up in the revelry, Rose clapped her hands and tapped her toes.

"Daniel, are you going to dance?" Wyatt asked after the first round ended.

"I'd rather be drawn and quartered."

Wyatt cleared his throat.

"Uh, that is...unless my lady wife cares to dance?" Daniel held out his hand to her.

"I would love to, but they are forming for an allemande." Embarrassing her husband wouldn't be the way to start their marriage.

Daniel cupped her elbow and led the way. "We'll manage."

Daniel more than managed. He accomplished the intricate steps to perfection. What a puzzle he was. Along with the nasal sound in his voice, she often detected the educated speech of the upper-class patrons who had purchased lace from her back in Ireland.

They performed a round and took the two steps that brought them within inches of each other. It was a flirtatious move—their faces close, their arms extended above their heads, their fingers clasped.

"You look lovely," he whispered.

They parted, then repeated their movements.

As the dance steps brought them closer, Daniel whispered, "I imagine this isn't the wedding you expected. And I regret that."

It certainly was not the wedding she had dreamed of. The guests seemed to be enjoying themselves. The food looked tasty, and the pine boughs and green ribbon table decorations added a festive touch. But she'd always thought she would at least know the man she married.

Performing the dance steps, Rose raised her arm to touch her fingertips to his. "I have to ask. Where did you learn to dance so handsomely?" The movement brought their faces inches apart. She longed to close the space between them and taste his lips. She lost a step.

He tightened his grip on her waist and brought them smoothly through the turn. "I thank you for the compliment. There's much we don't know about each other. I am more than eager to tell you."

To her regret, the music ended, and as they walked away to join her parents, Rose acknowledged to herself that she shared her husband's eagerness.

As they stood by Da and Ma, the McGregors approached Rose and Daniel to wish them happy.

"T'woulda been nice to have had the pipes at your daughter's wedding," said Mrs. McGregor.

Ma folded her arms across her waist. "Agreed, but we dunno want to break the law."

"What law is that, Mrs. Jackson?" Daniel rested his hand against the small of Rose's back.

"England considers the pipes a weapon of war and banned the use of them about eight years ago."

Mrs. McGregor scoffed. "Those caught playing them, as well as anyone who bore arms for Bonnie Prince Charlie, including my Douglas, are punished severely."

Mr. McGregor stood with his hands on his hips. "'Tis the

reason we came to this country. We pray for the day we're free from those kinds of laws...and of the king."

"Keep your voice down, McGregor. You're talking sedition," Wyatt warned. "There may be some here who agree with you, but my friend's wedding is not the place to speak of such things."

"Apologies, Mrs. Fordham...Mrs. Jackson." Mr. McGregor bowed first to Rose and then to her mother before he and his wife joined the other revelers.

Rose put her hand on Daniel's chest and scanned his face. "Some speak of a possible war between England and France over land. Now, it seems, we may be headed toward rebellion. What kind of country have I become a part of?"

He curved his hand around hers. "Whatever comes our way, we will face together. Now, let me see your lovely smile, lady wife. Today marks a new beginning."

Lady wife. The words sent joyous tremors through her heart.

Mr. Ward approached them. "My congratulations to the happy couple. I wanted you to have this as a small token of my wishes for a fine life together." He handed Rose a silver charm. "I purchased it on a voyage to the South Sea islands. It's engraved with a pineapple, a symbol for better fishing, good luck, and calm seas."

"It's delightful, Mr. Ward. I thank you kindly." Rose handed the charm to Daniel, who tucked it inside his coat.

"I considered giving you one of my hammocks but thought better of it," he said, his eyes twinkling.

They all shared a laugh until Wyatt came forward. "May I have the honor of dancing with your wife, Daniel?"

"You may, but bring her back to me quickly."

Rose allowed Wyatt to escort her to the dancers who assembled in two lines facing each other for a Scottish reel. She glanced over her shoulder at her husband. If only he enjoyed dancing as much as she.

"Thank you for your part in today, Wyatt. I'm so grateful you are in our lives." Stepping across the aisle and reaching out for his hands, she smiled at him.

"Well, if you want me to continue in your lives, you best not smile at me like that."

"What?"

"Your husband's face looks like a thundercloud."

"It truly does."

They both laughed, missing a step in the dance.

She had not long returned to Daniel's side after the dance when her da approached and made a gallant bow. "May I have this dance, my daughter?"

"Oh, Da." She gulped down a flood of emotions and wove her arm through the crook of his elbow.

"You look lovely," Da said, guiding them through the simple footwork of a country dance.

"Thank you, Da. And may I say you've never looked more handsome?"

They formed a circle with two other dancers and then pulled apart. "I'm proud of you, Rose. Not many young women could have endured what you have."

"I come from good stock."

The music ended too soon for Rose, and they stood for a moment, her da's arm resting across her back. His familiar warmth and security she had known all her life was being replaced by another. A sad, yet exciting thought.

She cupped his face. "I love you, Da."

He swallowed hard. His eyes spoke what his mouth could not.

By late afternoon, after chatting with each guest, dancing with several gentlemen, and pretending to eat the refreshments,

Rose gazed up at the clouds that glowed with a pinkish-orange color and let out a deep breath and some of the tension in her shoulders. Stress had taken its toll. Her cheeks ached from smiling. She searched the crowd for Daniel and found him standing with Wyatt. Beyond them, Nora hurried into the main building. What was she doing? Rose lifted her hem and followed.

Inside, she found her sister sitting on one of the benches. Her shoulders shook from crying.

Rose sat beside her and squeezed her hand. "What is it, dear one?"

"Please. I'm fine." Her pitiful expression belied her words.

"But you aren't. What can I do?"

"It's all of this." Nora waved her hand. "It's this dress. I truly don't want to ruin your day, but I'm miserable, Rose. When I overheard the beautiful words Daniel spoke to you during the ceremony..." She gulped. "Despite the circumstances of your marriage, I see nothing but hope and a fine life for you." She pressed a hand to her chest. "In my heart, I am happy for you. Truly, I am. But I miss my William. I miss his arms. I miss sharing my thoughts with him. I miss my baby. I've prayed so hard for courage...for peace. I don't know where I'm going to go from here. I have fallen into a hollow of grief, and I am lost."

Rose ached for her sister, but all she could do was listen and hold her hand. A shadow shifted, and Rose looked up. Daniel stood in the doorway. How long had he been there?

He strode across the room and squatted in front of them. "My words may not be sufficient, Nora. But please know, I consider you my sister now. Your unhappiness affects me deeply. You are not lost. You have the most excellent parents who cherish you, and should you decide to remain with them, I would understand. I know Rose agrees with me when I say that you will always have a place in our home, if you so choose. I would be honored to have you in my household."

Rose nodded, her throat so constricted she could not speak.

She was proud of her new husband for eloquently and gently saying everything she could not.

"You are kind, Daniel." Nora gave him a tremulous smile. "I canno' express how much your offer means. But I truly feel as if I have reached the end of my endurance...and it's frightening."

Rose and Daniel locked eyes, and her heart fluttered at the glimpse of worry in the brilliant blue depths.

"Life can be a challenge, but when faced with loved ones, it's not as daunting." He helped them from the bench and held out his arms for them to stand at his side. "Come, dry your faces, my ladies"—he caressed Rose's face with his thumb, capturing a lingering trace of tears—"and we'll brave whatever is in store."

They found their parents and stood arm in arm beside them, enjoying the music and the dancers until the sunset cast a brilliant canopy of orange across the sky.

Rose's posture began to sag. Daniel noticed, and with his hand pressed against the small of her back, started thanking everyone for a fine celebration. He escorted her away from the crowd toward the wagon where they would spend their first night together. Tsiyi tagged along behind them. The revelers called out to them, and Rose's cheeks grew hot.

As they neared the wagon, the hoot of an owl carried over the palisade wall.

Daniel stiffened, listening intently. The owl hooted again.

"Quickly." He grabbed her by the shoulders and gently shoved her underneath the wagon. "Stay here. Don't move." He motioned to Tsiyi. "Guard!"

"What's wrong?" The look on his face made her heart pound.

"Indians. I must warn the others."

CHAPTER 22

$\mathcal{W}$ith the hound pressed against her side, Rose peeked between the barrels as Daniel ran and shouted, "Indians! Take cover!"

At the edge of the crowd, he grabbed Nora by the elbow and shot a frantic glance around before he pulled her to the wagon and pushed her down beside Rose.

Rose hugged her, then crawled closer to the barrels in time to see hundreds of arrows arching over the fence and filling the sky. Flaming projectiles landed on the roof of the main building, setting the wooden shingles on fire. She gasped and covered her mouth as other arrows hit targets. First, it was Mr. Ward, then Petra and her parents, then the McGregors, then many of the settlers.

Daniel sped toward her parents, who struggled to escape the onslaught, but Rose's mother fell to the ground, an arrow piercing her neck.

"Oh, no, no, no!" she screamed as Nora scooted up beside her.

Clinging to each other, they watched their dear da bend on one knee to pick up their precious mother, only to be downed by an arrow to his back. He toppled over, covering his beloved's body with his own.

"God in heaven...please. This cannot be!" Nora yelled and then began to scream and scream and scream until she fainted.

Rose gathered her up into her arms and started rocking back and forth. Over and over, she relived the bloody scene that would undoubtedly haunt her for the rest of her life. She lay Nora down gently and returned to her vantage only to spy Daniel and Wyatt zigzagging across the compound with a rifle in each of their hands. Arrows rained all around them.

"Hurry. Hurry," she whispered, barely able to croak the words. Tension clawed at her chest and threatened to choke her. She grabbed Tsiyi around his neck and pulled his body closer.

Daniel and Wyatt reached the side of the wagon, and Daniel shoved one of the barrels aside. "Here." He handed her a powder horn and a musket. "Do you remember how to load?"

"I do."

Daniel had warned her that learning how to load a musket might one day be a matter of life and death. Never in her wildest dreams would she have envisioned loading a weapon and crouching under a wagon in her wedding dress.

For what seemed an eternity, sheltered behind barrels beside the wagon, Daniel and Wyatt fired at the enemy and passed muskets to her one after the other. Without hesitation, she loaded each one as she had been instructed. Her ears rang from the roaring volleys.

"Here they come, Daniel," Wyatt shouted. "There are too many."

Daniel captured her eyes with his and touched the knife at his belt. "I won't let them hurt you, Rose. I promise."

"I know, Daniel." She handed over a loaded musket.

A group of warriors crept toward the wagon, their faces painted black on one side with a white circle on the other.

Catawba. The hatred in their eyes gleamed as they crouched and advanced, slowly, stealthily, step by step.

Daniel fired his musket. One of them grabbed his chest, and his tomahawk flew through the air.

A bugle sounded loud and clear from outside of the fort, followed by hundreds of rifle shots.

"Soldiers!" Wyatt clapped Daniel on the shoulder. "The Indians are running away."

The chaos stilled to an eerie silence with only the *pop, pop* of a rifle in the distance.

Daniel peered at Rose between the barrels, his eyes glistening with unshed tears. "I'm sorry. I'm so very sorry about your ma and da. I wasn't able to save them."

With that, Rose began to sob. She lay down beside her sister and draped her arm over her unconscious body.

CHAPTER 23

They buried her parents beneath a stand of maple trees outside the fort. When they had first arrived at Fort Henry, Ma had remarked how the golden-orange leaves on those particular trees reminded her of Rose's hair.

The mourning party was small. Shaking uncontrollably, Rose stood at the graveside between Daniel and Mr. Kimball after the minister who had performed their wedding ceremony had spoken a few words. Tsiyi had pressed himself against her with his paw resting on her foot. His efforts to comfort her were endearing, but her despair was inconsolable. Mr. Kimball's right arm was in a sling from an arrow that had grazed the skin. Thankfully, he assured her, it was not a Catawba practice to poison their arrow tips with animal dung, so his wound should heal quickly. Wyatt had chosen to remain at the wagon to watch over Nora, who had remained unconscious after fainting.

After a brief prayer, the minister led the way back to the fort, where soldiers had dug a mass grave behind the barracks. With Daniel's steadying arm around her, they joined the mourners and watched soldiers lower the deceased into the grave. The bodies had been wrapped in various cloths, blankets, quilts, and lengths of canvas.

Of their wagon train, only seven had survived—Nora, Daniel, Wyatt, Mr. Kimball, Rose, and two of the single men. Sadness overwhelmed Rose as she recalled her encounters with the McGregors, the Ackermans, and Mr. Ward. And even though Petra had harmed Rose and her family, the vibrant young woman's life should never have ended so tragically. Memories of Rose's parents bludgeoned her, and she steeled her spine under the weight of it.

She clung to Daniel's arm as they walked away from the service. "We...each of us...began this journey with such high hopes." Including her sister, who now lay unconscious, her mind stricken by the horrors she'd witnessed. "I canno' bear it. I am undone," she murmured, pressing her hands to her face.

Daniel enveloped her in his strong, warm arms. Her body melted into his, and she felt comforted...safe.

"My heart is heavy with yours, Rose," he whispered.

His words made her tears flow even more. Finally, her crying spent, she stepped back and accepted the kerchief he took from his neck.

Survivors, many with dazed expressions, wandered around, trying to salvage what they could of their earthly goods. The sorrow surrounding them was palpable.

Daniel held her by her shoulders. "We must get away quickly. The Catawba could decide to come back and finish us. We can only take one wagon, so we should pack as much as we can in it, leaving room for Nora. Only the essentials. Wyatt has agreed to accompany us, since it is on his way to Fort McClain."

"I'm glad. It will be a comfort to have his company."

"He and I will purchase provisions, sell the extra horses, and see what can be done with the other wagon."

Da's treasured flax seeds. So much promise of a life never to be.

Rose pressed a hand to her heart. "Must we leave Ma's spinning wheel behind?"

"I don't know, Rose." Daniel searched her face and then lowered his head. "Let me see what we can do."

Going through her parents' belongings later that day was a nightmare. Familiar scents wafting up from her mother's storage chest brought back memories of her smiling and dancing at the wedding. Fingers of grief gripped Rose's chest, making it difficult to breathe.

Bracing herself, she chose her ma's favorite shawl and cameo pin and added a hairbrush and mirror that Nora would like. She placed them into a box along with her da's pipe, his game of draughts, and a pocketknife. She selected one last thing, the family Bible. She opened the cover and ran her fingers across the names inscribed over decades.

I'll have to add Ma and Da.

Would she and Daniel one day continue the list of names?

Grief and shock made the future too fuzzy to make out.

~

*E*arly the following morning, Wyatt drove the wagon out of the fort entrance. Sitting beside him, Rose waved goodbye to Mr. Kimball, who had pronounced this wagon train his last. He turned his steed onto the main road heading north toward Virginia and the farm he had purchased years ago. Daniel, who led the way on horseback, turned south onto the road that would take them to his cabin in the Blue Ridge Mountains, a journey of about five days.

"I'll sit with you a while, Wyatt, before I scoot inside to be with Nora," Rose said. "I need to be there when she wakes up. I was so pleased when Daniel told me you'd be with us."

"It suits me. It's on my way, and I truly want to see Nora and you safely to your new home."

"My new home. How strange it sounds. That I'm Mrs. Fordham now sounds even stranger."

He shot her a reassuring glance. "Daniel is a good man. Reliable. He'll provide you with a fine life."

The thought both frightened and thrilled her.

After a few miles, she slipped inside the wagon to join Nora, who lay as still as death. Rose began talking to her about anything and everything she could imagine, all the while searching for a movement, a flutter of eyelids, any signal that her sister was coming back to her.

Hours later, they stopped to rest the horses and eat.

Daniel helped Rose down from the wagon and offered Wyatt a small bundle wrapped in a piece of cloth. "It's bread and cheese. One of the settlement ladies fixed it up for us."

"It's about time." Wyatt unfolded the napkin. "My stomach was saying hello to my backbone."

Daniel handed Rose their food and took her by the elbow. "There's a nice spot up here a ways."

They stepped off the road and into a forest of pine and birch and cedar trees in myriad shades of green. Their path drew them toward the gurgling of water, and soon they entered a clearing with rivulets dancing and splashing down a rock-lined streambed. Branches of every shape, color, and size formed a canopy over the yellowish-brown stream. Some were stripped bare, while lacy yellow, orange, and red leaves clung to others. Thick layers of dark-red and brown leaves blanketed the banks.

Daniel motioned for her to sit on one of the moss-covered rocks. He rested his musket beside a tree and sat beside her. He opened the cloth and spread it out on the rock between them, along with his canteen.

"It's beautiful here. It reminds me of a coverlet my ma crocheted." Rose broke off a bit of the bread.

"Wait until you see the farm."

Rose chewed on the bread that was crunchy on the outside and soft on the inside. "Mm, this is good. Someone Irish made this soda farl. My ma...." She paused and stared at a leaf floating down the stream.

Daniel covered her hand with his.

She swallowed hard. "Tell me about your home."

"*Our* home," Daniel corrected. "It's on the side of Rodger's Mountain. Not at the top. Halfway. The cabin is larger than most. Growing up, I spent many hours watching the sun rise from the porch that wraps around it. I can't wait to show you the overlook nearby. It's a special place and means much to me. From there, you look down on a valley far below, and when you look out, it's like you can see forever. Mountain after mountain rolling away into the distance. A misty blue in the morning and purple at night. And the stars... It's like a glimpse of heaven."

My husband's a poet.

His words lit up his eyes. His face, lightly covered with whiskers, was relaxed. It was as if he was opening up a part of himself he kept protected.

"There's about three acres of farmland edged by a stream deep enough for swimming in places."

"What do you grow?"

"Corn, mostly. I plant it together with squash and beans. I plant them on the same mounds so the cornstalks support the beans and the squash spreads on the ground...holds the water and keeps the weeds away. The three sisters, the Cherokee call it."

"I'm excited to see it." Rose finished eating a piece of cheese and brushed the breadcrumbs from her lap.

A crisp breeze rushed across the stream, pushing Rose's hood from her head and sending a chill down her spine.

Daniel stood, took her hand, and helped her to her feet. "It'll get a lot colder as we climb farther up into the mountains." He secured her hood around her face. The guarded look had returned to his eyes. "I suspect we'll have snow soon. This cape won't be enough for winter. We'll have to see about some fur coats and lined boots. You have wool stockings and gloves?"

"I do."

"Best start wearing them," he said and led them back to the wagon. "There's a chest inside with extra blankets."

Later, after supper, Rose was sitting beside Nora when Wyatt greeted her from the back of the wagon. "Here." He lifted a bucket of water onto the wagon bed. "We got the water as warm as we could."

"How thoughtful, Wyatt."

"It was Daniel's idea." He pushed the bucket closer to her. "Have a good night." He ducked back outside.

Rose took a quick sponge bath and then bathed Nora the best she could. She turned her over onto her side and began massaging her back. As she kneaded the bunched-up muscles, she began to sing—Irish folk songs, hymns, a lullaby their ma rocked them to sleep with as children, anything she thought soothing.

"I pray you can hear me, dear one," she whispered. "Please, come back to me."

She curled up beside Nora and covered them with the extra blankets and fell asleep, only to awaken to the sounds of screaming. It was not until she felt herself being lifted onto Daniel's lap that she realized the screams came from her.

"Hush, now. I have you."

Rose trembled from head to toe and pressed her hands to her face to stop her teeth from chattering. "It was horrible. I-I was in the rapids again."

"Come." He jumped out of the wagon and held out his arms. She went to him, and he carried her to the campfire and laid her on his pallet.

Wyatt looked at them, the concern on his face exposed by

the firelight. He turned away onto his side and wrapped his covers up around his neck.

Daniel pulled her next to him and covered them with a blanket. Tsiyi lay beside her.

I am cared for.

With that thought, she sighed and fell fast asleep.

CHAPTER 24

The following evening, they made camp by the side of the road. With extra blankets draped across her legs, Rose huddled beside the fire, trying not to squirm. Wyatt sat nearby, pencil in hand with his sketchbook across this lap.

"Surely, there are more interesting things to draw than me." Why had she agreed to pose for him?

Wyatt frowned. "Stop fidgeting."

"I can't help it." She stretched her back. "When will Daniel return?"

"Soon, I suspect. He said the trading post isn't that far away." Wyatt put his sketches to the side, added another log on the fire, and wrapped a blanket closer around his shoulders.

Rose reached for the sketchbook. "May I see?" She sorted through the drawings. "These are excellent."

"They are rough..."

She held up a picture of Nora. "This isn't rough, Wyatt. 'Tis braw!"

"She's an easy person to draw."

"You have captured her perfectly." So perfectly, in fact, it made her wonder... Could Wyatt have a special tenderness for her sister?

He took back the drawing. "Thank you."

"And this one of Daniel..." She studied the portrait. "He's handsome. Rugged. Serious. May I have it?"

"Of course."

"You would make a marvelous portrait artist."

He stared off into the distance. "Maybe one day."

"'Lo the camp," Daniel called out from the road.

Rose's heart tripped. She was that happy to see him. She studied his every movement as he rode into the camp, unsaddled his horse, and added the mount to the tether line next to the wagon horses and Wyatt's horse and mule. He opened a bag of oats and spread them on the ground before squatting down in front of the fire and reaching his hands out to the flames.

"That was a long, cold ride." He rubbed his hands together. "Some of the folks at the trading post have sighted Catawba. I passed by many travelers who had loaded up their belongings and were heading toward shelter as far from the frontier as they can get."

Tsiyi came bounding up to the fire and lay down beside Rose, who began petting his ears and neck.

"What's our plan?" asked Wyatt.

"The horses are rested, and we have a full moon. I'd like to travel through the night. At least until we reach the turnoff to my home."

Though Daniel's voice was calm, Rose sensed the urgency of his words.

They got back on the road within an hour. The brilliant moon lit up the sandy trail ahead in an eerie glow. They rode for hours, stopping only for short breaks to rest the horses. Riding in a wagon had never been smooth, but the trail they had turned onto was apparently not heavily traveled, and each hole and bump battered Rose's already tender back. Her eyes grew unbearably heavy, and she dropped her head against Wyatt's shoulder several times.

"Oh, sorry." She sat up straight.

"Lean on me if you will, but I'm not sure your husband is happy about it." He chuckled. "He keeps looking back at us and scowling."

"Why—" She stopped and grabbed Wyatt's arm, pointing to a couple of men who appeared suddenly on horseback, coming from the road ahead. Rose's muscles tensed from head to toe. "Indians."

"Don't worry. Seems he knows these two."

Daniel approached the men and clasped each of their arms in turn. "*Siyo*," he greeted them warmly as Tsiyi danced around as if happy to see them.

Wyatt brought the horses to a halt as the men moved near and stopped beside the wagon.

"Rose, Wyatt, these are my Cherokee cousins, Gray Sky, the older, and Spotted Owl. They heard talk of a war party and have been scouting the forests near their village and our home."

Daniel had introduced them as his cousins, Gray Sky being the oldest, but he and his brother, Spotted Owl, could have been twins. Both had copper-colored skin, brown eyes with droopy eyelids, and angular noses—a combination that was at once handsome and fierce. Their heads were shaved except for a patch of soot-black hair at the crowns. Gray Sky wore three bell-shaped rings in one ear and decorated his top knot with raven feathers. Spotted Owl wore gold rings in each ear and had fastened owl feathers in his hair.

Their bodies, long, lithe, and muscular, were clothed in knee-length linsey-woolsey shirts. The sleeves were gathered at their forearms with wide silver cuff bracelets. Around their collars hung half-moon copper gorgets. Their leggings were made of fringed calico. Rose was familiar with the sturdy, waterproof fabric made from flax.

Daniel swept his arm toward Rose. "This is my *udalii*, Rose, and my friend, Wyatt. Rose's sister, Nora, is in the wagon."

Spotted Owl looked quizzically at Rose and spoke something in Cherokee. She thought she caught a word...*Rebekah*. Daniel responded, and the cousins looked at each other and shrugged their shoulders.

"It is good to meet Daniel's wife and his friend," said Spotted Owl. "And Nora?"

"She has been ill. Has not awakened for days," Daniel explained.

"Days? This I must see." Spotted Owl dismounted, went to the back of the wagon, and climbed up.

Rose swiveled around on the seat and peered inside. Spotted Owl sat beside Nora and took her hand, rubbing it gently. He spoke softly, then exited and returned to mount his horse.

"I have seen this deep sleep before. Only in ones who have suffered greatly. Maybe our Beloved Woman can help."

Gray Sky moved his horse away from the wagon. "I will go ahead to the cabin. Spotted Owl will spread the word among our village. We will make ready for your arrival."

Daniel nodded. "This is good."

"These are dangerous times, Daniel," said Spotted Owl. "You must remain alert."

Daniel nodded again, his expression grim.

The brothers waved and rode back down the trail.

"How long now?" asked Rose.

"A couple of hours." Daniel studied the sky. "We should arrive just about dawn."

As Daniel predicted, the sky was glowing a light pink when

they made a turn around a bend to a sight that made Rose gasp. Nothing, not even Daniel's descriptions, could have prepared her for the wondrous scene that greeted them.

The building, surely too large to even be called a cabin, was tucked away on the side of the mountain and backed up against a stand of cedar trees with layer upon layer of pines, oaks, and birch giants rising up the mountain behind. The sun seemed to set the tops of the firs on fire. A porch wrapped around three sides of the cabin that had a walkway to an adjacent barn.

A meadow encompassed acres of land with several fields now fallow. Harvested cornstalks pushed up through the dark-brown soil like bayonets. A stream meandered through the meadow and disappeared into a thick forest that circled the fields. And the colors—every shade of yellow, orange, and red —made her eyes widen.

Gray Sky stood on the steps beside an elderly Indian woman who was smiling and waving. They favored each other so much, they must be mother and son.

"Siyo," the woman greeted them. Her lovely smile lit her eyes and stretched the laugh lines that wrinkled her cheeks. This was someone who smiled often.

Wyatt helped Rose from the wagon, and Daniel dismounted to stand beside her. "Auntie." Daniel touched the small of Rose's back. "This is my wife, Rose. Rose, this is my Aunt Fawn."

She cupped Rose's face in her hands. "I am so happy to greet Daniel's *udalii*. Please, call me by my Christian name, Sara."

"It's a pleasure." Rose curtsied and smiled at the woman who studied her face with the most expressive dark-brown eyes. Though age had softened Sara's features and left streaks of white in her hair, she must have been quite beautiful as a young woman.

"You are tired and cold." Sara held Rose's hand as they ascended the stairs. "And you must be hungry. There's a nice warm fire, and I've prepared a meal."

Rose glanced over her shoulder at Daniel. "We must get Nora settled before anything else."

"My son told me of your sister and of your latest tragedy. My heart is heavy with yours." Sara pulled Rose inside, untied Rose's cape, took if off her shoulders, and helped her remove her gloves. She did those things with such tenderness, Rose had to fight against her sadness.

Wyatt carried Nora inside and followed Sara into a bedroom where he sat Nora on the edge of the bed. When he had left the room, Rose supported her sister while she and Sara removed her clothes except for her shift. They laid her down onto the feather mattress and pulled the covers up under her chin.

"Rest, my dear one," Rose whispered and then kissed her sister's forehead. "Have no fears. I'll be just outside."

Rose sat at the dining table that seated six and was situated in front of a fireplace as tall as Daniel. Filled with curiosity, she surveyed the room that held a willow rocking chair, a wooden wingback chair with a dark-blue seat cushion, and a footrest. A wooden worktable had been set up in the corner, its surface covered with cloth bags of sugar and flour and clay pots of various sizes that must hold spices. Bunches of dried herbs hung from nails above the table. Against the right wall and above the worktable, narrow stairs led up to a loft that spanned over the fireplace and across the back wall. To one side of the room sat a bureau decorated with framed portraits, a blue-and-white porcelain pitcher with a matching bowl, and a couple of lanterns. Above the bureau hung a shelf lined with candles that had been burned down to varying heights, along with a collection of seashells. Dark-blue curtains framed the oversized windows on either side of the front door. A braided rug in hues of blue and gray lay on the floor underneath the table. The feminine touches were undeniable.

Exhausted, she leaned her head on her elbow and watched Sara swivel an iron pot out from over the coals at the side of the fireplace and dip a porridge-looking mixture into a bowl.

She placed one of the bowls in front of Rose, who breathed in the sweet, unusual aroma.

"It smells heavenly. What is this?"

"*Kanuchi*. It's made from powdered hickory nuts boiled with rice."

Rose scooped up a bite with her wooden spoon. "Mm, it's delicious."

She finished the kanuchi quickly, scraping the bowl and savoring every last morsel. Her eyelids sagged, and she stretched her arms overhead.

"Come." Sara put an arm around Rose's shoulders and walked with her to the bedroom. "You must rest. It's been a long journey."

Just as Rose opened the door, Daniel entered the house, followed by Wyatt and the cousins.

"You're going to lie down, Rose?" Daniel asked.

Rose was so exhausted she could barely nod.

"We'll see you in a bit, then."

Inside the chilly bedroom, Rose quickly removed her clothes. She loosened the tie of the gathered neck of her shift and slid into bed next to Nora, the welcome warmth enveloping her as she pulled the covers up. It was not long before she fell asleep.

She awoke as the sunset cast an orange glow about the room. How had she slept so long?

The house was quiet. She donned her woolen socks and put on her robe and wrapped a shawl around her shoulders. A cheerful fire lit the main room and beckoned her to sit close in the wicker rocker. The aroma of rabbit stew wafted around her, making her mouth water.

The cabin door opened, and Daniel approached. "You had a good rest?"

"The best sleep I've had in ages. Where is everyone?"

"After Sara cooked the stew, the cousins took her home and will return soon. Wyatt is on the front porch, taking in the sunset." Daniel pulled off his moccasins, settled into the wingback chair, and propped his legs, ankles crossed, on the footstool. He pulled the cord from his queue, and his hair fell about his shoulders. What would it feel like, running her fingers through it?

He lit his pipe and took a puff from it. Tsiyi plopped down beside him and seemed to be studying the fire.

They sat in comfortable silence. In Ireland, her parents had often shared quiet times together before their fireplace.

Her parents. Her life had taken such a turn, she really had not had time to grieve. Melancholy pervaded her body, and she exhaled a deep breath.

Daniel raised his gaze to her. "Why the heavy sigh?"

"I was thinking of Ma and Da."

"I'm so sorry. They were fine people. Tell me about them?"

She began sharing memories, hesitantly at first, and then recollections of the times they had shared came pouring out. And, in truth, those memories were almost all filled with love and laughter and joy. They brought comfort, like wrapping up in a warm, soft woolen shawl on a cold winter's night. When she fell silent again, her heart felt lighter.

"And your parents?" Rose asked.

"My father was from a wealthy family in England. His father was a lord, but my father was the third son, so not many prospects. When he heard about the colonies and how a man could make his fortune trapping, he came over and learned the trade. On one of his trips, he met and fell in love with my mother—my *etsi*." He paused a moment and his expression softened. "Her name was Tallulah. As you know already, she was Cherokee. Well, together they made enough money to buy this land. They farmed it and shared the harvests with my mother's village."

"Where are they now?"

He put his pipe down on the table beside him and hunched his shoulders. "They died five years ago."

The stark memory of her parents' deaths silenced any words of sympathy she could have expressed.

He stared into the fire. "We share something terrible in common, Rose. I, too, saw my parents die."

"Oh, no." She held her hands out toward him.

"We were on our way downriver to a trading post. My mother and father were in the canoe in front, and my uncle and my cousins and I followed. Our canoes were full of hides from a few months hunting. It had been raining for days, so the currents ran swift. We knew that, but had traversed rapids before."

Rose's spine tingled and she leaned forward.

"A huge tree that was floating downstream...it seemed to come out of nowhere. It slammed into their canoe and turned it over. I never saw them again. We searched. But they were gone."

"My heart goes out to you, Daniel."

He leaned back into the chair. "I couldn't stay here. I took on a job as a scout with wagon trains. I returned several times during those years. The memories were painful, and I am thankful that my Cherokee family and friends kept the farm going. The job with Kimball was to be my last. It's been two years since I was last here."

The cabin door opened and Wyatt entered. He took off his coat and hung it on a hook by the door and then grabbed a dining chair and sat down between them. "You missed a glorious sunset."

Daniel took another draft on his pipe. "I'm happy to say that around here, most of them are remarkable."

Wyatt rubbed his hands together and held them toward the fire. "So what is our plan?"

Rose stopped rocking and cocked her head.

"My cousins will return tonight. Come early morning, we'll start working on the new rooms. I showed you the foundation and the fireplace that's been done already—"

Tsiyi sat up and stared at the door. Rose panicked for a moment until someone knocked and Daniel's cousins came through the doorway. They hung up their coats and sat on the floor with their backs toward the fire.

"Siyo, Rose." They spoke in unison.

"Siyo." She returned their greeting.

Daniel sat forward and leaned his arms on his knees. "I was explaining my plans for the addition to the cabin that I've been considering for a while. I sent word months ago to my cousins, and men from the village cut logs and piled them next to the barn. They gathered all the other supplies—planks, nails, tools —and stored them in other buildings."

"The snows will come soon. You can feel it in the air," said Gray Sky.

"That's why we must work hard and fast. Between the four of us, we could have the walls and roof finished in a week."

Wyatt nodded. "A week suits. After that, I'll need to be heading on to meet my surveying partners."

"Must you leave us so soon?" She liked Wyatt and enjoyed his friendship. Would his presence be good for Nora, once she recovered?

"Yes. I must. But I hope to return in a few months. Just to see how you and Nora are getting on."

"Good. I feel better about that." Rose tried to stifle a yawn. "I cannot believe after sleeping so much today that I'm still tired." She looked around at the men. "I don't want to be rude..."

Daniel stood and helped Rose from the rocking chair. "This is your home now. If you're tired, you must do as you please."

"Well, then. Good night, everyone."

"Sleep well," said Wyatt.

Gray Sky waved.

"*Osda usvi*," said Spotted Owl.

Rose smiled at Spotted Owl. She had some notion of what he had said, but she'd start learning Cherokee as soon as she could. She headed for the bedroom, followed by Daniel, who stopped long enough to pick up one of the buckets of water near the fireplace. He placed the bucket on the bedroom floor near a chest of drawers. "I tried to keep it warm."

"That was thoughtful of you. I'm getting used to sponge bathing, but I do long for a proper bath."

"I can't tell you how proud I am of the way you've come through all of this. I promise to make your life much easier in the future, Rose." He took her by the shoulders. "Try to get some rest. We will be making quite a lot of noise early on. But when we are finished, you and I will have our bedroom. We will finally become man and wife...as one."

Rose's pulse quickened, but she did not take her eyes from his. "Yes, Daniel."

"I know our marriage started out in a strange way. But if we both try, I feel we can make a go of it." He bent down and kissed her lips. "Sleep in peace." He shut the door behind him.

She pressed her finger to her lips. With the thought of sharing a bed with her handsome husband occupying her mind, how could she possibly sleep in peace? She bathed quickly and slipped under the covers next to Nora. She lay there a while listening to the muffled voices of the men. Someone must have said something funny, for they all laughed. The aroma of Daniel's pipe tobacco wafted in the air.

She leaned over and whispered in Nora's ear, "We are home, dear one."

CHAPTER 25

Someone was calling her name. Her mind fuzzy from sleep, Rose woke to find Nora sitting up in the bed.

"Where are we? I thought I heard you say we were home."

"Nora!" Rose cried and pulled her sister into her embrace. "Oh, thank you, Lord. Thank you. Thank you."

The bedroom door burst open, and Daniel and Wyatt ran inside.

As he skidded to a stop beside the bed, Daniel clutched his knife, which gleamed in the faint golden light easing past the curtains. "Rose? Are you all right?"

"Quite all right," she said with tears streaming down her face. "Nora has come back to us."

"This is the finest news." Daniel sheathed his knife and gave Rose a big smile. "We were just leaving to start work when we heard you call out." He held Nora's hand. "This is an answer to our prayers, dear sister."

"Thank you, Daniel." Nora's voice sounded faint but so dear.

He pushed back Rose's hair that had spilled out of its

mobcap and stroked her face with his thumb, drying her tears. "Can you manage while we get started?"

It was such a lovely gesture, it took all of Rose's strength to keep from turning her cheek and kissing his palm. "My heart is so light, I feel I could do most anything. You go ahead."

"I'm mighty pleased that you are well, Nora," Wyatt said as they left the room.

Rose hugged Nora to her and kissed her face over and over.

"Stop. You'll wear me out," Nora said playfully and then frowned. "How long was I...away?"

"Five days. But let's not speak of it."

"I can hardly put my mind to it." Nora shook her head and shivered. "The site of our ma and da...it's seared into my brain." Her shoulders shook and she began to sob. "Oh, Rose, our precious parents..."

They held onto each other as their shared grief overtook them. A sudden dread filled Rose. Would her sister succumb once again to the terrible sleep?

Finally, her weeping spent, Nora squared her shoulders. "I should like to get dressed. I don't want to be an invalid anymore."

Rose helped Nora to her feet and gently removed her shift.

She's nothing but a rack of bones.

She helped Nora bathe and put on a clean dress. She draped their mother's shawl around Nora's shoulders, crossed the ends in front, and tied them in the back. She quickly dressed herself before pulling woolen socks and latchet shoes on both of them. After brushing their hair with their mother's brush, they donned fresh mobcaps Rose found in one of her chests the men had stacked against the wall.

Nora's eyes filled with panic. "I feel a wee bit dizzy."

"You'll be better in front of the fire and once you've had something to eat."

Nora leaned heavily on Rose's arm as they approached the

fireplace. She groaned slightly as she dropped down into the wingback chair.

Rose lifted Nora's legs and propped them on the footstool. "Wait until you taste the kanuchi." She opened the lid of a large pot sitting beside the coals and spooned the mixture into a bowl and handed it to Nora. "Thank goodness, Daniel and the others left enough for us."

Nora ate a spoonful and sighed. "Heavenly."

"That's exactly how I described it. Aunt Sara offered to teach me how to make it. We can learn together." Her spirits soared with the thought. And the hammering outside brought comfort that her men were close.

"Aunt Sara?"

"Yes, we were joined by Daniel's Cherokee relatives. His aunt—his mother's sister—has been so kind, bringing us food and helping me care for you. Her two sons, Gray Sky and Spotted Owl, are not only Daniel's cousins, but they all grew up together here at the home of Daniel's parents. Sadly, his mother and father passed away about five years ago."

"No parents. What a terrible thing to have in common." Nora lowered her spoon.

They sat in silence while each dealt with the grief that assaulted them.

Rose cleared her throat. "Speaking of family, I must write to our cousins in South Carolina. Let them know about Ma and Da and that we won't be joining them."

"Yes." Nora bowed her head. "Things are very different than we planned. Do you wonder what became of Da's flax seeds?"

"I canno' let my thoughts go there." Rose swallowed hard and motioned to the kanuchi. "More?"

"No, I'm full. I noticed that Wyatt is here as well."

"Yes." Rose took their bowls and spoons and cleaned them in a bucket sitting on the worktable. "I don't ken when, but he'll leave us to begin his surveying."

Nora twirled the fringe of her shawl. "I'm sorry to hear that. He's a kind man." Genuine disappointment tinged her words.

"Aye. I'm happy that he and Daniel have become fast friends. And we are to call him Wyatt." She looked over her shoulder at the men's pallets neatly rolled up and stacked in a corner of the room. "This place is surprisingly tidy. They even washed their dishes. I'm beginning to realize the treasure I have married."

When there was no reply, she turned to find Nora dozing, but thank goodness, it was not in the scary, deep sleep, but rather a gentle, peaceful one. She took a blanket from the bureau and covered her sister, tucking it underneath her chin.

She rummaged through the crates and boxes stored underneath a tarp and dragged out her mother's spinning wheel.

Thank you, Daniel.

With trembling fingers, she stroked the fly wheel and the mother-of-all, calling to mind the times as a child she had sat at her mother's feet and watched her spin the flax fibers into linen while her mother's sweet voice sang a nonsense ditty...

Niddy noddy, niddy noddy,

Two heads, one body.

T'is one, t'aint one,

T'will be one by an' by.

Treasured and magical times for Rose.

Too weary to set herself a task, she passed the next few hours staring at the fire, napping, and watching her sister, who woke periodically to chat before dozing off again. Nora also woke long enough to acknowledge Daniel, Wyatt, the cousins, and Tsiyi, who came in to warm themselves by the fire and to quickly eat their meal, which they did in silence before leaving to work again.

Toward midafternoon, with a racket from the porch, the door burst open. Daniel and Wyatt came through the doorway hauling a large barrel that they placed to the side of the fireplace. Gray Sky and Spotted Owl followed them inside carrying buckets of water, which they poured into the barrel. They made several trips until the barrel was full.

"Madam." Daniel bowed and stretched his arm toward the barrel. "You requested a proper bath."

Rose laughed and clapped her hands like a child receiving presents on her name day. "I canno' believe it."

Daniel's eyes shone at her genuine response. "It will be easier to get in it if you use the footstool as a step. We'll leave you to it, then. Take your time. We still have much work to do before we lose the sunlight." He left, closing the door behind him.

Nora stood next to the barrel and dipped her hand into the water. "It's warm. Delightful."

"You go first, Nora. I know right where I stashed a bar of soap."

By the time Rose returned with the soap, several drying cloths, and clean nightclothes, Nora was immersed up to her shoulders.

"This is glorious." Nora scrubbed her hair with the soap and then ducked underneath the water to rinse. "Roses," she murmured. "Reminds me of Ma."

Not wanting to cry again, Rose avoided eye contact.

Much later, wearing nightgowns, robes, and slippers, they sat by the fire toweling their hair dry.

Nora combed her fingers through her waist-length, silky black hair. "I did not even ask what the men are building."

Rose blushed. "An addition...a bedroom for Daniel and me."

"Why are you blushing?" Nora's right eyebrow shot up. "You mean...you haven't...?"

Rose pressed her hands to her fiery cheeks. "With everything that has happened, there wasn't a proper time."

Nora's eyes twinkled. "Well. Well. Daniel doesn't seem to me to be the kind of man who would wait much longer. I'm sure the building will be finished much faster than normal," she teased. "I can see you're a bit anxious about it. Did Ma speak to you?"

Rose rolled her eyes. "In a vague sort of way."

Nora giggled and then sat up. "Wait. Does that mean the room I'm in will be mine? I'm to stay with you?"

"Of course, you goose. You're our family."

Nora choked up, and Rose sprang from the rocker, knelt, and leaned her head on her sister's lap. Nora played with the tendrils of her hair that were already coiling into curls.

Daniel knocked on the door. "All decent?"

"Come in," Rose called out and returned to the rocker.

Tsiyi, the first to enter, shook his fur furiously before coming over to sit at Rose's feet. The men removed their coats and settled themselves at the dining table. Daniel and the brothers wore deerskin leggings and breechcloths in contrast to Wyatt's homespun pants and woolen socks. They all had on linsey-woolsey trader shirts, though Daniel and his cousins had belts decorated with intricately patterned beads. Did Nora notice how good-looking each of them were? Though only one stood out to Rose.

Daniel pulled the rawhide string from his ponytail and scrubbed his fingers through the tresses. Seeing him perform such a customary gesture brought back the time she'd watched him sitting by the fire after rescuing her from the rapids. The memory awakened a disturbing yet pleasant reaction.

Gray Sky sniffed the air. "What is that smell?"

"Roses." Nora giggled. "Our mother taught us how to make soap from the flowers in her garden."

"My father used to grow roses," said Daniel. "He planted them beside the cabin near the barn. I wonder if they're still there."

147

"Wouldna that be wonderful, Rose?" Nora exclaimed. "Let's look tomorrow and see if some roots may have survived."

Rose swallowed hard. It was good to see her sister excited by something again. Like a shaft of flax that had been hatchelled over and over through beds of nails to become fine linen thread, her dear sister's natural resilience was coming back to life.

Gray Sky pointed to the spinning wheel. "What is that?"

Had he never seen one? "It's my mother's spinning wheel," Rose answered. "You take wool, or in my mother's case, flax, and spin it into thread. You can take that thread and weave it on a loom into cloth...linen...or, as Nora and I do, make it into lace."

Gray Sky's quizzical expression showed that he did not understand.

"Let me show you."

She opened several crates before lifting out the padded cotton arm over which was draped multiple bobbins attached with silk threads to a partially fashioned collar. She placed it and a piece of linen on the dining table.

"Going by a pattern we've already designed, we move the threaded bobbins over and under each other." She held up a finished collar. "And this is the result."

Gray Sky and Spotted Owl squinted at the lace. Wyatt and Daniel had also moved closer to get a better look.

She unfolded the linen cloth. "Our mother was known for making the finest cloth."

Spotted Owl rubbed the material between his finger and thumb. "Our mother would be happy to see this."

Daniel ran his hand across the spinning wheel. "This is small compared to ones I've seen in Philadelphia."

Rose stood beside him, close enough to feel the warmth emanating from his body. "My father made it especially for my mother."

Daniel looked down at her. "She was a tiny lady."

"People back home often thought she was one of the little people."

The brothers stared at each other with amazement.

"Little people?" Spotted Owl asked.

Rose was happy to explain the legend. "Yes. Men who are so small they barely reach our knees. They have beards...red...like my hair. They wear green shirts and pants. Black hats and shoes with gold buckles. Sometimes they wear green cloaks. They are known to mend shoes and often play tricks on people during the night. They hide so well no one ever sees them, but if you do, they must grant you three wishes. We call them leprechauns."

Rose chuckled at their wide-eyed astonishment and sat in the rocker as they began speaking rapidly in Cherokee.

Daniel poked the fire with a twig and lit his pipe from the flame. He took a long draught and then came over to stand beside her with his back to the flames.

"What are they saying, Daniel?" Rose asked.

"The Cherokee have little people too."

It was Rose and Nora's turn to be astonished.

"They are men...and women...who live in mountain caves. They look like Cherokee, though they only reach this high." He spanned his hand across his knee. "They are said to be handsome with hair long enough to touch the ground. Mostly, they sing and dance and drum, but sometimes they come onto people's land during the night and harvest their crops. If a hunter comes across a knife or tool in the forest, they must ask the little people out loud if they might have it. Our people tell our children about them to teach about living in harmony with nature."

"There are three kinds," Spotted Owl jumped in. "Rock People are mean and may even steal children, though they do so only because someone has tried to trap them. The Laurel

People... they make children laugh in their sleep or they play tricks—"

"When you think you have caught a big, big fish"—Gray Sky held out his arms as if measuring a fish—"but it becomes a stick! Very disappointing."

Everyone laughed at that. Rose had never heard Daniel laugh that hard. She liked the warm sound of it that came from deep within his chest.

Gray Sky continued, "The Dogwood People are kind and take care of others."

"Amazing," Wyatt commented. "That two cultures thousands of miles from each other should share such a legend." He paused. "While we're together, I want to announce that I will be leaving the day after tomorrow."

"Ach. I am fashed." How truly sorry she was to see him leave. "Husband? Do you think it a good plan for us to have a party tomorrow night...to wish Wyatt a safe journey?" Why she had addressed him in such a manner? But somehow, it felt natural.

The glint in his eyes further assured her. "Yes. It's a good plan, wife." He reached to the side to place his pipe on the mantel, exposing part of his thigh not covered by his leggings or shirt.

Rose gulped and looked away.

Nora tried to stifle a yawn. "I hate to go, but I must be abed."

"I will go too." Rose stood, but before she could reach her sister, Wyatt had jumped up from his chair and offered his hand to lift Nora to her feet.

Nora thanked him with a smile and let Rose help her to the bedroom. Daniel followed.

Saying goodnight to the men, Nora slipped into the bedroom, leaving the door ajar.

As Rose turned back to Daniel, he moved close, lifted a tendril of her hair to his nose, and breathed in deeply.

Rose's stomach quivered.

He let go of her hair and tipped up her chin with his fingertips, forcing her to meet his eyes. "Only a few more days and we will no longer have to say goodnight in this way." When she couldn't hide her panic, he touched her arm. "Do not fear, Rose. It is a part...a very nice part...of becoming man and wife. I would never harm you in any way."

The timbre of his voice was so soothing, she relaxed. "Thank you," she whispered, slipped into the bedroom, and leaned her back against the door.

Her heart pounded as visions of Daniel danced through her mind. Astride his horse. His piercing blue eyes as he held his wedding mantle over them. Pulling Nora across the compound as arrows flew around them. Sitting by a fire drawing the smoke across the top of his head.

I love him!

She could not pin down the moment it had happened, but she knew in her heart of hearts that this was the kind of love her ma had harbored for her da.

Joy flooded her body, and she hugged her arms about her. But doubts quickly overcame her delight. Daniel was thoughtful, tender at times. And yet he kept his guard up. Why?

Until she discovered the answer, she would be wise to hide her love.

CHAPTER 26

*A*unt Sara came to the cabin after breakfast with a basket full of unexpected ingredients—dried berries of many kinds, honey, hickory nuts, and buttermilk.

Nora whooped with joy when she saw the buttermilk. "Now I can make Wyatt's favorite blackberry scones."

Sara had also brought beautiful gifts—moccasins and body-length capes with buffalo fur on one side and circle patterns on the other. Rose's robe pattern and the intricate beadwork on her moccasins were blue and Nora's were red. Sara explained that on very cold days, the capes were meant to be worn with the hair next to the skin. When Rose tried to thank Sara, she let them know that Daniel had arranged for the gifts.

Rose donned her new cape and twirled around to expose the lining. "I'm going to collect some eggs. How many do we need?"

"Four, if we have them," answered Sara. "Hens might not be laying. Tsiyi scared them with his barking. Daniel called him twice to leave the barn."

Rose grabbed a basket and left the cabin, stopping at the top step to once again appreciate the view. This morning, the rising sun had tinted the sky a brilliant orange, giving the puffy, flax-fiber clouds pink-and-orange-tinted edges. The stream gurgled louder from the torrential rain that had fallen during the night.

Rose made the short walk to the barn and pushed the single-entry door to the side.

"Top of the morning, ladies," she greeted the three hens that had huddled together in their straw nests.

Just as she stepped forward to open the coop door, Tsiyi charged in, barking louder than she had ever heard him.

Daniel came running behind him and stopped in his tracks. "Don't move."

He slid his knife from its sheath and hurled it toward her. It landed next to the toe of her shoe, slicing the head from an orange-and-black-striped snake.

She clasped a hand to her heart, and Daniel strode over to her. "You're all right, Rose. Come, fetch the eggs, and I'll walk back to the cabin with you."

Tsiyi ran over to sniff at the snake's carcass, and Rose reached down to scratch his ears. "Good boy, Tsiyi. Thank you. And you, Daniel."

Inside the cabin, Rose removed her cloak and handed the basket of eggs to Sara. She slumped in a chair. Her heart continued to hammer as Daniel opened a chest that had been stored next to the bureau.

He pulled out a beaded strap and held it up. "Come here, Rose."

She stood beside him and lifted her arms as he secured the belt around her and arranged the knife and sheath on her right side. "The beading is beautiful."

"It was my mother's." He motioned to Nora. "You're next."

With a quizzical expression, Nora joined them and allowed him to fasten a knife and sheath at her waist.

He surveyed them with his fists resting on his hips. "Wear these at all times. I'll try to teach you the best way to use them."

He must have spotted the obvious panic in Nora's eyes, which led him to add, "Don't worry, Nora. You and Rose, as each day passes, will learn more about what it takes to live here. I pray that you both will come to love it as much as I. We are not to live in fear, but the wilderness can be dangerous, and we" —he motioned to Sara, who rested her hand on her own knife sheath—"all of us...must keep vigilant."

"Thank you, Daniel." Though Rose and her sister compared the beadwork on their belts, unease stirred again in her middle. These were deadly weapons they now carried. Would they ever have an occasion to use them?

"Now that you are armed, there's an important lesson I must give. Follow me," he said over his shoulder as he walked past the dining table to the right-hand wall of the cabin.

Exchanging leery glances, they trailed behind him.

"You see this?" Daniel pointed to one of the planks.

Rose stared at the place he was pointing to, then glanced at Nora, and they both shook their heads.

"It's a bit different from the rest." He pushed on the board and shoved it aside to reveal a hidden passageway. "That"—he pointed to floorboards next to the workbench—"is the trap door to the root cellar. Never, never go there if there is an attack. Indians are familiar now with them, and it's the first place they will search. This is the way."

Rose gaped as Daniel slipped through the passage and motioned for them to follow. Inside, they stood at the top of a stairway.

"There are steps that lead to a tunnel. My father built this cabin not long after the Yamasee made war on English settlers, so he added this as an escape. Pulling on this knob closes the door." He slid the door shut, throwing them into complete darkness.

"Oh, my." Nora giggled nervously.

"I'll lead." He pushed past them. "There are five steps. Feel them with your feet."

Hanging onto Nora, Rose counted each step they descended.

"I always keep flint and candles to the right here. See if you can feel them."

Rose reached out her hand that brushed over Daniel's chest.

He grunted. "Over a bit more."

She found the flint box that was now familiar after Daniel had showed her how to use it. She scraped the flint, but it took several tries before she created a spark that she blew to life on the flint cloth.

"Now, light a candle."

Rose found a candle and held the wick against the burning flint cloth. A small flame sputtered and grew until it lit the tunnel around them.

He led the way down the passage that was so small even she and Nora had to stoop.

"This will go on for a time and will end at the springhouse."

The farther they walked, the lighter the tunnel became, until the candle was no longer necessary. When they reached a wooden wall that could only be the back of the well house, Rose blew out the flame.

"If you ever have need of this passage, wait here. Listen carefully. Make sure there's no one close before pushing the wall to the side. Like this." He shoved the wooden plank entrance aside.

They entered the springhouse kept cool by a small tributary that broke away from the stream and flowed underneath the building, providing a place to store milk and food. To Rose's relief, they climbed out into the sunshine.

Daniel walked between them. "Can you remember to do this again?"

Rose nodded. She could, though she dreaded the thought of it.

Daniel turned away and left them to finish his work.

"Were you afraid?" Nora asked as they climbed the cabin stairs. "I know how you hate small, cramped places."

"I don't ever feel afraid with Daniel nearby. But I shudder to think of going through that passage without him."

That evening, the party—Aunt Sara, the cousins, Wyatt, Nora, Daniel, and Rose—sat down to eat the meal the women had prepared. Daniel, Wyatt, Nora, and Rose drank freely from ale tankards and made toasts to Wyatt, which became sillier and sillier. Sara and her sons sipped on cider and water. Gray Sky tasted cider for the first time and made such a face the others could not help but laugh. When all had their fill, the women cleared the table while the men lit their pipes.

Rose sat in the rocking chair, and Daniel scooted across the floor to sit next to her. Nora snuggled in the wingback chair and Wyatt settled on the footstool beside her. Sara and her sons sat on blankets on the floor in front of the fireplace.

"Friend Wyatt," Sara began, "there is no word in Cherokee for goodbye. Instead, we say 'we will see you again.' My sons and I have a gift for you—a song we sing when a loved one is far away."

Gray Sky brought out a rivercane flute. Spotted Owl placed a small leather-covered drum in his lap and began to tap on it with his hands. Sara began singing. Her low, melodic voice drifted through the air with a melancholy that reminded Rose of Irish tunes back home, tunes which often brought grown men to tears. Rose closed her eyes, enjoying the music and the soothing back and forth of the rocker. The song ended and Wyatt started clapping, and was soon joined by the others.

"You have a fine voice, Sara," Wyatt commented. "Thanks to each of you for the special gift."

Wyatt looked at Rose and winked. "We have another fine voice in the room. Will you gift me with it?"

Nora sat up. "Please, Rose. I only wish I had my lyre, but I'm sure Daniel considered it a nonessential."

"One moment." Rose jumped up and ran to the bedroom and minutes later returned with Nora's lyre. She avoided looking Daniel's way.

When they had decided upon a song, they began, Rose singing the lyrics accompanied by Nora's artful strumming. Nora seemed happy and her eyes twinkled. Sharing this moment with her dear sister brought Rose such joy, she felt she might burst.

When they had finished, Daniel leaned forward and looked up at Rose, his eyes glowing. "Ladies, that was beautiful. Rose, I heard you singing once when we were on the wagon trail, but you were inside the wagon tending to Nora."

"Thank you for your gift, ladies." Wyatt turned to Daniel. "And now, my friend, what is your gift for me?"

Daniel chuckled. "My gift is that I will not sing."

The others laughed.

"Come on, Daniel. What talent do you have for us?" asked Gray Sky.

"How about a story? Will that do?"

"Yes, that will do." Wyatt grinned.

Daniel put down his pipe and rose to station himself to the side of the fireplace, half in shadows in front of Nora. He stood quietly for a few moments and then began. "There was a young boy of eight summers who spent his days roaming the woods, swimming in the river, playing his flute, and making blow darts from rivercane and thistle. Upon hearing of his father's plan to take him on his first hunt, he was excited but also frightened. Would his bow aim true, or would he bring shame upon his father's house? Would the gods of hunting—Nu'nta, god of fire, and Long Person, god of the river—show favor upon him?"

The somber, low tone of Daniel's voice gave Rose chills. He was looking right at her with his penetrating blue eyes, wrapping a web of mystery around her.

"He joined his father and the other huntsmen in four days of rituals. Following their lead, on the first day at sundown, he swam in a pool of water and sang an ancient chant. The second sundown, they swam and chanted again. The third day, he fasted. A hard task, since he had never gone without food. The next day, he was happy to cook a meal and eat it and then spread the ashes from the fire across his chest. He enjoyed the meal, but the ashes itched."

Gray Sky and Spotted Owl laughed.

"Fear circled around him like a vulture, stood at his sleeping pallet, and shook him awake during the night. It was his mother who saw the fear in his eyes that had grown as wide as a spotted owl's, and she spoke of it with her husband."

Spotted Owl poked Gray Sky and nodded his head as if proud to be mentioned in the story.

Daniel held his arms out to them. "It is here that I must explain...the boy's mother was of the Cherokee. The father, though he joined in the rituals and respected the Cherokee ways, was of the whites and shared their belief in a God of three persons—Father, Son, and Holy Spirit."

Rose nodded, liking where the story was headed.

Her new husband continued. "The evening before the hunt, the father told his son of a great warrior, a young boy of fourteen, one who attended his family's sheep high in the mountains. One night, a bear came and stole away with a lamb. The boy chased after the bear, killed it, and rescued the lamb from its powerful jaws."

Rose sat up, sensing something familiar in Daniel's story.

"There came a time when the boy's people faced a great and

powerful army, among whom was a giant who stood as tall as the tallest fir tree on the mountain. The soldiers, including the boy's older brothers, were filled with terror.

Delighted that she'd been correct, she met Daniel's eyes and smiled. He returned her smile with a wink.

"But the boy believed with all his heart in his people's Great Spirit. He trusted in Him. Prayed and sang to Him in a voice as pure as the sunrise. In return, the Great Spirit granted him strength and courage and a heart as fierce as a lion. Armed with these gifts, the boy offered to slay the giant. Some laughed at him, but his king agreed."

Rose glanced around the room. Each person was leaning forward, captivated.

"So with a shepherd's staff, a sling, and five smooth stones in his bag, and armed with the most powerful weapon of all, his faith, the boy went to meet his foe. This fearsome giant came forth with his hands on his hips, looked down on the boy, and laughed." Daniel took up the stance he'd just described, then dropped his arms. "But the boy stood his ground, placed a stone in the sling, swung it around his head, and let it loose. The stone flew through the air and slammed the giant in the middle of his forehead. Conquered, he fell to the ground with a mighty rumble."

"Good," said Spotted Owl.

"After sharing this story with his son, the father took five pebbles from his pocket and gave them to the boy, who stored them away in the sacred medicine bag he wore around his neck." Daniel reached up and clasped the leather pouch that lay against his chest. Rose sighed, for he'd just revealed a small part of the secret contents. "To this day, as a grown man, when facing troubles and fears that seem as tall as the tallest fir tree on the mountain, he seeks out the place from which his courage springs."

Rose's face shone with pride as she clapped along with the others. *My husband is a storyteller.*

Wyatt stood and held out his hand to Daniel. "Thank you, my friend, for that gift. I will treasure the memory of it."

Daniel clasped Wyatt's hand and sat back down next to Rose.

"Words cannot express how much this evening...how much each of you...means to me. So I won't express it in words. I'll do it with my own gifts." Wyatt walked to the dining table and pulled something from his satchel. His sketchpad.

"Sara, Gray Sky, Spotted Owl..." He handed them each one of the sketches.

They peered at the pages and whispered among themselves in Cherokee.

"Thank you, Wyatt." Sara put a hand to her heart and showed the drawing to Rose.

It was magical to watch her friends come to life on the paper. Wyatt had not only captured their likenesses, he'd portrayed Sara's noble wisdom and sweetness, Gray Sky's light-heartedness, and Spotted Owl's fierce and generous nature. What a diligent study of character he was, even in so short a time.

"And now, Daniel and Rose." He gave a piece of paper to Daniel.

When Daniel turned the portrait toward her, his expression was so intense and the picture so surprising, she gasped and looked up at Wyatt with all the gratitude she had inside. Before her was a masterpiece, a recreation of their wedding day. Daniel, his emotions guarded, resplendent in his hunting frock and buckskins with his mantle draped across his shoulder, stood with his arm around her. She wore her wedding dress, and her hair was braided with gentians. Her eyes held an expression of hope mingled with a bit of fear.

"It's amazing, Wyatt." Choking up a bit, Rose pointed to the portrait. "And there is our Tsiyi, lying at my feet...noble and fine. If he had a voice, he would be saying 'These are my people whom I will guard with my life.'"

"And last, this is for you." Wyatt handed Nora her portrait.

She studied it for a moment. "This is how you see me?"

Wyatt nodded.

Nora flipped the paper around to show the rest of them. Nora, dressed in her nightgown, robe, and slippers, was sitting next to the fireplace, drawing her fingers through her newly washed hair. And the expression on her face...this was a lovely, delicate woman who had suffered much, but who was enduring with grace and courage.

How could Wyatt, with a few strokes of a pen and pencil, capture so many emotions and expose another person to the world with such honesty and insight?

"God has given you a great gift. Wyatt, you must pursue your art," Nora whispered.

"When the time is right, Nora."

Rose peered between them. When the time was right for art or Nora?

At the end of the evening, as Rose was about to enter the bedroom, Daniel came up to her and handed her Nora's lyre.

She started to explain. "I'm sorry. I know you had strict rules about packing only those things that are essential—"

Daniel pressed a finger to her lips. "Do not worry. Anything that brings my wife as much joy as this is truly essential."

Rose choked up. "Thank you, Daniel."

It was all she could do to close the door between them.

CHAPTER 27

$\mathcal{A}$fter breakfast, Rose, Daniel, Nora, Gray Sky, and Spotted Owl stood on the cabin steps and waved goodbye to Wyatt. Afterward, Rose went inside, and Daniel and the cousins went around to the back, but Nora remained on the porch until Wyatt rode completely out of sight.

Nora entered the house and retrieved her book from the dining table. "I might read in my room for a while."

"Enjoy your book." Rose sensed that her sister sought solace and time alone, something neither of them had experienced in months. "I'm going up to the loft. Daniel mentioned that his family's things are stored up there, and I'm curious to see what they are."

Upstairs, Rose discovered a treasure trove of trunks, crates, and wooden boxes. Beside one of the larger trunks, she found a stool that would fit perfectly beside her rocking chair. She slid it in front of the trunk, sat down, and lifted the lid. She gave a little cry, for it stored many of Daniel's childhood toys and clothing. She picked up a tiny nightshirt and a pair of moccasins not much bigger than her thumb. She laid them on the floor beside her. What a handsome baby he must have been, whose startling blue eyes would've melted his mother's heart.

She opened a piece of silk to reveal a sterling-silver baby rattle and one made from a gourd and seeds. Laying side by side, they created a poignant representation of Daniel's beautiful heritage. She unfolded a piece of paper that had Daniel's mother's receipt for molasses drops. She slid it inside her underskirt pocket.

Shuffling aside hand-sized wooden horses and a miniature bow and arrow, she found a strange object and lifted it up to study it.

"It's a cradleboard." Daniel stood behind her.

"Oh, I didn't hear you." She jumped up and faced him. Did her pulse race from being startled or being near him?

He took the cradleboard from her. "Women put their babies on the board." He turned it over. "You see, here is a foot board, and this the headboard. They place the baby inside the deer-skin pouch and lace them up with the rawhide strings. The fox fur covers the head in winter. My mother was partial to blue jay feathers, so these are for decoration."

"I love blue jay feathers too."

He plucked one from the cradleboard, moved closer, pulled off her mobcap, and put it in her hair. "There. It suits."

She patted the feather, and with her face only inches from his chest, her gaze traveled from the scarf around his neck, to his chin, to his brilliant blue eyes. Feeling bold, she glided her hands over his shoulders and around to the rawhide string holding his hair. She freed his hair and combed it with her fingers, pushing it around his neck. It was silkier and curlier than she expected. If only she was close enough to smell it.

Daniel grabbed her wrists.

Rose sucked in a soft breath. "Am I not permitted?"

His throat muscles tensed as he swallowed hard. He let go

of her and held his arms out to his sides. "Do with me as you will."

Responding to his invitation, she drew her hands gently across his forehead and over the tiny scar at his temple.

I will have him tell me how that happened.

Next, she traced his thick sable brows that curved over his eyes, now hooded from her sight. Her fingers traveled down his long, straight nose to his nostrils that flared from his heavy breathing. With one finger, she followed his sable mustache that outlined his lip. How would those lips taste—the top one thin and the bottom full with a fine bit of hair underneath? Rising up, she sought to find out. She nibbled first the left corner of his mouth and then the right.

Daniel groaned, grabbed her wrists, and captured them behind her back. He covered her lips with his and kissed her with a hunger that set her insides on fire. He released her wrists, and she wrapped her arms around his waist. He pulled away and searched her face, then nibbled at her lips just as she had done. He took several deep breaths and pressed her cheek against his chest.

"Rose...Rose," he whispered in a voice deep and hoarse.

The front door banged open.

"Where is everyone?" Gray Sky called out. "How does a man get fed around here?"

Her face flaming hot, Rose picked up her mobcap that had fallen on the floor.

Daniel helped her straighten her hair. "Up here."

She leaned over the banister and waved down to the cousins, knocking the feather out of her hair. It floated slowly through the air and landed on the floor below.

"Should we go back outside?" Gray Sky asked and poked Spotted Owl's side.

Nora came out of her bedroom. "No, no. Everything is

ready." She winked at Rose. "Especially for those who have worked up an appetite."

"Looks as though we're in for some ribbing." Daniel's eyes sparkled as he offered the crook of his arm to help Rose down the stairs. Halfway down, he whispered, "Later, my sweet Rose."

Their meal was a jolly affair full of good-hearted banter that assuaged Rose's embarrassment, but not the tingly feeling that played havoc with her spine each time she caught her husband's gaze.

~

*M*idafternoon, a wagon pulled up in front of the cabin. Daniel greeted the drivers and oversaw the unloading of a bed, mattress, three rocking chairs, a table, and a bulky, very heavy crate.

"What is all this?" Rose asked, watching the men haul the pieces up the stairs and store them on the porch to the right of the cabin.

Daniel carried one of the rocking chairs onto the porch. "Furniture for our bedroom. Also, I thought Nora would like a chair for her bedroom."

"But how did you manage?"

"Remember when we were on our way here, and I got supplies from a trading post? There was a couple selling their things for enough money to go back home to Virginia. They were afraid of Indian attacks and wanted to get away fast. So I bought all this and arranged for delivery. They hadn't been in the wilderness long, so everything is almost new."

Rose surveyed the rope-sprung bed just large enough for two. "I wondered how we would sleep."

He raised an eyebrow.

"I mean...it was nice of you to think of Nora."

Daniel waved goodbye to the men, and Nora came out to the porch.

Rose folded her hands behind her back. "Daniel?'

"Yes, Rose?"

"I know I may be asking much, but is it possible...as far as I'm aware there isn't a church nearby. Might you have enough materials to build a small chapel?"

Nora clapped her hands. "What a lovely idea. With every-thing that's been happening over the past weeks, I've neglected worship. Although, to be honest, I haven't been sure what day of the week it is."

"It would be my honor, ladies, to build you a chapel. In the meantime, let me show you the most beautiful cathedral that God himself built. Follow me."

They walked across the meadow to a pathway that mean-dered through a thick forest and ended at the edge of a cliff. Standing between them, Daniel hooked their arms through his and escorted them to the edge. From their vantage, far in the distance, mountains seem to roll over and over like a billowing blue-and-purple coverlet. A valley hundreds of feet below nestled among acres and acres of trees that had burst forth in flaming oranges and reds. Flowing through the valley was a river that sparkled like a thread of molten silver.

The magnificent sight filled Rose with such awe she felt she might burst. "I don't have the words."

"It's marvelous," said Nora. "No wonder you call it God's cathedral."

"I come here when I thirst."

Rose knew he did not mean a physical thirst. "Thank you for sharing your special place."

Daniel cleared his throat. "It's yours now."

They remained awhile and then headed back home.

Just before supper, Daniel broke through the back wall of

the cabin to create a doorway into the bedroom. He brandished a hammer. "Almost done."

"May we see?" Rose asked, resisting the urge to push back the tendril of sweaty hair that curved around his cheek.

He beat her to it, shoving it behind his ear. "Maybe tomorrow. I want to completely finish, to clean up and bring the furniture in."

After dinner, Rose and Nora sat in front of the fireplace and watched the men hang a door to the bedroom and then haul in the furniture. Nora left her long enough to show them where she wanted the rocking chair in her bedroom.

She returned and sat on the edge of her chair. "You're very quiet, staring so deep into the fire." She reached out and covered Rose's hand with her own. "The cousins plan to leave in the morning, and I am going with them."

Startled, Rose blinked.

"Sara has invited me to stay with her a few days, and I accepted."

"But why?"

Nora smiled. "I should think it obvious."

Oh. Rose gulped. Tomorrow would be her real wedding night.

CHAPTER 28

*R*ose hugged her sister and bid farewell to Gray Sky and Spotted Owl. "Thank you for your hard work. You are welcome here anytime. Think of this as your second home. And please"—she hugged Nora again and pulled together the sides of her robe—"please take care of her." Her stomach clenched. She and her sister had not been separated for a long time.

Daniel patted the small of her back. "She will be well taken care of. We have their pledge to us."

His words did not lesson the pain she felt upon letting her sister go.

Gray Sky lifted Nora onto the back of Spotted Owl's horse, slipped the strap of Nora's rucksack over his shoulder, and mounted his horse. As they entered the forest, Nora waved goodbye. The gesture released a dam of emotions Rose could not contain. She whirled around and buried her face on Daniel's chest.

He held her until she stopped trembling and then pushed her away gently. "All will be well." The words echoed the ones her father had given her before the wedding.

"You do understand, Daniel? Nora isn't only my sister, she's my best friend. She's my only link to my past, to Ireland, to my ma and da. And she has suffered so much."

"You realize that you suffered along with her, and just as much? You've taken care of her so well, I was surprised to learn that she is four years older than you."

Rose's bottom lip trembled. "She was always so delicate. It is only natural that I care for her."

"It's one of the things I admire about you."

A frigid wind blew across the meadow. Rose shivered and gathered the robe tighter.

Daniel studied the clouds that hovered over the mountains. "I think we're in for snow soon. Let's get you back inside."

Rose spent the day trying to concentrate on lace making but became frustrated with her mistakes. She dozed off twice. Her nervous thoughts about her wedding night had kept her awake most of the night prior. The thumping, banging, and scraping noises coming from the bedroom made her wonder what Daniel was doing.

Nora had already prepared their supper that sat in pots on the hearth keeping warm. Next to the pots, leftover scones nestled in a tin underneath a cloth. She was reaching for the butter bowl on one of the shelves over the worktable when she spotted a bottle of whiskey. She held it up to the candlelight and swished it around.

"Two wee drams. Maybe three for some Dutch courage."

She knocked back one drink and coughed. The potent liquid burned all the way down her throat and into her stomach and with immediate effect. Her arms became heavy, and a calm settled over her like waves rolling up to the shore. She heard Daniel coming and hastily stashed the whiskey back on the shelf.

His hair, loose around his shoulders, was wet as if he had recently bathed. "Are you ready?"

Um, no. Maybe another whiskey is in order.

"To see the addition?"

Oh, *that* ready.

"Certainly." She held out her hand and let him lead her through the doorway.

Inside against one wall was a bed with blankets and a bison robe piled on top. Next to that sat a side table with a candle and holder and a pottery vase filled with gentian flowers. A cedar chest was pushed up against the foot of the bed. Facing the bed on the other side of the room stood a fireplace, the flames dancing a merry welcome. Daniel had tacked their portrait above the mantel. Two rocking chairs, side by side, faced the fire. Tsiyi was sound asleep atop the deerskin rug lying on the floor underneath the rockers.

"It's...it's charming. More than I could have expected." She rocked one of the chairs back and forth.

"If you want to rearrange..."

"I'm not used to anything grand, Daniel. My family lived simply, but I did ken the quality of the furniture here—the bureau, the wardrobe in the bedroom, the dining table."

He frowned. "Reminders of another world." After a quiet moment, Daniel waved his hand toward a door to their right. "Now, this is something I don't think you expected."

She opened the door to another room almost as large as the bedroom. Seeing her mother's spinning wheel in one corner made her heart skip. In another corner, Daniel had placed the bathing barrel with steaming water and a footstool with a bar of rose soap. Her robe and chemise lay on a chair beside the barrel, and her slippers were tucked underneath.

"Nora helped with your clothes."

"Oh, my. I certainly did not expect this. What is that?" she asked, pointing to a black metal object underneath the room's only window.

"It's a cast-iron stove. It's the newest kind. It uses wood or coal. And you can even put a kettle on it when you want coffee. The room is for when you want to work, bathe, or"—he cleared his throat—"for a baby when we start a family."

So many thoughts raced through her mind. She visualized a workroom with a loom and shelves piled with woven linens and cords of flax fibers hanging from pegs on the wall. Or, as Daniel had hinted, a nursery. With that daunting thought, she took in the anticipation on her husband's face as he waited for her reaction.

She walked straight toward him. She wrapped her arms around his waist and pressed her body tightly to his. "It's braw and warm and homey and so much more than I deserve."

He tipped up her chin with a finger, and the gleam in his piercing blue eyes told her how much her words meant. He leaned down and kissed her with an intensity that made her legs weak. She reveled in the feel of his arm muscles against her fingers. She was lost in the smell of him...his warmth...his solidness.

He ran his tongue across his lips. "Have you been drinking, Rose?"

"I-I...only a wee dram," she stuttered.

"Dutch courage?" His eyes twinkled and then became serious. "I've said it before. I would never hurt you. Yes, we began this journey in a difficult way. But, if we try...together...we could make this a happy union."

Unable to speak, Rose nodded.

"Now, take your bath." He pulled her mobcap from her head and caressed a strand of her hair. "I'll serve our supper." He walked to the doorway. "I'll be waiting."

Rose entered the tub and lathered her body with the rose-scented soap. The warm water and aroma should have relaxed her, but failed. She stepped out of the bath and dried with a towel, then, with trembling fingers, donned her nightgown, robe, and slippers.

She opened the door to find Daniel so near, she nearly jumped back into the bedroom. Waiting, indeed.

Soon they were seated at the dining table, he at one end and she at the other—the way Nora had set the places.

"This won't do." He moved to sit by her side. "Better."

He spooned the venison stew into bowls and topped the servings with wild onions and mushrooms.

The intoxicating aroma swirled around her, and she took several sips of the broth. "Mm. This is good."

"Yes, Nora did well."

"Sara is a good teacher. She's a kind person."

"She is that. She was the one who consoled my mother the year my father took me to England."

Intrigued, Rose put down her spoon. "How old were you?"

"Fourteen and completely intimidated by the huge buildings and the crowds of people. My reception, at first, was warm. You see, I was an oddity, and there's nothing London society likes better than an oddity."

Rose tried to imagine her husband as a fourteen-year-old dressed in London fashion. He was probably as stunning and handsome as he was now.

"The newness wore off, and I began to hear the whispers... half breed. The fact that I was the mixed-race offspring of the third son of a lord didn't help."

She covered his hand with hers. "How painful that must have been for one so young."

"Don't feel sorry. I gave back as good as I got. Was in several fights. I hated that place and the pompous people with their never-ending rules for behavior. How I missed my mountains and forests. Sometimes, I would disappear, but my father knew right where to find me—in a park somewhere, up a tree. I ruined many a pair of fine pants."

Rose giggled.

"It's nice to see your smile."

When they finished the meal, Daniel started gathering the dishes. "Sara made kanuchi."

Rose pressed her hands to her stomach. "As much as I have come to love it, I can't. Let me do that." She reached for a bowl.

"No, you sit in your rocker, and I'll just put these in the bucket."

Rose settled down in the chair and pushed away the lace-making bolster. Daniel soon joined her, but instead of lighting his pipe and getting comfortable, he perched on the edge of the chair.

"Rose, I want us to always be honest with one another. Don't you?"

She nodded, but her stomach tightened. What would he say next?

"I honestly cannot wait any longer for us to be as one." He held his hands out and lifted her up from her chair. "Are you ready?"

"Aye, Daniel."

He whooped, swept her into his arms, and strode to their bedroom.

~

*H*ours later, Rose woke to Daniel standing beside the bed, gently shaking her shoulder and calling her name.

"You must see this." He pulled away the covers, grabbed her chemise from the floor, and glided it over her head. He knelt down and put her slippers on her feet.

Wearing his full-length rabbit fur coat, he led her to the front door. "Close your eyes."

Out on the porch, he turned her back to him, opened his coat, and enveloped her inside it. "Open your eyes."

Heavy flakes of snow fell in white sheets, looking much like the lace Rose fashioned. A blanket of snow covered the meadow that reflected the hazy light of the moon. Across the stream, the mountains seemed to go on forever, like layer upon layer of white cotton clouds.

She exhaled a frosty plume. "It's the most beautiful sight I have ever seen."

They watched the snowfall in silence until she turned to discover that he was naked underneath the coat. She ran a finger across the shiny line above his left breast.

He clasped her hand and kissed her fingers. "You have made your mark upon me."

Emboldened, she started nibbling along the scar.

"Back to bed, wife?" he asked, his voice shaken.

"Oh, aye, husband."

CHAPTER 29

*R*ose came to know what it felt like to be truly attuned to another person. Her deep love for her husband precluded any embarrassment or awkwardness in their coming together, which became as natural as breathing. One glance, one smile, one touch could spark their desire like a tinderbox.

They were lying in bed one evening, holding hands, when Rose felt compelled to speak up. "Daniel?"

He lifted her hand to his lips. "Yes?"

"Please...don't think I'm silly, but..." She hesitated.

He rolled up onto his elbow to scan her face.

"Well, sometimes when we are like this...well, it seems uncomfortable with Tsiyi in here."

"What?" He sputtered, clearly astounded. "He's sound asleep."

"But sometimes he isn't and...he's such a proud fellow, I would never want to embarrass him."

"Oh, Rose." He choked on the words and started laughing so hard the bed shook and tears rolled down his face.

But from then on, Daniel made Tsiyi sleep in the main

room. Once, when they were headed for bed, she could've sworn she caught an expression of gratitude in the dog's eyes. She shared that thought with Daniel and was rewarded once more with his raucous laughter.

When tending the livestock or hunting took him away, she yearned for his nearness. Even more, she longed for their times sitting together in front of the fire in their bedroom with Tsiyi asleep on the floor between them. It was during those times that her husband opened up and shared more about his youth and his family.

He seemed to take pleasure in watching her make lace and laughed when she grumbled at her mistakes. She often caught him staring at her while she was doing the most common tasks —cooking, sweeping the cabin, and mending his shirts and socks. He took particular pleasure in watching her braid her hair.

"It seems to have a life of its own," he commented one evening as she prepared for bed.

"Do you know I overheard you talking to my father about it?"

He raised an eyebrow.

"You said that the man who tried to kidnap me may have singled me out because of my mop of red hair."

He grinned. "If I recall correctly, I said '*glorious* mop of red hair.'"

She grinned back. "You're right and I forgave you."

"I also recall that your father stated that you have a temper to go with it. But I've seen no evidence of that."

"And you don't ever want to."

He snorted.

They shared this idyllic time together for a week until Nora returned. Though her presence curtailed some of their freedom, they took pleasure in searching out secret meeting places. The game added another dimension to their intimacy, for

Daniel enjoyed sharing the wonders of his world with her. She felt his gaze upon her many times as he waited for her reactions, and she never disappointed. It was evident that her husband knew and cherished every inch of the mountain, and he desired for her to love it as much as he. To her joy, they explored a myriad of footpaths.

One led to a giant hickory nut tree.

Daniel swept his arm out. "Each October, we can come here and gather the nuts—"

"And I can make them into kanuchi." Rose clasped her hands together.

"Yes," Daniel said with a smile. "We both love kanuchi, but the nuts can also be made into a soup with sweet potatoes."

Another path spilled out onto a row of spectacular climbing trees.

"That one...there... is my favorite." Daniel pointed to a tall oak. "When the weather turns warm, we can climb each of these trees, and you can choose your favorite."

Once, they came upon a willow tree that sparked Daniel to show her places to gather items for her medicine kit.

"Here, you'll find cottonwood bark for coughs and sweet gum bark for sore eyes and burns. We'll have to wait for spring and summer to harvest many of the plants you'll need, such as chamomile flowers and blackberries."

She was particularly delighted to discover the apple orchard on the property across the road. She spotted what looked like a crystal apple clinging to a branch.

"How amazing," she exclaimed.

"We call it a ghost apple. Some apples don't want to let go of the tree, and when the first frost comes, ice forms around them. The apples rot and drop to the ground, leaving behind apple-shaped ice."

One morning, the sun shone so bright, it warmed the nip in

the air and chased away the clouds, leaving the sky a brilliant blue.

"Come. I want to show you something." Daniel's expression was particularly eager.

With Tsiyi circling around them, they walked upstream along the riverbank until they came to a patch of cane. To go around it, they had to move away from the river west on a trail that wandered deep into the forest. The dense trees almost blocked out the sun, and the air became damp and cool.

"How far are we going?" Rose asked, following Daniel's footsteps. How was he so sure of a path that was undetectable to her?

"Not much farther. Believe me, it will be worth it."

Soon Rose heard the distinct sound of moving water, not like the rapids, but more like a steady, heavy rain. They came upon a waterfall with multiple tiers that started at a top level and spread in a wide, inverted *V* shape. White frothy veils of water splashed over partly shiny, partly moss-covered slate-gray boulders. At the base of the waterfall, the curtains of water emptied into a shallow pool with stepping stones crossing from one side to the other.

"What say you?" he asked in a voice raised enough to be heard over the falls.

"It's so beautiful, Daniel. It fills me with...I canno' describe it..."

He pressed her back against his chest and wrapped his arms around her. "Peace? Well-being? A sense of something far greater than ourselves?"

"Yes. All of those things."

They remained quiet, enveloped in the glorious sights and sounds and smells, reveling in the beautiful gift of nature.

"This isn't the best part." He swept her up into his arms and proceeded to walk across the stepping stones to the other side of the pool. "The water only reaches my ankles now, but in the spring, it will be deep enough for us to swim."

He put her down and led her up an incline to the third tier of the falls and a rock that jutted out from the wall.

"We have to squeeze around. So be careful. Tsiyi, stay," he ordered and waited for the hound to flop down.

Following Daniel's lead, she hugged close to the shelves of rocks that offered natural handles to grasp. Once around the outcropping, they were able to stand on a shelf that provided a breathtaking view of the forest with more wintry shades of brown, silver, and green than Rose could count. Dormant vines, still thick, crisscrossed in and out of blue-green firs, brilliant emerald-green pines, ashen-limbed birch, and massive beech trees with their dried beige leaves still clinging on.

"Now, we must stoop under this curl of water." He guided her into a cave the water had cut into the boulder.

From there, they could stand up and see through the water that tumbled out and over in front of them.

Rose laughed out loud, filled with a joy she could not contain. "It's marvelous!"

He chuckled at her response. "I knew you would love it."

But did he love *her*? She met his eyes, her heart racing, but he turned to lead her back out.

Everything seemed so right. Daniel was tender and cared for her every need, but he had not made that final declaration. Was something holding him back?

CHAPTER 30

*D*aniel stood at the precipice of his mountain cathedral and breathed in the crisp, cold air. He could not think of a time in his life when he'd felt such happiness.

Rose constantly amazed him with her talents, her kindness and gentleness. Her impish sense of humor often made him laugh out loud. He adored her curious nature and her enthusiasm for exploring their mountain and all its natural gifts. Her passion matched his, and their lovemaking took him to heights he had never dreamed of. He enjoyed her company and looked forward to their quiet times together seated in front of the fire. He missed her terribly when farm work and hunting took him away.

He removed his hat and held it in front of him and bowed his head.

"I humbly thank You, Lord, for bringing me this treasure, for she truly is worth far more than rubies. Help me to be a good husband. Grant me wisdom in my decisions. As always, I pray that You will guide me in my thoughts and deeds."

He donned his hat and started down the path to the cabin,

his heart light, anticipating spending time with his Rose. He had reached midway on the path when he heard someone behind him. He whirled to find Rebekah, his childhood friend.

Tall and lithe, with her ebony hair bound in two braids flowing down the sides of her lovely face and over the front of her deerskin tunic, she made a charming picture.

"Siyo, Daniel." Despite the soft greeting, her nut-brown eyes reflected her pain.

"Siyo."

She held her hands in front of her in supplication. "Why? Why did you abandon me?"

She looked so wounded, his heart went out to her. "Rebekah, we were never promised to each other. We shared an affectionate childhood, and I will always have fond memories." Indeed, they had spent years together as youths with the cousins, roaming the forest, playing games, climbing trees, and swimming in the river.

"Fond. I don't accept fond." She set her jaw and stiffened her arms by her sides. "You love me. I know you do. I waited years for you to come home to me. I even turned down offers of marriage."

When her entire body trembled, Daniel frowned. "I certainly didn't expect you to do that, Rebekah. I never approached the grandmothers, nor did I ever pay a bride price."

"But there was an understanding." Her voice broke, and she clasped her hands to her face. She dropped her head onto his chest, her shoulders shaking from her sobs.

The sadness in her eyes pierced him as he gently pulled her away. "I'm sorry I hurt you, Rebekah, but you must accept that I am married now. I'm bound to my wife."

She jerked her head and stared at him with a quizzical expression. "'Bound'? Why would you use such a word? Did you not marry for love?"

"Let's not speak of this anymore. What's done is done." He should profess his love for Rose, but that would surely upset her even more.

"I will not accept this, Daniel. We were meant to be together, and if there was a reason other than love for you to marry, I intend to find out."

The angry glint in her eyes concerned him. "Go home, Rebekah. Build a life of your own."

"I'm going." She crossed her arms across her chest. "But you'll see. We will be together. I will make it happen."

Daniel shook his head. "No, Rebekah. Don't come back here, unless it's to meet my wife."

He turned away and slowly made his way home, battling the thoughts that roiled in his mind.

Should I tell Rose? No, nothing will come of it. She has suffered much, and I don't want to concern her.

Rebekah had issued a warning. Something spoken in the heat of emotion? Or something to fear?

CHAPTER 31

"*I*'m going to see what's holding Daniel up," Rose called out to Nora and threw on her coat, fur side in to combat the frigid weather.

On the porch, she leaned against the railing and looked across the meadow toward the mountains that never ceased to stir something deep within her. She breathed out heavily, enjoying the cloud that formed in the air.

A movement drew her eyes to two people on the cathedral path. A young Indian woman pressed her hands to her face and dropped her head onto Daniel's chest. He took her by the shoulders and gently pushed her away. Rose's mouth dropped open, and her gaze riveted on the two of them.

After a brief conversation, the woman hurried down the path, and Daniel, his shoulders drooping, strode toward the cabin.

Who was she?

As long as Rose could remember, she'd possessed keen insight, an internal compass that guided true. That insight had stirred when Daniel first introduced her to his cousins as his wife. The announcement had clearly surprised them. Though they had spoken in Cherokee, she remembered picking up on one word—*Rebekah*.

Was that Rebekah in the woods?

Not wanting her husband to see her, she scurried back into the cabin. She leaned against the door and tried to calm her breath that came in painful spurts. Her stomach churned. She hung up her coat and pinched color back into her icy cheeks.

What should she do? It could have been a perfectly innocent meeting. Perhaps the girl was a family member upset by something. Somehow, Rose did not believe that. She would wait for Daniel to broach the subject.

What if he didn't?

~

To Rose's dismay, Daniel chose to keep silent about his disturbing visitor. His decision stung and caused her pain as intense as any she had ever suffered. As the evening wore on, her hurt turned to anger.

Daniel furrowed his brow as he assessed her. "You're quiet. Are you unwell?"

"I'm fine." Rose pushed her feet against the floor, rocking the chair faster.

He rose from a dining chair and stretched his arms over his head. "I'm for bed."

He beckoned to Rose, who sunk deeper into the chair. "I'm staying with Nora for a wee bit."

He leaned over and kissed her forehead, but she kept staring at the fire. He left, shutting the bedroom door behind him.

Nora looked up from the book she'd been reading. "Is anything wrong, Rose?"

"Don't fash."

Putting aside her book, Nora came to her and searched her

face. "I know you well. I'll no' try to make you speak of it. You'll share it with me when you're ready. Good night, dear sister."

Rose huddled in her chair, fighting against the countless emotions that assaulted her heart, shredding and tearing it apart like flax fibers. She finally fell asleep, only to feel Daniel wrapping his arms around her and carrying her to bed.

The following day, Rose's anger seethed. Her one-word responses to Daniel filled the house with tension. Avoiding confrontation, he went hunting, returning in time for supper, which they ate in almost complete silence. After the meal, he plopped down at the table to clean his musket.

"You need to put a cloth underneath," Rose snapped. "You'll get oil everywhere and ruin the table."

Daniel jerked his head up. "I've been cleaning muskets this way since I could hold one in my hand."

"Fine, then." Rose slammed one of the dishes into the cleaning bucket.

Nora, who had been sitting at the table with Daniel, stood. "I feel like reading this evening. I took one of your books, Daniel. If that is agreeable?"

"Of course, Nora. At least two of us here are agreeable."

"*Pfft.*" Rose blew out a breath, dried her hands, and headed for the rocker.

"I'll bid you good night." Nora waved goodbye at the bedroom door and closed it behind her.

"You're as cross as a bear with a thorn in its paw. Whatever is the matter? Have I done something—"

"Ha!" she interrupted, shaking from head to toe. "Have you, now?"

He sprang up from his chair. "Stop this. You're being childish."

Rose jammed her hands onto her hips. "You of all people know I am not a child."

He glanced away.

"I'm going to bed." She yanked off her mobcap and stomped to the bedroom door. "You might want to take the time to consider your actions of late."

Much later, Daniel slid into bed beside her. He reached over and splayed his hand across her stomach.

"I'm tired, Daniel," she snapped.

He lay still a few minutes before he jumped up from the bed and threw on his night shirt. He came around to her side, ripped the covers away, and gathered her into his arms. He plopped her onto one of the rocking chairs and sat facing her.

"Talk to me, Rose."

She glanced away, to the embers smoldering in the fireplace, ready to burst into flames if poked just right. Much like her.

Daniel heaved a heavy sigh. "I won't have secrets in my house."

He had poked her just right. "Really? Does that apply to us both? Or only me?"

"What?"

"Who was the woman with you on the path?"

His shoulders slumped. "You saw?"

"So you're not even going to deny it?"

"Her name is Rebekah. We've known each other since we were children."

As she had thought. "And?"

He ran his hand through his hair. "Up until my parents died, many assumed...even me...that we would marry."

His words hurt so much. Near tears, Rose gulped. "Then I came along and spoiled everything for you." He reached for her hand, but she pulled away. "Do you love her?"

"Yes, but—"

He was cut off by a loud banging at the front door.

"Daniel!" Gray Sky yelled from outside.

After a split second when she tried and failed to process her husband's response, Rose tossed on a robe and rushed to open the door with Daniel. Nora, her face flushed from sleep, came out of her bedroom, throwing a shawl over her nightgown.

Gray Sky and Spotted Owl hurried inside, their faces etched with worry, their chests heaving from exertion.

"Our women have been taken," Gray Sky blurted.

Daniel startled. "Who took them?"

"Slavers. Maybe." Gray Sky rested his hand on the tomahawk in his belt. "We're not sure."

A muscle in Daniel's jaw twitched. "When?"

"An hour ago. Many of our men are on a hunting party and won't return for days. The ones not staying to guard the village have gone to search. We need you to lead us, my friend."

Daniel hurried to the bedroom while, in the front room, Rose raced around gathering anything she thought might be of use.

"Can I help, Rose?" Nora tied the ends of her shawl together.

"Fetch one of those rucksacks from the hooks over there." Rose filled a canteen from their water bucket.

She and Nora stuffed the sack with the canteen, jerky, biscuits, and whatever food they could find.

Daniel reappeared, dressed and sporting his hatchet, powder horn, and an extra knife. "How many were taken?" he asked, grabbing a musket and pulling his coat from a peg.

"Five," Gray Sky answered. "Adsila, Dyani, Catori—she is only twelve, Daniel."

Daniel clenched his jaw.

"Spotted Owl's intended, Odina." He paused. "And Rebekah."

Daniel shot a glance at Rose, who struggled with memories of her own kidnapping. He strode over to her and caressed her cheek. "Wear your knife. Keep muskets close by. Be alert. I'll have someone from the village check on you." He bent down, searched her eyes, and kissed her. "We must talk when I return."

She clasped the front of his coat. "Don't think o' me. Find those women. May God grant you safe travels."

He and the cousins hurried away with Tsiyi close behind. Rose stood on the porch until the men rode out of sight, a prayer on her lips.

CHAPTER 32

*B*efore entering the forest, Daniel made the mistake of looking back at the cabin where Rose huddled with Nora in the doorway. Their interrupted conversation had shattered her and dimmed some of the light in her eyes.

Why hadn't he explained? Yes, he had been caught up in the urgency of rescuing the kidnapped women. Every moment counted. But he should have taken time for Rose. *I love you with all my heart, my precious wife.* Speaking those words could have allayed her misgivings about Rebekah. And yet he had never done so. He had shown his love in a thousand different ways but had failed to express it.

What an idiot.

Part of him longed to turn around, but thoughts of the terrified women held him in check, and he prodded his horse into a gallop.

At the edge of the village, Daniel, Gray Sky, and Spotted Owl, traveling with five others, picked up the trail of the kidnappers.

Gray Sky pointed to hoof and footprints. "Looks to be about

four of them. They're on horseback and forcing the women to walk."

Tsiyi left Daniel's side and sniffed at the prints.

"Agreed," said Daniel. "They've got more than an hour's head start but can't travel fast with the women. Thank God for the full moon. We may have a chance of catching up."

Unfortunately, a couple of miles from the village, they found evidence that the group had divided—one, including two of the women, moved north, and the other, with the remaining women, traveled west.

Daniel rested a knee across his saddle. "We'll split up— Gray Sky and Spotted Owl with me. We'll go west. Leave trail markers—three stones, branches, notches on trees. If either of us comes across something, send a rider to find the others."

Gray Sky switched his horse's reins from hand to hand. "And if we do find them? What do we do with the kidnappers?"

"Frankly, I don't care." Daniel raised his voice. "We've no official law to hand them over to. They reap what they sow. It's the women we need to worry about."

With that uppermost in Daniel's mind, he joined the cousins in their trek west. The farther into the mountains they rode, the colder the weather. Many times, the way grew so treacherous, they had to dismount and lead the horses.

After four days on the search, the first pale-pink rays of the sunrise had colored the forest when they came to a stream.

Gray Sky pointed to rocks that had rolled down the embankment. "They crossed here."

"Let's stop." Daniel dismounted. "Our horses need rest."

"The kidnappers haven't stopped. The women must be exhausted." Spotted Owl drank heavily from his canteen. "From the tracks, one stumbled and fell. How long will the men put up with it?"

His words reminded Daniel of tracking Rose and her kidnappers and how many times they had punished her for falling. He pulled jerky and biscuits from his rucksack and handed them to the cousins and fed pieces to Tsiyi.

What was Rose doing? Sitting in front of the fire in their bedroom brushing her hair? Making her morning coffee? Had he hurt her even more by hurrying off to track his former sweetheart?

Even if he had, even if she'd been angry and confused, she had rushed to gather everything he might need for the journey. Bless her. He didn't deserve that precious woman. But he'd spend the rest of his days making sure she knew how much he loved her.

"You're deep in thought, Daniel," Gray Sky observed, feeding the horses leftover biscuits and some of the oats he carried with him.

"Thinking about my wife. Hoping we find our women soon, and I can go back home."

Spotted Owl mounted his horse. "Let's get back on the trail."

"Sorry, Spotted Owl. I've been thinking only of myself. Rose was taken from the wagon train by Catawba, so I know some of the pain you're feeling about Odina."

Spotted Owl set his jaw and prodded his horse across the stream. "I'll hunt for supper. Catch up with you."

He returned soon after with two rabbits tied to his belt. "I'll gut them when we stop."

Hours later, after riding another ten miles or so, they came across a small farmstead.

"'Lo the cabin," Daniel called out.

Tsiyi moved toward the rickety building.

"Stay," Daniel ordered.

A young woman came to the door holding the hand of a toddler. Angry red spots covered their emaciated faces. They both had beads of sweat on their foreheads, and their cheeks had turned blood red from fever.

"Don't come no closer. We got smallpox here," said the woman, rubbing one bare foot across the other.

"Where's your husband, missus?" Daniel asked, searching his rucksack for food he could share.

"Mrs. Kelly. And my husband left out for hunting this morning."

Spotted Owl dismounted and offered the rabbits. "Here, ma'am. You need them more than us." When she hesitated to come forward, he added, "Do not worry. We had the pox as children."

Her eyes filled with tears as she accepted his offering. "Thank you."

"I wish we could do more." Daniel secured the rucksack on the back of the saddle. "Have you seen a group of people...two men and three Indian women?"

She picked up her little boy and wrapped her tattered shawl about them. "Yes, they was here a few hours ago. Didn't heed my warning about the pox and came busting in here looking for food. My young'un was crying, and one of the women picked him up. She put him down real quick when one of the men slapped her. I was glad to see 'em leave."

Daniel shared a glance with Gray Sky. "Thank you, Mrs. Kelly. I hope you and your son get well fast."

After leaving the settlers' cabin, they had traveled hours when dark clouds covered the sun and a misty rain started to fall.

"Where do you think they're headed?" asked Gray Sky, his voice full of frustration.

Daniel guided his horse across a stream and up an embankment. "My guess is the Ohio Valley. There's lots of trappers and hunters working the frontier. Many need a wife or helper and are willing to pay whatever it takes." He pulled a piece of canvas from his saddlebag. "We've got to stop."

Spotted Owl tugged his coat up around his neck. "This rain will wipe out tracks."

"I know, but we'll sort that out once we've had some rest. Besides, it'll be night soon, and with no moon to help, we might lose the tracks, anyway."

After securing the horses, they tied the corners of the canvas to trees and sat on the ground underneath its shelter.

Daniel lay back, covered his face with his hat, and motioned for Tsiyi to join him. "Try to sleep. We'll get moving again first thing in the morning."

They rose before the sun, but the rain had erased any traces of the kidnapping party.

After two more days of futile searching, zig-zagging through forests, following Indian trails, and backtracking for any signs, Daniel wondered if they would ever see the women again. Moving north, they had left North Carolina and had skirted around the foothills of the Allegheny Mountains. He had been away from Rose ten days, and his longing for her multiplied with each day that passed.

"Look! Here!" Gray Sky called and pointed to the ground. "Three pairs of moccasin prints. Where are the horses?"

Daniel jumped off his horse and studied the footprints. "You reckon the women escaped somehow?"

Gray Sky rocked in his saddle and peered through the woods ahead. "Don't make sense."

"They're close, I can feel it." Spotted Owl prodded his horse and followed the fresh tracks.

A couple of hours later, they came upon a derelict cabin with vines growing into the windows, and the door that had fallen from its hinges lay on the ground. Coughing came from inside. Tsiyi growled, and the fur stood up on his back.

Daniel slid from his horse, pulled his knife, and crept toward the open doorway. Spotted Owl and Gray Sky shadowed him. Daniel peered inside, and once his eyes adjusted to the dark, he saw Dyani, Catori, and Rebekah huddled together on the dirt floor, so quiet they barely breathed.

Rebekah lifted her head and squinted. "Daniel? Is it really you?"

Inside, Daniel knelt beside them, and his chest tightened. They weren't not rising because they were exhausted, but because they were raging with fever.

Gray Sky pounded his fist against the doorway. "The pox."

"Get water." Daniel, too, balled his hands up and ached to hit something...anything.

Spotted Owl disappeared a moment, then came running back and held the canteen for each of the women to drink their fill. Dyani clasped the canteen against her breast and refused to let it go.

Daniel cleared his throat at the pitiful gesture. "We'll be right back." Outside, he approached the cousins. "We'll need to build a fire. Get them warm and dry again."

Spotted Owl released a huff. "Those animals left them to die out here."

Daniel grimaced. "This isn't the time for anger. We must build up their strength."

"How?" Gray Sky asked.

Daniel scanned the woods. "We need something for broth —rabbit, squirrel, turkey."

"I'll do that." Gray Sky mounted his horse and rode away.

"We need birch bark shavings to fashion bowls."

Spotted Owl nodded. "I saw some not far away."

"I'll gather firewood and look for limbs and branches to make travoises."

Daniel entered the cabin once more, where the women sat up and stared at him with such hope it made his heart ache. "Dyani, Catori, Rebekah, we're going to take you home. But first, we have to get you well enough to travel."

They blinked at him, obviously too tired and too sick to stand.

"Don't worry. I'll be outside getting wood for a fire." There were enough holes in the dilapidated roof to draft the smoke. "If you need me, call out. And Tsiyi will guard you." He motioned for the dog to sit at the door.

Outside, shaken, he leaned against a tree and took deep breaths.

Thank you, Lord, for bringing us here. Help us get them home, please.

Though he and his cousins should be immune to the disease, how long would nursing the women back to health take? They couldn't risk taking them back to the village. Given the way he'd left Rose, was every day apart from her slowly widening the gulf between them?

Regardless, he had no choice. He mustered his strength and set about keeping his promise to the sick women who now needed his protection even more than his wife.

CHAPTER 33

$\mathcal{A}$lmost three weeks since Daniel's departure, Rose pushed back the curtain from one of the front windows to watch the snowfall. "At last. It's stopping. Do you think Kamama and Woya will brave this weather to visit?"

The two sisters had arrived almost each day since Daniel and the others left to search for the missing women. When they were unable to come, their brother would appear on horseback, skirting around the edge of the property. She deeply appreciated their vigilance. Daniel was true to his word.

Nora leaned forward in her chair and put her book down on her lap. "Not much has stopped them so far. But you need to come away from the window. You'll catch cold."

Rose remained where she was. "Do you ever think it strange that we don't have a calendar? That in this wilderness, we have to guess what day it is? I know exactly what day Daniel left, but today might even be Christmas Day, for all we ken."

"I never thought of it that way."

"Christmas has always been a somber day of worship for us. But Daniel is Church of England. Can't we celebrate for him?"

196

Nora came to her side. "We need a wee bit of joy. Let's do it. Do you remember what they do?"

"They decorate with greenery and ribbons and bright colors. Candles...lots of candles." Rose thought a moment. "They bake wonderful cakes and cookies. And presents, they exchange presents. What about a nativity scene or a puppet show?"

"Let's not get too carried away." Nora moved away from the window and clasped her shawl tighter. "What day shall we make it?"

"Three days from now? That will give us time."

"It will be our first Christmas without our parents. Without my husband...my boy." Nora gulped and her eyes filled with tears.

Grief chose that moment to stab Rose's heart. It hurt. She hugged her sister while memories of their ma and da and their loving family filled her mind.

Rose broke their embrace and caressed her sister's cheek. "Our parents were such pleasant, contented people. They took great joy in making sure we were happy too."

"Yes," Nora agreed. "When I picture them, I see them smiling. Like the first time they held their grandchild."

"Or when trying to eat squirrel."

Nora laughed through her tears. "Or dancing at your wedding?"

"Then let's follow their lead. Let's determine to make this Christmas a happy time. Agreed?"

Nora brushed the tears from her eyes. "Agreed."

Heartened, Rose threw on her robe. "I know just where to find some holly."

"You're not going out now?"

"It's stopped snowing. Don't worry. I won't go far. I'll stay on the path to the cathedral."

Rose picked up a rucksack and hurried out the door.

Outside, she breathed in the crisp, fresh air. She almost danced her way down the path. She came upon the holly bushes, and using her knife, she cut the branches that had the most berries. Several times, the sharp leaves penetrated her gloves, making her wince. But she could already picture them nestled among fir branches on her dining table and across the mantel. It would be worth the trouble.

At the crack of a twig, she hunched her shoulders. Coming out alone may not have been a good idea, but she felt a strong urge to visit the overlook before heading back home.

At the edge of the precipice, she dropped the rucksack and scanned the valley below. The mountains had taken on a mantle of glistening snow that hid many of the bushes and underbrush. Evergreen trees bowed under the weight of big puffs of snow. Ice gathered on the trunks of trees and on the leaves scattered beneath her feet.

She'd bent down to examine the waxy green leaves of an unfamiliar bush when she was shoved violently. Throwing her arms out in front of her, she flew through the air, fell onto one of the boulders, and rolled over and over down its slippery surface. She landed on a shelf about ten feet from the top of the ledge. Rose peered down the cliff side, and her breath came in short bursts. Had she rolled another foot, she would have toppled over and plunged several hundred feet down the mountain. Dazed, she closed her eyes. Thank God, nothing was broken.

She sat up, moving carefully since everything around her was slippery with ice. A gust of wind shot over the ledge and buffeted her back and forth. Shaking from head to toe, she pulled the robe tightly around her, hugged her knees, and dropped her head down on them.

Who pushed me? Did they really mean to kill me? Are they up there now, looking down on me, waiting for me to die? Is Nora in danger too?

Anger burst full blown and permeated her body.

The hate necessary to want to take her life was daunting. Who would do this?

Rebekah. But she was among the captives. It must have been someone close to her—a family member or friend.

Fear, anger, and dread took turns roiling in her mind. After a time, her attacker must have fled. She needed to find a way back, but behind her, layer upon layer of solid rock offered no bushes, no clumps of grass to grab on to. Straight ahead, the edge of the shelf promised sudden death. She was trapped.

"Help. Someone, please, help." Was anyone near enough to hear her? She called out again and again, until her throat hurt.

Her mind began to drift to the many things she had experienced in the past few months. She had been uprooted from the only home she had ever known in order for her father to seek his dream. She had endured a harrowing sea voyage only to arrive in a land that stole the lives of her brother-in-law and nephew. She had been kidnapped and almost drowned in a raging river. Her memories were forever scarred after witnessing the deaths of her parents. Her husband whom she adored with her entire being might still be in love with another.

Reliving the past. Isn't that what one does when facing imminent death?

Would she allow her memories to rob her of hope? No. By God's grace, she was still alive. His presence had sustained her through many tragedies and dangers. Her faith in Him assured her that all would be well—in life *or* death. She drew strength through the knowledge that, here in this beautiful cathedral of God, she was alone, but not alone.

She was not sure how long she had waited when the sun slowly began to sink behind the mountains, and the temperature was dropping with it.

A voice called from some distance away. "Ro-o-o-se!"

Nora.

"Here! I'm here!" she yelled.

"Ro-o-o-se." This time it was Kamama and she was closer.

"Please," she called out, "help."

A moment later, she looked up to see Nora leaning out over the precipice, her expression one of complete terror.

"Rose, dear one. Are you all right?"

"As all right as one can be stranded on the side of a mountain." Rose, whose teeth chattered from the cold, sounded braver than she felt.

"Kamama is going for a rope. We'll lower it down and haul you up." Nora shivered. "How did this happen?"

No need to worry Nora any more than she was already. "I lost my footing."

Before long, a rope was lowered over the edge, and Rose reached out and grabbed the looped end and draped it over her head and underneath her arms.

"Ready?" Kamama called out.

"Ready."

The loop tightened around her ribcage, and she struggled to breathe. Her feet left the ground, and for a few heart-stopping moments, she dangled in midair. She clamped her eyes shut as she was slowly dragged up the side of the boulder. Once she reached the top of the cliff, Woya grabbed hold of her and pulled her to safety.

"Come away," Kamama ordered with a shaky voice. "We are too close to the edge."

Rose scooted across the ground until Nora pounced on her and hugged her close. "You mustn't ever do anything like this again. I canno'"—she gulped— "canno' lose you." Nora's eyes were wild with fright. "Promise me."

"I promise."

On the way back to the cabin, Rose lifted up a silent prayer of thanksgiving and pled for strength and wisdom. But the question remained—who had tried to kill her?

CHAPTER 34

Following the signs Daniel had left along the way, two riders from the other search group found them days later and announced that they had uncovered the trail of the men who held Adsila and Odina captive.

Daniel rejoiced at the look of relief on Spotted Owl's face. His friend wanted to jump on his horse and leave right then, but Daniel held him up. They needed a plan.

He and the cousins met outside the cabin. "The way I see it, the women are in good enough shape to travel. Gray Sky, if you and these men would see them home, Spotted Owl and I will join the search for Adsila and Odina." Though his beloved new wife waited at home, Daniel, as the leader and most experienced tracker of the searchers, must see the rescue through.

Everyone agreed and set about making the women comfortable on travoises.

Her lovely face now pale and emaciated, Rebekah stretched out her hand. "You're leaving me, Daniel?"

For days, Daniel had done his best to avoid Rebekah, though it proved difficult in such close quarters.

Nevertheless, he smiled at her. "You're in good hands. Before you know it, you'll be home." He motioned to the riders. "You left us signs?"

One of them nodded. "It's about a week's ride east at the fork of the Chance River."

Another week away from Rose.

The thought bothered him, for he had awakened that morning from a terrible dream that something bad had happened to his wife. The dream left him moody and unsettled the rest of the day.

Daniel mounted Wadulisi and waved goodbye to Gray Sky and called for Tsiyi, who came to his side. "Let's get going."

Trudging through the mountains on horseback called for a steady, skilled, patient rider. The horses shied away from treacherous places that threatened their sure footing. They often balked at crossing deep streams with fast currents. The arduous trek necessitated more frequent rests for the horses which struggled to breathe in the higher altitudes. The going was slow, and Daniel's patience was wearing thin.

Finally, they picked up on the trail signs and had followed them several days when they came upon a cabin. A man was seated on the front porch, propped on the back legs of his chair with a musket resting across his legs.

"Mornin'. How can I help you?" he asked with a suspicious expression that belied his warm greeting.

Daniel took measure of the man, who seemed cautious, but friendly enough. "We're looking for two men and two Indian women."

The man sat up and leaned forward. "What are they to you?"

"The men are slavers. Stole the women from our village, and we aim to get them back."

The man slumped his shoulders. "I don't think that's going to happen."

Daniel's spine tingled. "Why is that?"

"I hate to be the one to tell you, but a couple a days ago, when I was huntin', I came across the bodies of two Indian women. They'd been shot. Maybe a day before I found them, so the animals hadn't gotten to them yet."

Daniel and Spotted Owl locked glances. The fear in Spotted Owl's eyes was intense. Daniel yearned to say they might not be Odina and Adsila, but in his heart, he knew they more than likely were.

"That don't mean they was your women, though," the man said. "What'd they look like?"

"One had a tattoo of a bird. Here." Spotted Owl touched his arm just below the elbow. "And a beaded belt with a mountain pattern." He swallowed hard. "Her name—Odina—means *mountain*. She was to be my wife."

The man stood and leaned his musket against the cabin wall. His expression was stern, but his eyes held sadness. "Yep. Sounds like them."

Spotted Owl's entire body seemed to melt from his grief. He turned his head away and stared into the forest.

"Seemed they was treated worse than animals. They had rope burns on their ankles as though they'd been hobbled. I suspect they'd tried to run away."

The man's every word made Daniel sick to his stomach.

"I gave them a decent burial." He pointed toward a path leading away from his cabin. "That way. You'll come upon an overlook. It's a nice place. I laid them to rest there."

Daniel had to force himself to speak. "We thank you for your kindness."

The man nodded, sat back down, and tilted his chair against the wall.

Daniel and Spotted Owl guided their horses up the path to the fresh burial places at the edge of a cliff. The man was right —it was a nice view of the mountains that rolled, one into the other, like a blue silk coverlet that had been lifted and settled to the bedrock.

Standing beside the graves, Daniel put his hand on his friend's shoulder. "I'm at a loss. I grieve with you. My heart is heavy."

Spotted Owl blew out a sigh. "Thank you, Daniel. She's at peace now, and I don't have to spend the rest of my life wondering where she is." He pressed a hand to his heart. "Can I have time for ashes?"

Daniel nodded, stepped away, and sat on a boulder at the brink of the overlook. Tsiyi lay beside him, and he ruffled the hound's ears and waited for the fire Spotted Owl built from leaves and twigs to cool down.

How was Rose managing? Hopefully, his Cherokee family had watched with care over her and Nora. Was she eating well? He recalled her reaction the first time she tasted kanuchi. The times she had giggled at his response when she jumped in bed and warmed her cold feet on him. Was she wearing socks? He pictured her concentrating so hard making lace and mumbling when she made a mistake. And the expression of awe when they stood inside the waterfall. He trembled with the thought of her lovely hair splayed across his pillow, her silken body and her molten blue eyes at the pinnacle of their passion.

Spotted Owl had just lost the opportunity for a marriage like Daniel's. Mentally shaking himself, he joined his grieving friend and bowed his head while he scooped handfuls of ashes and spread them over his head.

Daniel arranged three stones in a circle by the grave, signifying the end of the trail. Spotted Owl removed a feather from his headdress and buried it on top of the gravesite.

"Let's go. Get you back to Rose," said Spotted Owl, avoiding eye contact.

They mounted their horses, and Daniel took one last glance

at the tragic gravesite. The glorious panorama of mountains reminded him of his own cathedral overlook.

I'm coming home, my darling.

CHAPTER 35

Rose stood at the window, again watching the snow flurries that added another inch to the porch bannister. As far as she could see, days of snowfall had covered the landscape in a solid white blanket. Skittish, she hadn't ventured out in the two days since the attempt on her life.

"Here come Kamama and Woya." Rose flung open the door and greeted the sisters warmly. "You must be freezing."

Nora helped them with their coats, and Rose ran to her bedroom and dragged the extra rocking chairs next to the others. The women hung their coats on pegs and settled before the fireplace.

"I cannot believe you came out in this weather." Rose put another log on the fire and handed them blankets.

Kamama draped a blanket across her knees. "We promised Daniel we would watch. We keep that promise, especially after what happened."

Rose shrugged away the goosebumps that ran up and down her arms. "May I offer you some coffee? With much sugar...as we did last time?"

"Yes, please." Woya gave Rose a huge smile. Coffee with sugar had become her favorite.

"Any word of Daniel and the others?" Rose poured coffee into pewter mugs from a kettle she'd placed next to the fire. "It's been weeks since he first left us."

Her voice was calm, but her insides quaked. She feared for her husband and desperately regretted the way they had parted. Her morning prayers had become repetitious pleas —*Lord, please, let Daniel find the women, and please bring him back to me. Grant me patience and strength.*

"Sadly, no," Woya answered, taking the mug Rose offered. "Tracking will take time."

"We may never see our sweet friends again." Kamama's expression was so sad, Rose hugged her.

"Let's not abandon our hope." Nora spoke gently. "We'll keep ourselves busy. Rose and I thought we would show you how we make lace."

Woya and Kamama found lace-making fascinating and were even more amazed by the spinning wheel. After that day, they spent several afternoons watching Rose spin flax while Nora made swaths of lace. They caught on quickly and even shared their own handiwork—hand weaving, beading, and basket weaving. Rose enjoyed basket weaving the most and became proficient enough to fashion a new egg basket. Nora was drawn more to the intricate patterns of beading.

In addition to bringing her threads and reeds, Kamama presented Rose with bread and corn. "It's for the little one," she said. "You must eat more."

"I don't understand." Rose searched their faces.

Kamama folded her arms and rocked them back and forth. She circled her fingers across her middle and pointed to Rose. "*Usdi.*" She rocked her arms again.

Nora's eyes glistened with unshed tears. "She thinks you're with child, Rose. And I believe maybe you are."

Rose pressed her hands to her stomach. Could it be?

"Have you missed your courses?" Nora asked, studying Rose's belly.

"I-I," Rose stuttered. "Twice. And...I did have to loosen my stays this morning. I truly thought I was gaining weight from staying inside so much." She laughed. "And from all the kanuchi I've been craving."

She ran into her sister's outstretched arms. Joy and fear took turns washing over her.

What would Daniel say? If he loved Rebekah, would he resent their child? Another thought rammed home. What of the person who pushed her over the cliff? She laid an arm across her stomach. *Don't fear, little one, I will keep you safe.*

Later, after Kamama and Woya left, Rose went to the barn to gather eggs in the basket she had woven. As she headed back to the front porch, a group of men on horseback stopped on the cabin road. One broke away and approached her. It was Gray Sky. Her heart leapt.

He dismounted. "Siyo, Rose."

"Daniel?" she croaked.

"He is well."

Thank you, Lord.

"But they still search. We found three. But not Spotted Owl's woman or Adsila."

"It saddens me to hear that. Won't you come in?" She shielded her eyes from the sun to see the three men who accompanied him. They each dragged something behind them, but she could not make out what. "Bring your friends."

"We cannot. We return with the women." He scowled. "But we must keep them away. I don't know...build a shelter?"

"Why?"

"Smallpox."

Rose closed her eyes to the terrible news.

"I don't know who will care for them. The Cherokee were a

great nation once with many clans. The white man's diseases have wounded us. We must keep the women away from the others, especially our old people, our treasures."

Rose thought only a moment. "Bring them here."

Her offer seemed to amaze him. "But it's smallpox."

"Nora and I had it when we were children. We are safe." A jarring thought came to her, and she blurted, "What about Daniel? And you?"

He pointed to a mark at his temple. "We, too, had the pox when young."

"Gray Sky signaled to the others, who left the road and drew near the cabin.

Rose hurried to tell Nora, and they dashed to the workroom, where they shoved the spinning wheel into the corner by the bathing barrel and cleared their supplies. Nora started a fire in the cast-iron stove and gathered all the covers she could find. She even took the deerskin rugs from the bedroom and main room floors.

Rose rushed outside, where the men lifted the women from travoises. She directed them to the workroom but faltered at Gray Sky's grim expression.

"What is it?"

"Here are Dyani and Catori." He motioned toward the women nearest him. "And she"—he pointed to the third woman—"is Rebekah."

Even though pale and sickly, Rebekah remained quite beautiful. Her almond-shaped eyes were the color of cattails. Her nose was long and regal, and her lips were full. Rose understood Daniel's attraction. Truly, she was a striking woman—though at this moment, she stared at Rose with palpable anger.

Lord, I asked for strength and wisdom. I ken Your answer.

After putting the women in the workroom, the men declined a meal, carried away the travoises, and waited outside for Gray Sky.

"I left Daniel in the Ohio River territories, over a hundred miles away. I will see my mother and then meet him and Spotted Owl in a place we agreed." He paused. "You are well, Rose?"

"I am well, though I miss my husband."

"And he you. I do not know how long this will take before the Great Spirit tells us we have done enough, though I cannot see my brother giving up the search for Odina." He held out his hands. "I think if it was you, Daniel would travel to the ends of the earth."

Rose clutched her stomach. If only that was so.

"I promise, my brother, Daniel and I are pledged to look out for one another." He motioned toward the workroom. "Thank you for this."

Rose waved as the men rode away and then entered the workroom, where Nora struggled to remove Catori's tattered, filthy clothing. The young girl was so weak, she could barely sit up.

"What will they wear?" asked Nora, pulling Catori's shirt over her arms.

"I have an extra shift. Do you?"

"Yes."

"Wait. I remember seeing some clothing stored in the loft. I'll see if there's anything we can use."

Upstairs, she threw open trunks and boxes and found several shifts and nightshirts that must have belonged to Daniel's parents. She paused at the top of the stairs and recalled the stirring kiss she and her husband had shared there. She missed him so much, she ached with it.

Lord, keep him safe. Bring him back to me, please.

She and Nora soon had the women bathed and dressed and lying comfortably on pallets.

"From my memory, these women are in the later stages. They

must have already endured the rash on their tongues and in their mouths...fever...vomiting," Rose whispered as they stopped in the doorway. "But it's clear that travel weakened them."

Nora's body slumped. "Yes. That's the way it was with my William and my baby."

Rose hugged her sister as they both relived the nightmare weeks in Philadelphia. "Let's pray they don't get pneumonia. We must make them drink. Tea? Or water?"

"Water at first, I think. Maybe chamomile tea later." Nora peeked back into the room. "Will they be fortunate like us and have only a few marks? I do hope so."

"That may be the least of their worries." Rose frowned. "Did you see the bruises? They were terribly mistreated."

Nora gulped. "We will care for them as we would each other."

Kamama and Woya, both of whom had the pox as children, joined them the next day, and, for the following few days, they all took turns caring for the women, though Rebekah shunned Rose each time she neared. Catori, the twelve-year-old, was plagued with nightmares and often woke up screaming. Rose learned from Kamama that slavers often raided Indian villages and kidnapped women they sold to trappers in the wilderness. She also found out that Catori had not been touched. As a virgin, she would have brought a huge price. Even so, it would take her a long time to heal from what she must have endured and witnessed.

Rebekah's mother visited one day and stood at the bottom of the porch stairs. Rose greeted her but remained on the porch.

"I must know how my daughter is." The woman jabbed her fists onto her hips.

"She and the others are doing as well as can be expected."

"I fear for her. If you do her harm..." She raised her fist.

Rose pulled in her chin as if she'd been struck. "Why would I wish to hurt her?"

The woman stared at her with undisguised loathing. "Why would you not?"

Kamama joined Rose on the porch. "Go away. I'll not have you bothering Rose. Take your hatred elsewhere."

The woman departed, leaving Rose with the answer to who may have tried to kill her.

The day finally arrived when the women were well enough to return to the village. Catori and Dyani hugged Rose and Nora and thanked them for their care. Rebekah walked straight out the front door without acknowledging them.

"Watch that one. She means you harm," Dyani whispered.

Rose had sensed that already. More than once, she had caught Rebekah staring at her with eyes that seethed with hatred.

They had not been gone long when Rose glanced out the window, checking on the pile of smoldering clothes the women had been wearing. A movement in the distance across the meadow caught her eye. A large group of men stealthily made their way to the cabin. Terror shot through her body.

"Nora! Catawba!"

CHAPTER 36

"*H*urry!" Rose threw some jerky into a rucksack, grabbed a pistol, and ran to open the passage.

Nora pulled one of the robes from its peg and scrambled through the doorway. Rose handed her the pistol and slipped inside, closing the panel behind them. Wrapped in total darkness, they huddled at the top of the stairs. Rose's heart pounded so hard she almost missed the sound of breaking glass. Nora clamped her hand over her mouth. Rose swallowed hard and rested a hand on her stomach.

If we had hesitated any longer...

Slowly, searching for each step with the toes of their shoes, they descended the stairs. Rose felt around for the flint and the candle but was so afraid of making any noise she stood still, straining her ears to catch sounds inside the house. The men whooped and mumbled, then overturned furniture thumped and pottery and glass crashed.

Rose motioned for them to move along. Brushing her hand along the cool clay wall, she continued on until she felt it safe enough to scrape the flint. Sparks flew momentarily, lighting up

Nora's face that was white as parchment paper. After several tries, Rose lit the candle and breathed a sigh of relief.

As they crept along, she could not fight the sense that they had gone much farther than when Daniel led the way. Finally, a faint light shone ahead, and she blew out the candle. They reached the back of the springhouse, and as Daniel had instructed, they waited, listening intently for intruders. At first, she heard only the gurgling of the stream that flowed underneath the building. Then men's voices carried from behind the wall.

Nora dropped the pistol on the clay floor with a *thump*. The men stopped talking.

Lord, help us.

The men started conversing again, and soon their voices faded away.

"I'm so sorry," Nora whispered through chattering teeth.

Rose took the pistol and slipped it into her under-pocket. She motioned for them to sit, and they cowered together and waited. They remained still, afraid to move a muscle. Rose's back stretched so taut, she thought it might crack. Unable to endure it any longer, she carefully opened the panel and stuck her head through. Satisfied that no one was near, she crawled into the springhouse, followed by Nora, who shook so hard she could barely stand.

"Let me go first." Rose mounted the steps that led to the outside. At the entrance, she peered at the clearing ahead and then back toward the cabin. "They haven't set it on fire...yet."

"I pray they don't. All reminders of our family are in there."

Rose hugged her. "We are family and we can build new memories."

They crouched out of sight of the cabin.

"I say we make for the village. But I'm not sure which way. When you visited, do you remember how you got there?"

Spurts of cold air punctuated each of Rose's words, and she rubbed her arms against the chill.

"No. But I do remember one of the young boys saying he could put his toy canoe in the river and it would float past our cabin."

"Brilliant." Rose pulled Nora close and kissed her forehead. "We'll follow the river."

Using bushes and trees for cover, they crept through drifts of snow to the riverbank. There they threw the robe over their shoulders and headed upstream, skirting around the deeper piles of snow that invaded their shoes and stockings.

Rose's feet and hands grew numb. "How far do you think it is?"

"I'm not sure...about an hour or more on horseback."

"Miles, then." Panic bubbled up inside.

As they continued, Rose's nerves took hold. She glanced over her shoulder often. What would they do if she did see Indians following?

They had not trekked far when they came upon a dense patch of cane and swamp.

"We'll have to make our way around it." Rose motioned to their left. "This place seems familiar. I think Daniel took me this way once when we were exploring."

Bypassing the swamp steered them farther away from the river. The sky shifted from blue to purple, casting a pall over the forest around them. Rose grimaced at the footprints they had left in the snow.

"Goodness," she exclaimed. "We could not have left a more obvious trail." In their panic, she had forgotten to cover their tracks. Daniel wouldn't be happy with her.

"What can we do about it?"

"Let me think. But, right now, let's just run."

"What's that noise?" Nora tilted her head.

"It's a waterfall." Along with another sound that sent shivers down her spine. "The Indians are following us, and they're close. Hurry, hurry."

Rose grabbed the cloak, threw it over her arm, and started running so fast, her feet barely touched the ground. Soon they stood at the edge of the waterfall.

"Follow me," she whispered.

They ran several yards up and down the embankment, hopping across rocks and scrambling over fallen trunks until their footprints overlapped each other.

"I don't know how long that will fool them, but let's get over to the waterfall."

With Nora close on her heels, she jumped from rock to rock, crossing the shallow pool that reached her mid-calf. Pushing through the water that soaked the bottom of her dress, she remembered how Daniel had held her in his arms.

"Careful here. It's slippery," said Rose as they scrambled up the incline. "Watch what I do."

She went first, squeezing around the boulder that jutted out from the slate wall. She dropped down into the cave behind the rushing water that roared from the latest rain. Faint from holding her breath, she held her arms out to help Nora, who trembled so hard she fell to her knees.

Rose pressed her finger to her lips and motioned for Nora to back up as far into the cave as possible, where they huddled against the wall. Her heart hammered so hard, Nora could probably hear it. They waited until she grew impatient and crept forward to peer though the cascading water.

Five men—and one seemed to be looking straight at her. She watched, frozen, as the men wandered up and down the edge of the pool, following their scrambled footprints. Finally, one of them signaled for them to leave, and one by one, they skulked away, glancing over their shoulders.

Relief flooded her body, and she slumped down on the floor of the cave. "They're gone," she muttered.

Nora joined her and put an arm across her shoulders. "I've never been so frightened in my life. I'm guessing Daniel showed you this."

"Yes, he brought me here one day, and I remember him saying it isn't that far from the village."

They descended to the bottom of the falls and continued west, terrified of all the snaps and cracks of twigs that echoed through the trees.

"We must stop soon. It's too dangerous for us to go on in the dark," said Rose.

"I'm so cold. Can we light a fire?"

"We canno' risk it. But we'll build a shelter and keep each other warm." Her sister's pale and weary face made her heart squeeze. "You take the robe and sit there at the base of that tree. I'll cut branches and make a shelter."

"You know how?"

"I remember the one Daniel made for us when he rescued me." Rose unsheathed her knife and began cutting limbs from a fir tree, shaking the snow off before throwing them onto a pile.

Speaking his name hurt. She yearned for his comforting arms, penetrating blue eyes, and sable-colored hair that flowed across his shoulders. She pressed her arm across her stomach.

What does the future hold for us? Will I even survive to see him again?

She completed the lean-to, and they crawled inside. They clung together and draped the robe around them. Rose divided pieces of jerky between them, which they ate in silence and downed with the last of the canteen water. They peered through the small entrance as night took over day. A full moon shone through the trees, transforming the mounds of snow into a sparkling blanket. Nora spoke an evening prayer over them. Rose was so weary, she welcomed the sleep that enveloped her.

~

*R*ose and Nora awoke the following morning to the sight of a raccoon sitting up and watching them from the lean-to entrance.

"Oh, my!" Nora spoke so loudly, the startled raccoon scurried away. "It's nice and warm in here. I almost don't want to leave."

"Come on. The sooner we get going, the sooner we'll be there."

They moved outside and Rose stared up at the sky. "We were going north, then west to avoid the swamp. Then north again when we passed the swamp. So we need to go..." She held her arms out and scanned from one direction to another. "Truthfully, I have no idea. I don't hear the river anymore."

"We need to go that way." Nora pointed.

"What makes you say that?"

"Because Daniel gave me a lesson once. He told me that if I was ever alone in the woods to imagine I was walking on a map. Every now and then, draw an arrow in the ground pointing in the direction I was headed. And...before I bedded down, I was to draw an arrow in the dirt, or lay downs sticks. That way, I wouldn't backtrack or go in circles. So..." She motioned to an arrow on the ground made of branches.

Rose gave her sister a huge smile. "I love you."

They had traveled for what seemed hours when Rose thought she heard the river again. She glanced at Nora, whose body wilted with each step. "Let's rest a while."

They were about to sit down by a huge oak when snowflakes started drifting down through the treetops.

Lord, please, help us.

Nora peered from beneath the robe. "It's coming down fast, Rose. I can hardly see."

"We need to stop and build a shelter, but..." Rose hesitated and blinked the snow from her eyes. "Do you see that?"

"I do."

A few yards away stood a dilapidated cabin. The front door barely hung onto its hinges, and vines grew along the outside wall and into the windows.

Rose peeked inside, making sure there were no varmints. "I think we'll be all right here."

They scurried inside. Rose slid the door to and then plopped down on the dirt floor beside Nora and drew in a weary breath.

She pointed to the fireplace. "Look. Someone left a pile of wood."

She searched her rucksack and found the flint box. She gathered a pile of rotten leaves for kindling and lit a stick that she held over the wood. Smoke from the stick curled up through the chimney.

"It's drawing!" she exclaimed and then shoved the burning leaves and stick into the kindling at the bottom of the woodpile, which soon came to life.

With the robe thrown over their shoulders, they removed their shoes and soaking-wet stockings and hung them on a branch near the fire.

Nora wiggled her bare feet next to the flames. "I can feel my toes again."

They shared the last bit of jerky and waited for their clothes to dry.

"Lovely and toasty," said Rose, donning her stockings and shoes. "But we're out of water."

Rose carried the canteen to the door, scooped snow into it, and placed it next to the fire. They settled down and watched through the cracks in the door as the drifts piled up around the cabin.

Lying on her side underneath the buffalo robe, Nora sighed.

"When I think about our lives back in Ireland, I'm astounded. Would you ever have thought we would be lying on a dirt floor, in a cabin that's about to fall around our ears, in the middle of a strange forest, hiding from hostile Indians?"

"We are in a much different world."

"You realize, if it wasn't for Daniel, we never would have made it this far. He's taught us so much." Nora flipped over onto her back and rested her head on her arm. "I can't wait to see his reaction when you tell him about the baby."

"You think he'll be happy about it?"

"Of course, you ninny. He adores you, as he will his child."

I'm glad one of us thinks so.

Rose settled beside her sister underneath the robe. "It's a nice thought, but first, we have to make our way out of this."

She gave over to her exhaustion and quickly fell asleep despite the whistling of the wind through the cracks in the cabin.

She woke the next morning to Nora poking her in her side.

"Rose," Nora whispered. "Someone's outside."

Blinking away sleep, Rose sat up and listened. She sprang up and unsheathed her knife. Sometime during the night, the door had fallen off its hinges, and a group of Indian women watched them from the opening. She planted her feet on the ground and held up the knife, ready to defend herself.

"Rose," someone called out. "You are safe."

Aunt Sara pushed her way forward.

Terror and relief changed places so fast, Rose's heart thundered in her ears. "Oh, Auntie. I'm so very happy to see you." She sheathed her knife and ran into the woman's embrace.

Nora threw on the robe and joined them, and they held on tight, laughing and talking at the same time.

Rose cupped Sara's face in both hands. "How did you find us?"

"We heard about the raid and started searching for you.

Someone saw the smoke from your fire. You're not far from our village." Sara accepted a blanket from one of the women and wrapped it around Rose's shoulders. "Come, let's get you to my home."

They were walking away when Rose overheard two of the women talking excitedly to each other.

"What are they saying?"

"They say you greeted us with a knife, like an angry bear with your hair on fire. That is your name now—Fire Bear—Atsila Yona."

Rose exchanged smiles with the women. A Cherokee name...a sign of belonging. When her husband returned, would his welcome be as warm?

CHAPTER 37

$\mathcal{D}$aniel, Spotted Owl, and Gray Sky reached the bend in the road to Daniel's farm, and his heart leapt.

Almost home.

The long and treacherous journey was about to end.

"I won't stop," said Gray Sky, who had found them not far from the gravesite of Odina and Asdila. "I'm going ahead to the village."

"I'll see you—" Daniel stopped. "Something's wrong. There's no smoke coming from the chimney."

They galloped down the snow-covered road and across in front of the cabin. Daniel slid from his horse and caught a glimpse of a pile of burned clothing on the snow. He took the stairs two at the time. The sight of the battered front door gave him a sick feeling.

Inside, he stepped around overturned furniture and bits and pieces of shattered glass, pottery, and contents of crates that had been ripped open.

"Rose. Rose," he called out.

With Tsiyi on his heels, he ran to the bedroom, where the rocking chairs had been upended and lay atop the wedding portrait that had been ripped from the wall. In the workroom, he found the pallets where Rose and the others had cared for the sick women. Gray Sky had informed him of her generous act of kindness, and Daniel loved her more than ever for it.

He returned to the main room, where Gray Sky, holding a lighted candle, stood at the opening of the root cellar. The rug had been rolled back and the door flung open.

"Let me take a look," said Gray Sky, his expression grim.

His heart thumping, Daniel waited at the top of the stairs. *Please, don't let him find anything.*

Gray Sky returned in a couple of minutes. "Nothing." His eyes met Daniel's. "Not even a crumb left. Whoever broke in here took all the food." He placed the candle on a shelf beside the dining table.

"They must have been in a hurry," said Spotted Owl. "Looking for food, guns, and ammunition. Probably not the ones who took our women."

Daniel released a breath. "Thank God, they didn't set the place on fire."

He spotted a discarded tin on the floor with bits of molasses candy strewn around it. Rose had made his favorite candy. He remembered her expression the first time she'd tasted it after coming to his defense with the store owner who had begrudgingly served him. His emotions threatened to overflow, and he swallowed hard.

"No bloodstains anywhere." Gray Sky surveyed the tumbled mess. "A good sign."

Daniel's body shook. He stepped outside and sat on the first step of the stairs, his elbows on his knees and his face buried in his hands. "Where can they be?"

"Gray Sky and I will search the barn and the outbuildings." Spotted Owl briefly rested his hand on Daniel's slumped shoulder.

When they returned a few minutes later, they had found no

signs of the women. The chickens were gone, but the goat and cow remained, more signs that the raiding party was in a hurry.

"Where's Tsiyi?" Daniel looked around for the dog that rarely left his side.

Spotted Owl stuck his head inside the doorway and frowned. "He's in here, scratching at the wall."

Daniel sprang up and hurried inside. "The escape passage. You good boy."

He pushed the entry boards aside, lit a candle that had rolled onto the floor, and slipped inside. At the bottom of the stairs, he saw that some of the flint was missing as well as a candle. Followed by Gray Sky and Spotted Owl, he hurried through the tunnel to the springhouse and stepped outside but found no signs of Rose and Nora.

What was I expecting? It's been weeks.

They took the tunnel back to the house, where Daniel righted a chair and sat down at the dining table. "I don't know where to start. I assume they've been taken, so we must find the raiding party." He turned and looked at the pegs beside the door. "Why is only one of their robes missing?"

If only one was taken, where was the other?

Daniel jumped up so fast, he knocked over the chair. He strode back outside, leaned against the railing, and scanned the snow blanketing the fields. He snatched off his hat and scraped his hand through his hair. So many emotions roiled inside him —frustration, anger, fear, exhaustion. They swirled through his body, rumbled in his chest, and escaped in a primal roar that echoed throughout the valley.

Gray Sky put a hand on Daniel's shoulder. "Let's not lose hope, my friend. Right now, you need rest. When you rise, we'll make a plan. Go ahead and lie down a while. My brother and I will tend to the horses and prepare food."

Daniel had to admit, he was so tired, every bone in his body ached. He went to the bedroom and threw himself across the bed. He gathered Rose's pillow close and inhaled, reveling in her scent, and fell into a deep sleep.

He awoke to Gray Sky shoving his shoulder. "Daniel. Wake up. We have news."

Daniel shook the cobwebs from his mind and sat on the side of the bed. "What?"

"It's Burning Tree. He's outside. Someone witnessed a small band of Catawba traveling down the Catawba River into South Carolina. Most likely, headed for their main village."

Daniel stood with his arms ramrod straight. "And?"

Gray Sky put his arm on Daniel's shoulder. "There are two white women with them. One with red hair."

CHAPTER 38

heir first day in the Cherokee village, Sara offered to take Rose on a tour. Outside Sara's cabin, they waved goodbye to Nora, who had joined women gathered around a fire hand beading. Nora returned their wave, her eyes bright with eagerness to learn a new skill.

Rose stopped a few feet from the cabin. "Sara, Nora and I have talked about our stay here. We are both anxious about returning to our home. It's terribly isolated, and without Daniel...well...the thought of the two of us staying there by ourselves is frightening." She held out a hand to Sara. "But we don't want to take advantage of your hospitality."

Sara clasped Rose's hand in both of hers. "You are family. Not guests. You must stay as long as you need."

"Thank you. Thank you." Rose pulled her aunt close and hugged her tightly.

"Now, you will see your new home." Sara linked her arm with Rose's, and they proceeded down a path that had been cleared of snow.

Rose estimated the settlement comprised about thirty cabins and close to eighty men, women, and children. The cabins were one- or two-room dwellings with frames fashioned out of rivercane, logs, and vines plastered over in a mixture of clay, grass, and deer hair. Cedar shingles covered the roofs, giving the homes a pleasant, sweet aroma. Holes had been cut in the ceilings to draw out the smoke from fires that provided a warm, cozy feeling.

Sara waved to a group of women sitting outside one of the cabins. "Siyo," she called out.

The women waved back, though they studied Rose with open curiosity.

"They are weaving baskets, mostly from rivercane. Some use white oak and some honeysuckle. These cane strips"—she motioned to a pile atop a rivercane mat—"have been wet in warm water for ease in weaving. Some, as you see, are being boiled with black walnut to dye them a darker color."

Rose recalled the basket that held the gentian flowers Daniel had gathered for her wedding bouquet. Her stomach tightened with longing. The gesture and his note had revealed a tenderness about him that was endearing.

Rose leaned over the boiling pot and sniffed. "It smells a wee bit like kanuchi."

One of the ladies beckoned to Rose. "This will carry water." She held a basket up for Rose to see that it was two baskets woven together at the lip. "You would join us?"

"Thank you. I would love to learn, but my auntie is helping me explore the village today."

Rose and Sara bid them goodbye and wandered down a path that took them past young women who winnowed wheat while they watched after children gathering firewood. Their path emptied out onto a stream where young men crafted blowguns from hollowed-out lengths of rivercane. Several young men fashioned darts from sharpened cane and thistle for the fletching.

"We use these to hunt small game, like rabbits and squirrels," Sara explained. "As a young boy, Daniel was quite a marksman, always sharing with me his bounty of squirrels. They are one of his favorites, you know."

The mention of squirrels brought to mind the bittersweet memory of her mother's first encounter with cooking them. "Maybe you will teach me the best way to prepare them. I so want to make him happy, Auntie."

Sara smiled at her. "Of course, Rose. And you will."

Rose approached one of the young men. "May I try the blowgun?"

Before handing it to her, he gave a quick demonstration that landed the dart in the middle of a target set up several paces away. Rose tried twice, and the boys laughed good-naturedly when the dart rolled out of the cane and plopped onto the ground.

"Oh, my, this takes much stronger lungs than mine."

Sara chuckled. "You see how they hollow out the joints with hot coals?"

Rose nodded.

"One day, Daniel and my sons were acting like silly chipmunks, throwing the coals at each other. One hit Daniel in the head. You have seen the tiny scar at his temple?"

"I have. I intended asking him about it." She sighed and cupped her hands across her belly. "Thank you, Auntie, for sharing these wonderful stories of Daniel. Hearing them soothes my heartache."

They walked back up the path to the cabins and passed a young girl carrying a basketful of water. "Siyo, Atsila Yona," she called out.

"Siyo, little one." The friendly greeting and her new Cherokee name raised Rose's spirits.

They made way for a group of men, who passed them and disappeared into the dense forest.

"A hunting party," Sara explained. "Depending on their

skills and if others have been hunting, they may be away as long as two months."

Daniel has been gone even longer.

As they ventured past more cabins, it became clear to Rose that everyone kept busy. Even when they gathered for conversation or gossip, the men, women, and even the children kept their hands actively engaged in mending, beading, weaving, flint-knapping arrowheads, or fletching arrows.

Sara stopped suddenly. "We must turn back."

Rose raised an eyebrow.

"That"—she pointed to a dwelling at the end of the path— "is the cabin of Rebekah's mother. It is not a good thing for you to go near it."

As they retraced their steps, Rose assured herself that she would definitely avoid that part of the village.

～

*T*he next morning, Rose sat cross-legged on the hide-covered dirt floor of Aunt Sara's cabin, watching her teach Nora how to hand weave a belt. Rose and Nora wore the clothing the Cherokee women had graciously given them— knee-length, long-sleeved calico shirts, wrap-around deerskin skirts, leggings, and moccasins. They both had parted their hair down the middle and wore it in two long braids. What would their parents say if they could see their daughters now?

She pressed a hand against her slightly swollen belly. *What would they say about this?*

They would have been wonderful, proud, loving grandparents. By Nora's reckoning, she was close to three months along.

I carry a child underneath my heart. My beloved's child. Is it a girl with his sable-colored hair and generous nature? Or a boy with eyes like gentians and a commanding presence?

Where was Daniel? Was he well? Did he think of her?

"Don't be sad, Rose. Daniel can take care of himself," said Sara, stirring the cook-fire coals with a stick.

"Did you read my mind?"

"Anyone can see how much you miss him."

"What was he like when he was a boy?" Perhaps hearing more about him would ease her loneliness.

"Much as he is now—serious and brave. He spent time with his father hunting and fishing and learning the ways of the forest. He adored his mother and often sat at her feet listening to her stories."

So that was where he got his fine storytelling from.

"He loved kanuchi, so much that he often helped me powder the hickory nuts. He never minded the jokes from the other boys about doing the work of women."

Rose laughed. "Yes, he still loves kanuchi."

Sara's eyes lit. "He was curious about everything. Asked so many questions of the elders that they would tire and send him along to bother another."

Rose and Nora giggled.

"Oh, and he loved to climb trees." She pressed a hand to her chest. "How many times did his mother and I almost swallow our hearts when we heard him calling to us from the tallest of oaks? My sister believed he must have been part eagle."

Rose laughed, remembering the time he had helped her climb the willow tree. What a delight that they shared such a simple joy.

"Tsiyi came into his life as a puppy when Daniel was fifteen winters. They moved together—Daniel, my sons, Rebekah, and Tsiyi. Where you saw one, you saw the others."

Rose's lips turned down at the thought of Rebekah.

"You frown, Rose. That you are wary of her is good." Sara started rolling up a length of yarn. "Her hate for you has become a sickness, more so since the things she suffered when she was taken away." She closed her eyes. "After you came here, her mother sent her to visit others of our clan who live upriver."

Ah. That was why the girl had been curiously absent since Nora and Rose arrived.

"Sara," Kamama called from outside. "Are you ready?"

"What does she mean? Ready for what?" Rose asked.

Sara stood and folded the weaving into a cane basket. "We must gather our belongings. This evening, we will all go to the longhouse, where we will spend many nights."

"The entire village?" asked Nora, who folded her own mat and put it into the basket.

"Yes. Winter is baring its teeth. Freezing winds come. We will be safer and warmer together."

Hauling rucksacks and baskets, they greeted Kamama and Woya outside a few minutes later. They waved to others along the way as they trekked the short distance to the birch-bark-covered structure that sat on a mound in the center of the village. It was many times the size of Sara's cabin and two stories high. Canoes leaned against the front tunnel-like entrance that emptied out into a huge room with support poles lined up every few feet. Four roaring fires down the center warmed the entire building. Although there were draft holes in the roof, smoke lingered in the air.

Each family gravitated to what must have been designated areas. Sara directed them to a place in a corner near one of the fires. Rose and Nora followed her lead, spreading deerskins and cane mats on the dirt floor, covering them with a pile of buffalo skins and blankets, and arranging their belongings next to the wall. When they were settled, they sat and watched the other families arrange their living areas. Everyone was so organized, amenable, and helpful, Rose felt a glow, a sense of belonging to what was quickly transforming into one family. Soon everyone was accounted for, and someone closed the entrance door.

A striking woman with a regal bearing occupied a choice

spot in the middle of the room. Several of the young maidens gathered around her. Rose leaned close to Sara to ask, "Who is that?"

"She is our Beloved Woman. One who in younger days fought for our people against our enemies and was known as War Woman. She attends war councils and offers advice on how to win battles. Even our grandmothers go to her for counsel." Sara started scrambling through the baskets. "Oh. I forgot my weaving."

"I'll go." Rose stood and wrapped the buffalo cape around her.

One of the women opened the door to the room, graciously walked with her through the entrance tunnel, and opened the outer door. Outside, Rose breathed in the air that was so frigid it hurt her lungs. She hurried toward Sara's cabin and was about to enter when a heavy cloth bag dropped over her head. Filled with terror, she fought to pull it away, but someone grabbed her wrists and tied them tightly in front of her. They pulled on the rope so viciously, Rose stumbled and fell to the ground.

"Get up," the person hissed and yanked her to a standing position.

Gagging on the cloth that clung to her nose and mouth, Rose coughed and sputtered as she was yanked along. The sound of water told her she was being led to the river.

"I know it's you, Rebekah," she called out.

The bag was ripped from her head, and Rebekah stood before her with an expression so wild, so demonic, that Rose trembled.

"So. You know."

In a moment of pure desperation, Rose yanked the rope from Rebekah's hands and ran toward the longhouse. "Help!" she screamed.

Rebekah hit her from behind with such force that she fell to her knees. She grabbed Rose by her braids and dragged her to the riverbank, where Rose fell onto tufts of snow that remained from the last storm.

Rose's breaths came in jagged spurts. "Don't do this. Daniel loves you."

"I know he does. He has been mine since we were children. But he is bound to you. He will honor that despite his feelings for me. You must disappear." She tugged on the rope, hauling Rose into the freezing current.

"I'll go away. Please. I'm with child." Rose frantically searched around her for a weapon—a rock or stick—but the rope bound her too tightly.

"My mother told me." She sneered. "More reason to be rid of you. With you gone, he will come to me. I will give him many children." Rebekah slid a knife from her belt and raised it, ready to strike.

"Please, I beg you." Rose lifted her arms in supplication, but when Rebekah thrust the knife down toward her, a fury stronger than Rose had ever known raged within. She screamed and shoved the mad woman away.

Something swished by her, followed by a loud thump.

The tip of an arrow protruded from Rebekah's chest. She slumped over and fell onto Rose, tumbling them both deeper into the river.

Frigid water swirled over Rose's head. She lunged her feet against the river bottom and surfaced, gasping and floundering. On the bank, the Beloved Woman stood grim-faced, bow in hand. From behind her, Sara and Nora ran to Rose, untied her hands, and dragged her to shore. The last thing she remembered before passing out was Rebekah's body floating away, face down in the water.

CHAPTER 39

*R*ose spent that day and the next alternately crying and sleeping. She feared for her baby, but Sara assured her that her child remained safe and secure in her womb.

Rebekah's mother left quickly for another village after her daughter's burial. Did the villagers blame Rose for Rebekah's sadness and death and her mother's departure?

Her worries were assuaged when many came to her side with gifts of sunflower seeds, dried berries, and bowls of kanuchi. One little girl gave her a dolly made of cornhusks. Another left an ebony hawk's feather at the foot of her pallet.

The Beloved Woman even gifted her with a bear-claw necklace. "For your courage, Atsila Yona."

For days after the assault, Rose wanted to do nothing but eat and stay burrowed beneath her pile of hides and blankets. She had to prod herself to get up and help with tasks.

One evening, she and Nora sat by the fire learning how to roll handfuls of bean mush into cornhusks that they would steam later. Rose sighed and sat back on her heels. "Auntie, I'm so tired all the time. They should call me Sleeping Bear rather than Fire Bear."

Sara chortled. "It has much to do with the baby. Some women can't keep food down and others sleep. You are fortunate to be the sleepy kind."

That evening, a sound dragged Rose from her drowsiness. She lifted her head out of the covers that muffled her ears.

Daniel!

Across the longhouse, he spoke with Sara. Rose desperately wanted to run to him but held back to hear what he had to say. Why had he been gone so long?

Tsiyi left Daniel's side and came to lie beside her. She reached out and scratched his ears.

"Auntie," Daniel said in a hoarse voice. "She has disappeared. What shall I do without her? My heart is broken. She is the other half of me. The one meant for me." He dragged his fingers through his hair. His eyes were hollow and his cheekbones angled as if he had lost weight. "I went to our cabin. It had been ransacked. I assumed she and Nora had been taken. We followed a lead about two white women...one with red hair...being taken by the Catawba to South Carolina. We caught up with the small raiding party and saved the women, whom we took to a nearby fort." He balled up his fists. "I had convinced myself it was Rose and Nora. But my hopes were dashed. I have never suffered such pain." He dropped his chin onto his chest. "I have searched everywhere. My Rose is not to be found."

Sara put a hand on his shoulder. "Steady, dear one. You have not found her because you did not search in the right place." She swept her arm toward Rose. "She is here."

Daniel stood rigid as if poleaxed and then followed Sara's direction.

"Rose," he shouted and ran toward her as she raised herself on her pallet.

"Daniel."

They spoke as one with a sound so full of joy many in the room laughed and cried.

He swept her up out of her covers and into his arms and began to rain kisses all over her face. She returned his caresses and kissed his eyelids, nose, cheeks, and finally, his lips.

"I can't believe you are here." She burrowed her face into his neck and breathed in his wonderfully familiar smell.

Nora sat up, dazed from sleep. "It's about time, Daniel Fordham. My sister has been impossible to live with without you." She grinned. "And I have missed you also, dear brother. You must promise us all that you won't go away again." She turned away and covered her head with the blankets.

"I will make it my life's goal." He gently placed Rose on the pallet, sat beside her, and pulled her onto his lap.

"There is so much to tell you," Rose began.

"There is, but right now, I want only to look at you." He tugged on one of her braids and scanned her shirt and leggings. "Quite the Indian maiden, I see," he said with a gleam in his eyes. His glance fell to her waist, and he splayed his hand across her stomach, his expression questioning.

She placed her hand over his. "That is one of the things I must tell you. I am with child."

He clasped her to him so hard she could feel him shaking. He leaned down and whispered in her ear, "My beloved. My treasure. I love you so."

Rose wrapped her arms around his neck. "I have yearned to hear those words. I have loved you for so long."

"I will whisper to you the words in Cherokee..."

He kissed her with a hunger so overwhelming, it sparked her own craving that had lain dormant for many months.

"Daniel. My Daniel." She cupped his face in her hands. How could she tell him that she had been the cause of his childhood sweetheart's death? "I-I..."

"What is it, my heart? Something troubles you."

"It's Rebekah."

"Must we speak of her now?"

"I bear a burden. You promised on our wedding day that we would share...that our burdens would be halved."

He sat up and clasped her shoulders. "Not here. Come." He picked up a blanket and threw it over her shoulders.

"Stay," he said to Tsiyi, who had started to rise.

They passed by a family who lay together awaiting sleep. Their little girl sat up and called out, "Where does he go with Atsila Yona?"

Rose waved at the child and spoke softly. "All is well."

She followed Daniel into the passageway. He closed the inner door behind them and walked with her toward the outer door. There he held her close, and when she looked up at his face, she was once again captivated by his beautiful eyes, now full of adoration.

Would that adoration remain once she told him? She would hesitate no longer.

"It saddens me to have to tell you...Rebekah is dead."

His pupils contracted, intensifying his eyes to dark blue.

"And it's because of me."

The wrinkles in his forehead deepened.

"She loved you. In her mind, you belonged to her. It was a strange passion...a sickness of sorts. One that turned into a hatred for me so strong that she wanted me gone."

"Gone?"

"Dead. I think her mother hated me too. So much, she tried to kill me...she pushed me over the mountain ledge."

His arm muscles grew rigid, and his face hardened like a stone.

"But I didn't fall from the cliff. I landed on a shelf. As I lay there, I brought to mind visions of you...pictures of the many times you wove in and out of my life. I recalled the night you told me you loved Rebekah, and I ached from that knowledge."

"No. No. You must let me explain—"

She pressed a finger to his lips. "Let me finish. When I was rescued, I wasn't angry. Rebekah loved you so much, I think her mother was willing to do anything to make her happy. I forgave her. And you know why?" She caressed his cheek. "As I lay stranded on that precipice, with the wind whistling about me, threatening to push me over or freeze me, I came to know hope. In our beautiful cathedral of God, I felt the blessed assurance that though I was alone, I was not alone."

He leaned his chin on the crown of her head.

"The day came when Rebekah heard that I was with child. It was too much for her to bear, and she came after me. We had gathered here in the longhouse, but Rebekah found me alone. She attacked me...dragged me to the river." She closed her eyes against the memory. "She raised her knife to kill me...our baby. But the Beloved Woman killed her instead."

He groaned. "I should have been there for you. I vowed to keep you safe."

"She is dead and I feel responsible. You loved her. If my father had not forced you to marry me..."

He clasped his hands on her hips and moved her away to scan her face. "Come here. Let's sit on the bench."

He sat down and gathered her into his arms to sit on his lap and wrapped the blanket around them. "Listen to me and listen well. Yes, I loved Rebekah, but with the feelings of a young boy for the familiar, for the expected. At first, I resisted you...that I will admit. I felt obligated to Rebekah, although I had never formally approached her parents or offered the bride price. But you were not to be resisted." He kissed her eyelids and then her mouth. "Also, I worried if you were really aware of what being married to me would entail."

"Because you are half Indian? It matters not to me. Nor did

it matter to my da. He never once mentioned your race." She remembered something that made her smile. "Do you know what did matter to him about you?"

He shrugged.

"That you are Church of England."

They both chuckled at that.

"Seriously, though, Daniel, did I not show you how I felt when I confronted that terrible man at the store who called you a half breed?"

He hugged her closer. "You were magnificent. But defending me against those who act out their prejudice isn't the same as being married to me. Believe me, you—we—will be confronted with ugliness...hatred, even. And so will our children." He leaned down and kissed her stomach.

She ran her fingers through his hair. "I love you so much, Daniel. With you by my side, I'm willing to face anything."

He sat up and stared deep into her eyes. "I pledge with everything in my being that I will make up for all you have suffered. God has graced us, my love. My heart is so full of gratitude for His mercies, I might burst."

They held each other for a time until Daniel asked, "I have to know. Why did that little girl call you Atsila Yona?"

"Ha! It is quite a story. When Nora and I fled the attack on our cabin, we headed for the village. You would have been so proud of Nora. She remembered what you taught her about walking as if we were on a map. Anyway, one night when the snow was falling so heavy we almost couldn't see, we came upon an abandoned cabin. We woke to strange sounds, so I jumped up, unsheathed my knife, and stood at the ready. Women from the village who had been searching for us were gathered outside. One of them said I looked like a bear with its hair on fire."

Daniel threw back his head and laughed, then kissed the top of her head. "I can see we have much to share with each other. But"—he stifled a yawn—"my lovely Fire Bear, I must admit, I am an exhausted bear."

They stood, and he pulled her close as they returned to the main room where most everyone had retired for the night.

At their family place, Daniel lay down on his back and clutched her to his side. He reached over and threw the blankets over them. For a delicious while, they murmured sweet words of love, they touched and whispered. He leaned down and spoke such endearing words to their child that Rose wanted to weep. But she had had enough weeping in her life. This was a blessed time of comfort and joy and peace.

Daniel turned onto his side and pulled her against him, tucking his knees under hers. Wrapped in her lover's arms, with their faithful Tsiyi curled at her feet, she fell asleep with a prayer of thanksgiving on her lips. At last, the long, winding road of their love story had led them home.

EPILOGUE

*R*ose and Daniel stood together looking out from the cathedral precipice onto the valley as the sun burned away the morning mist.

"You do not use the cradleboard?" asked Daniel, surveying the sling she had fashioned out of a length of linen to carry their son, who snuggled against her breasts.

"Maybe in a few weeks, when we harvest our crops, I'll put him in the cradleboard. But for now, I want to be able to look at his beautiful face."

They had named their month-old son Connor Wohali—Connor in remembrance of Rose's father, and Eagle because of their own passion for searching the mountaintops for the best and highest trees to climb.

Daniel leaned down and kissed his son's tiny head.

Rose glanced over her shoulder at the open-air chapel Daniel had built for them to worship in on Sundays or occasions when they needed to spend time alone or quench their spiritual thirst. Magenta and white morning glories bloomed on vines climbing along the walls of the pergola. Seated on a bench inside, Nora and Wyatt were immersed in conversation.

"I'm happy Wyatt is here," Rose said.

"Me too. He says he came to see Connor. That may be part of his reason, but I think we all know his real aim."

"His feelings must be true for him to have waited for Nora's mourning time to end." Rose ducked her head. The remembrance of her sister's loss always led to thoughts of her parents.

Daniel put his arm across her shoulders and pulled her close.

"Have you talked with him?" Rose tilted her head to peer up at him. "If they marry, where will they live?"

"He has his eye on property in the Ohio Valley."

Her heart dropped. "So far? Wouldn't it be ideal if they lived close by?"

He smiled. "When you look at me like that, my lady wife, I canno', as you often say, deny you anything."

She returned his smile.

"The decision is not up to me, but I'll approach him about it when the time is right."

"Thank you. I dinno think it possible to love you any more than I do."

"I'll remind you of that the next time you scold me about cleaning my musket on the dining table."

Rose laughed lightly at that. Then, looking outward, she pointed. "Look, there, beside the river. It's a wagon train. So far away, the wagons are the size of ants."

"I imagine we'll be seeing more of them as time passes."

"Siyo," Gray Sky called out as he and Spotted Owl joined them. "Are we ready?"

"Ready?" Rose tucked Connor's hand back into the sling.

"We want to show you something." Daniel's expression was as serious as she had ever experienced. "Something sacred. A secret known to only a few."

Rose's pulse raced. "Should I leave Connor with Nora?"

"No. He will be fine with us, and this involves his birthright."

Rose waved goodbye to Nora and Wyatt and walked alongside Daniel on the path leading to the river. There she and Daniel and Tsiyi got into one canoe, and the cousins manned another.

She had so many questions but sensed that this should remain a quiet journey. Her imagination raced as fast as the current.

What was she about to witness?

They moved into a branch of the river she had not traveled before. The tributary dumped out into a lake at the bottom of a mountain so high, Rose had to lean back to view the top. On the other side of the lake, Daniel guided them toward a line of boulders. He maneuvered them in between two of the largest ones.

"You need to duck, Rose," he said as they moved underneath a canopy of bushes.

It was not until they had passed through the limbs that she spotted a cave entrance just large enough for the canoe to pass through. Inside, the light grew dim, barely illuminating rock formations that reminded Rose of pillars in a cathedral. Other rocks hung from the cave ceiling like giant icicles.

Daniel lifted the paddle out of the water and allowed a current to push them along.

The only sound besides her quickened breath was the *drip, drip, drip* of water from the paddle. The farther they progressed, the colder the air became. Darkness so impenetrable she could not see her hand in front of her face overtook them. At last, Daniel lit a lantern and set it at the front of the canoe. She glanced behind her to see that the cousins had lit a lantern as well.

They approached a fork in their path, and Daniel guided them to the right. After a short while, he extinguished the lantern, and she thought she could see a light ahead. It grew bright enough for her to wave to the cousins.

Connor stirred.

"All is well, my love. Ma is here."

He snuffled and relaxed once again.

At a landing where the black water splashed up against a flat rock, Daniel assisted her to stand beside him and then secured the canoe to metal rings hammered into the rock. At least someone had been there enough to have prepared a docking place.

Daniel pointed to a path that slanted upward between a line of boulders. At the end of the path lay a village that was almost an exact replica of Aunt Sara's. In the distance, a waterfall spilled out into a narrow river that flowed between footpaths and rows of cabins.

She stood in awe, unable to speak.

What was different about this village? It was abandoned. And most stunning of all, it had been created inside an enormous cave with a hole in the ceiling large enough for the sun to shine through.

"Oh, Daniel! Am I dreaming? Have you brought us to a fairytale land?"

"No, my love, it's very real. Come, let's sit over here while the cousins make sure all is in order."

Gray Sky and Spotted Owl, accompanied by an inquisitive Tsiyi, visited each cabin as if conducting some sort of inspection.

He pressed a hand to her heart. "You must promise upon our love not to tell a soul what I'm about to tell you. Not even Nora."

She nodded, still unable to take in what she was seeing.

"Five years ago, three of our grandmothers...they have all passed since...awoke from dreams and visions they had experienced during the same night. When they shared with each other, they found that they had had identical visions—terrible dreams of our people being herded like cattle, forced away from our village...decimated. The visions held death, horrible sadness, and tears...many tears."

She put her hand on top of his.

"The prophecies were considered so profound that our elders decided we must be prepared for such an event...plan an escape and create a place to escape to." He swept his arm toward the village.

"When?" she barely managed to whisper.

"That, we don't know. It might be in our lifetime...and it may not. But the cousins and I have been given the task of coming here three or four times a year to ensure that everything is as it should be in case our people must flee at a moment's notice. Should it not come to pass in our lifetime, our sons will take on the mantle when we are gone."

"I swear I won't tell a soul, my husband. And I promise, I will help prepare our son for this task." She lay her head against Daniel's shoulder. "I will pray with all my heart that the prophecies won't come to pass."

The cousins returned and, their task completed, they all returned to their canoes and rowed back through the cave. She thought of Sara and the family and friends at the village. She studied her precious son, a quarter Cherokee, and was overcome with sorrow. How would she and Daniel keep him safe and secure?

A shaft of light darted across the water in front of them, illuminating the way. Rose's spirits lifted. There was a plan in place in case of trouble or danger against her people, and she and Daniel and their son were an essential part of it.

Their canoe broke through the shadows of the cave and into the sunlight. Rose's heart overflowed with the hope that, no matter their plan, the God of love and grace had an even better one.

Did you enjoy this book? We hope so!
Would you take a quick minute to leave a review where you purchased the book?
It doesn't have to be long. Just a sentence or two telling what you liked about the story!

Receive a FREE ebook and get updates when new Wild Heart books release: https://wildheartbooks.org/newsletter

Don't miss the next book in the The Great Wagon Road Series!

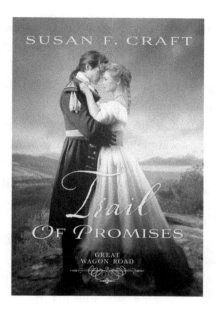

Trail of Promises
By Susan F. Craft

June 15, 1753

Strolling alongside her family's covered wagon through a dense forest with more trees than she could name, Tessa Harris dragged a stick across weeds that draped onto the edges of the trail. Though it was only early morning, the air already sweltered, and she welcomed the tufts of mist that moistened her arms. The emotional burden she carried weighed her down as heavily as the humidity.

Today marked her nineteenth birthday as well as the second anniversary of her mother's death. Both had passed without mention. Had her mother been alive, she would have awakened Tessa with laughter and a silly ditty. Name day presents and cakes would have awaited her at the breakfast table.

A gray rabbit thrashed through a nearby bush and scurried so close to her toes, she hopped back. She dropped the stick and adjusted the strap of the rucksack slung over her shoulder. The canvas bag held her sketchbook, charcoal, and pencils. She never allowed it far from her reach.

Her father, Thomas Harris, drove their wagon with the ease born of many years' experience as a limner traveling from town to town seeking commissions for portraits. But his tall, lean form hunched on the bench. Last night's drinking had left his usually handsome face bloated and his mood testy.

She moved closer to the wagon. "Father?"

"What is it?" he snapped. He did not look at her but concentrated on the team of horses.

Should she engage with him or let him be? Despite his moroseness, she missed his companionship.

"How far have we come since leaving Philadelphia?"

He continued looking ahead. "Around a hundred miles."

"So three hundred more to go?"

He grumbled and jerked the reins. "Give or take."

His terseness precluded any further conversation. Tessa walked on in silence until they reached a section of the trail so narrow it caused her to squeeze closer to the wagon. Her father angrily shoved away a pine branch that threatened to slap his face. The brim of his black felt hat flopped over his forehead as if to shelter his stoic expression and the grief lines etched on either side of his mouth.

He abruptly pulled back on the reins, bringing the wagon to a halt. "Tessa, you'll have to take over."

Tessa's spirits slumped.

"Why have you stopped, Miss Harris? Is something wrong?" a voice called out behind her.

She turned as Stephen Griffith, the owner of the wagon that

followed hers, prodded his coal-black stallion toward her. The master and his horse made a striking picture.

"Good morning." She curtsied.

During their short acquaintance, they had made only fleeting, casual conversation, but his engaging smile that lit his eyes and his friendly manner appealed to her. Her pulse fluttered each time he came near.

"It's my father. He's unwell and I must drive." Avoiding his gaze, she concentrated on pulling the worn leather gloves from her belt and slipping them on.

Mr. Griffith dismounted, stroked his horse's jaw, and murmured, "My fine Knight." The horse nuzzled his shoulder before Mr. Griffith looked up at her.

"One of my brothers would be happy to drive for you. Although Francis and Adam have both become proficient this past week, they quarrel over who will drive. You would be doing me a favor by allowing one of them to assist you."

"That's kind of you, but I can manage. Father and I traveled many miles as we moved from one commission to the next, and I often drove our wagon." She chuckled. "I got quite good at dodging holes in the road, especially in remote country villages."

Without acknowledging Mr. Griffith's presence, her father slapped the reins around the brake and climbed inside the wagon.

His rudeness mortified her. "Do forgive my father—"

Mr. Griffith stepped closer to her. "Please, there's no need to apologize."

He was so tall, Tessa had to lean back to gaze into his warm brown eyes.

No, not just brown. Sienna. Burnt sienna.

Considered individually, each of his features was unremarkable. A square jaw covered by a cropped dark-brown beard. Long nose. Full lips shadowed by a thin mustache. Dark, feathery eyebrows that framed his golden-brown eyes. And curly sable-brown hair he wore loose, flowing over his ears and resting on his collar. Taken all together, though, his was a handsome, arresting face. Although his arms, exposed by his rolled-up sleeves, were tanned from many hours in the sun, Tessa could tell that his complexion was naturally pale.

He cleared his throat. "Is something amiss?"

Tessa blinked and flushed over being caught staring. "Oh, do forgive me. I tend to get lost studying people. Have you ever had your portrait done?"

"Me? No. Definitely not. My younger brothers said you allowed them to see samples of your work. You're brilliant, according to them."

She fiddled with the strap of her rucksack. The two young men had shown genuine interest in her work. "What a nice thing to hear."

He glanced up the trail at the cloud of dust stirred by the last wagon that had rounded the bend. "Let's not let the others get too far ahead."

He slipped the rucksack from her shoulder, clasped her elbow, and helped her up onto the wagon seat.

Tessa wrinkled her nose at the knee-high cloud of dust already lingering in the air. Today, hers and Mr. Griffith's wagons were the last in line. The farther the train ventured during the day, the higher the dust cloud would grow.

"You have a kerchief?" he asked and handed her the rucksack.

"I do." Tessa reached into the side slit of her petticoats and pulled her scarf from her under-pocket. "Thank you for your kindness."

She waited for Mr. Griffith to step back before slapping the reins and driving the horses forward. Closing the gap that had formed behind the previous wagon, she fought the misgivings that crowded her thoughts. How could she manage if her father persisted his drinking? Driving the wagon, settling down each evening with the eight other families, building a fire, cooking the meal, caring for the horses, and preparing the bedrolls underneath the wagon exhausted her so much that she often retired without speaking a word to anyone. Some nights, too spent to sleep, she lit a candle and worked on her sketches.

Carrying the burden of their family drained her mentally. She needed her father. A master portrait artist, at one time, he had charmed his female subjects, perusing them with his intense cobalt-blue eyes that delved into their personalities, bringing them to life on canvas. His wife's death had cast a pall over his artistic passion. Drink had doused the fire in his eyes.

When their ship docked in Philadelphia weeks prior, Tessa had hoped the adventure of a wagon train and the promise of a new portrait studio in the South Carolina colony would lift his spirits, but the opposite held true. His moods swung between anger and melancholy with increasingly rare expressions of more tender emotions between.

Did her father not see how his behavior frightened her? How alone she felt, uprooted from everything familiar and dropped into a world of strangers and sights and sounds so alien from their home in England?

Her prayers had become fervent pleas for her old father to return to her.

How sad to compare what was real with what she wished life to be. Even so, she had to put on a brave face. And one day, she'd see her father smile again.

A deer bounded from the woods and streaked across the trail, startling the lead horse. It reared up and gave out a scream that sounded almost human.

Tessa pulled back on the reins with all her might as the wagon rocked back and forth. A loud *crack* and the wagon careened to the side. She shrieked as she was tossed into the air.

ABOUT THE AUTHOR

Susan F. Craft retired after a 45-year career in writing, editing, and communicating in business settings.

She authored the historical romantic suspense trilogy *Women of the American Revolution—The Chamomile, Laurel*, and *Cassia*. *The Chamomile* and *Cassia* received national Illumination Silver Awards. *The Chamomile* was named by the Southern Independent Booksellers Alliance as an Okra Pick and was nominated for a Christy Award.

She collaborated with the International Long Riders' Guild Academic Foundation to compile *An Equestrian Writer's Guide* (www.lrgaf.org), including almost everything you'd ever want to know about horses.

An admitted history nerd, she enjoys painting, singing,

listening to music, and sitting on her porch watching geese eat her daylilies. She most recently took up the ukulele.

AUTHOR'S NOTE

Sadly, despite the fervent prayers of many, events were already occurring that would eventually lead to the fulfillment of the prophecies.

The Trail of Tears was a series of forced displacements of approximately 60,000 American Indians of the "Five Civilized Tribes" between 1830 and 1850 by the United States government.

In May 1838, without any warning, Federal troops rounded up an estimated 12,000 Cherokee at gunpoint and forced them to march to a designated territory in Oklahoma. No one knows how many of them died, but the journey was especially difficult for infants, children, and the elderly. A missionary, Doctor Elizur Butler, who accompanied the Cherokee, estimated that over 4,000 died—nearly a fifth of the Cherokee population.

About 1,000 Cherokees in Tennessee and North Carolina escaped the roundup. They gained recognition in 1866, establishing their tribal government in 1868 in Cherokee, North Carolina. Today, they are known as the Eastern Band of Cherokee Indians.

Although the cave that Rose and Daniel were caretakers for was fictitious, I like to think of the Cherokees who escaped the roundup, some whom could have been Connor Wohali's children and grandchildren, as living in such a place—safe and comfortable.

Black Willow bark was used for the treatment of back pain, headaches, and inflammatory conditions. Mr. Jackson had arthritis in his hands, so he would chew on the twigs and drink the tea his wife prepared from the bark. In this novel, I attempted to explain that Rose and Daniel climbed black willows and not weeping willows.

The Jacksons were flax growers and weavers headed for an area in northeast South Carolina called the Waxhaws that came to be known as Rock Hill. I based them on President Andrew Jackson's family, who emigrated from Ireland. Presbyterians, they wanted to escape persecution and tariffs from the ruling Anglicans. Among other accomplishments, Andrew Jackson's mother, Elizabeth, was known for her excellent flax weaving.

I offer my sincere appreciation to the Oconaluftee Indian Village in Cherokee, NC. They have recreated a 1760s village with traditional dwellings, work areas, and sacred ritual places. During the numerous times I visited the village, the sights, sounds, and smells enthralled me. I witnessed the people making a canoe, sculpting pottery, hand-fashioning beadwork, weaving cane baskets, and forming thistle into darts for a blowgun. As a history nerd, I could not have been happier.

I also thank the Cherokee Nation for the fabulous videos, *Cherokee Word of the Week*, where Cherokee words are spoken, spelled out, and defined.

Thank you to Ghost Farmer Productions and the Museum of History NSW for the video *Loading and Firing a Musket in 1776*.

And, of course, I extend heartfelt gratitude to my Lord, from Whom all blessings flow.

Soli Deo gloria.

Want more?

If you love historical romance, check out the other Wild Heart books!

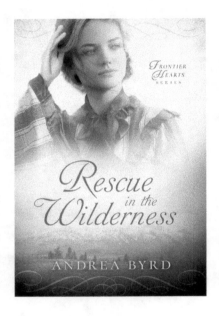

Rescue in the Wilderness by Andrea Byrd

William Cole cannot forget the cruel burden he carries, not with the pock marks that serve as an outward reminder. Riddled with guilt, he assumed the solitary life of a long hunter, traveling into the wilds of Kentucky each year. But his quiet existence is changed in an instant when, sitting in a tavern, he overhears a man offering his daughter—and her virtue—to the winner of the next round of cards. William's integrity and desire for redemption will not allow him to sit idly by while such an injustice occurs.

Lucinda Gillespie has suffered from an inexplicable illness her entire life. Her father, embarrassed by her condition, has subjected her to a lonely existence of abuse and confinement. But faced with the ultimate betrayal on the eve of her eighteenth birthday, Lucinda quickly realizes her trust is better placed in his hands of the mysterious man who appears at her door. Especially when he offers her the one thing she never thought would be within her grasp—freedom.

In the blink of an eye, both lives change as they begin the difficult, danger-fraught journey westward on the Wilderness Trail. But can they overcome their own perceptions of themselves to find love and the life God created them for?

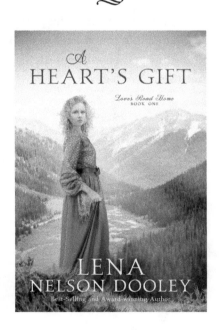

A Heart's Gift by Lena Nelson Dooley

Is a marriage of convenience the answer?

Franklin Vine has worked hard to build the ranch he inherited into one of the most successful in the majestic Colorado mountains. If only he had an heir to one day inherit the legacy he's building. But he was burned once in the worst way, and he doesn't plan to open his heart to another woman. Even if that means he'll eventually have to divide up his spread among the most loyal of his hired hands.

When Lorinda Sullivan is finally out from under the control of men who made all the decisions in her life, she promises herself she'll never allow a man to make choices for her again. But without a home in the midst of a hard Rocky Mountain winter, she has to do something to provide for her infant son.

A marriage of convenience seems like the perfect arrangement, yet the stakes quickly become much higher than either of them ever planned. When hearts become entangled, the increasing danger may change their lives forever.

~

Lone Star Ranger by Renae Brumbaugh Green

Elizabeth Covington will get her man.

And she has just a week to prove her brother isn't the murderer Texas Ranger Rett Smith accuses him of being. She'll show the good-looking lawman he's wrong, even if it means setting out on a risky race across Texas to catch the real killer.

Rett doesn't want to convict an innocent man. But he can't let the Boston beauty sway his senses to set a guilty man free. When Elizabeth follows him on a dangerous trek, the Ranger vows to keep her safe. But who will protect him from the woman whose conviction and courage leave him doubting everything—even his heart?

Printed in the USA
CPSIA information can be obtained
at www.ICGtesting.com
JSHW062132010324
58201JS00009B/43